NEMESIS
INTO THE SHADOWS

CATHERINE MacPHAIL

NEMESIS
INTO THE SHADOWS

BLOOMSBURY

First published in Great Britain in 2006 by Bloomsbury Publishing Plc
36 Soho Square, London, W1D 3QY

A CIP catalogue record of this book is available from the British Library

ISBN 978 0 7475 8268 7

All papers used by Bloomsbury Publishing are natural, recyclable products made
from wood grown in well-managed forests. The manufacturing processes conform
to the environmental regulations of the country of origin.

Typeset by Dorchester Typesetting Group Ltd
Printed in Great Britain by Clays Ltd, St Ives Plc

3 5 7 9 10 8 6 4

www.macphailbooks.com
www.bloomsbury.com

To Daniel David Small

FRIDAY, 4 AM

I stirred in my sleep. The cold was seeping into my dream, turning the fire that surrounded me in my nightmare into flames of ice. Tendrils of ice reached out to me, licking at my fingers, encircling my ankles, holding me back from running. And I had to run. There was just a desperate urge inside me to run, to hide. To keep on hiding.

Had I had this dream before? There was something familiar about it. The ice-cold fire, and the sound. A rhythmic thumping somewhere in the distance. Like the beat of a war drum. Something else to be afraid of. Warning me. Louder and louder. Closer and closer it came, dragging me from my dream.

I jumped awake. Cold concrete soaked through my clothes, through my skin and deep into my bones. I bolted upright. Where was I? Why could I never remember anything but the dreams? Since when? I couldn't remember.

I was in a stairwell, a dark stairwell, with just a dim wink from a flashing bulb to lighten the shadowy corners. On a landing. And there were stairs going down and down and down. I didn't want to think how far down. Too scary. I wasn't alone. I could hear coughing, echoing from somewhere below me, unhealthy, grating, racking coughs. Another derelict sleeping rough like me in the only warmth they could find: the stairwell of this tower block.

Now something was coming back to me. The town by the river. I had arrived here yesterday. But from where? I didn't know. I could remember someone pointing out the tower block on the hill. Wellpark Court. Telling me this was a place where the junkies and the derelicts came to sleep at night. For warmth. For shelter.

I was no junkie. Was I a derelict? I didn't know what I was. Or who I was.

I had no memory. No memory before yesterday. Except for the nightmares.

Thump. Thump. Thump.

I tried to shake my head free of the noise, but it was still there.

Not a dream.

Real.

But what was it?

My legs were stiff and sore as I stood up and moved to the door that led to the landing. I listened silently. The noise was coming from somewhere beyond that door. And suddenly I recognised what it was. The lift doors, trying to close, and then opening again. Open and close. As if something was blocking them.

I pulled at the door. I didn't step through, not right away. Just in case there was someone waiting there, watching for me. There was a door into one of the flats ahead of me. 153, a brass number plate proclaimed. I was on the fifteenth floor. It was coming back to me – walking up the stairs, past junkies and the homeless. Stepping warily over them, hoping no one would notice me. Trying to find a landing that was empty, one that no one else was sleeping on. I hadn't travelled up on the lift. I was afraid of lifts. That much I knew. Couldn't step into one and not think of the drop below me. The drop into nothingness. I was afraid. Always afraid, it seemed to me. Always wary of what I might find. And though my mind was still fogged with the nightmare, hidden deep in some recess of the memory I no longer had, I knew that many times before I had been in danger.

Open and close. Open and close. Thump. Thump.

Common sense told me to ignore the sound, but I didn't seem to be strong on common sense. The landing turned in an L shape and I had to take another reluctant step to peer round the corner to see the lift. Directly facing it were two more doors into flats. 155 and 157. Now I could see what was stopping the door from closing.

Someone's arm.

It lay outstretched on the ground, immobile. I almost stepped away. An old drunk, I thought, who had had too much whisky and had collapsed. Comatose. Not my business.

Until I saw the blood.

Still, I didn't move closer. I waited and listened. A door was swinging shut, footsteps taking the stairs two at a time to the ground floor. Someone running from this? I held still, waiting for the sudden rush from one of the houses. Other people alerted by the sound. But no one came out on to the landing. No doors opened.

Either no one had heard, or, having heard, decided it was wiser to ignore it. No one wanted any trouble. I took a step forward, still ready to run. For one awful second I thought that there was only the severed arm, sliced off by guillotine-like lift doors. It was almost a relief to see that the arm was still attached to a man, lying inside the lift. He was on his back, his mouth open. His white shirt was soaked in blood. Was he dead? At first I thought he must be. There was so much blood. No one could survive losing so much blood. But suddenly the man stirred. He let out a painful moan and his eyes fluttered open.

I froze to the spot as the eyes focused on me. Stared at me. I couldn't drag my eyes from his. The hand, outstretched on the ground, beckoned me closer. I didn't want to move. If anything, I wanted to run. But something drew me nearer. The man's lips were moving as if he was trying to speak. With each painful muttering blood gurgled from his mouth. I stepped inside the lift, bent down towards the figure, trying to make out his words, but there was no sound, just the gurgle of blood.

This is crazy, I thought. I should be running. Running away from this. I almost took a step back, would have taken a step back, when all at once the outstretched arm shot into life, reached up and, with a strength I wouldn't have believed, pulled me close. Dragged me down towards his face.

I tried to pull away, but the man for all his loss of blood – could there be so much blood in one man? – had strength. The strength of the dying, for in the man's eyes I could see death. And even in that second I wondered how I could know such a thing.

His teeth were stained red with blood. He mumbled something I couldn't understand. A jumble of words I couldn't make out. I wanted to break free. I was afraid. Was this still part of my nightmare? I hoped that any second I would wake up. But the fingers curled around my coat were real, the smell of so much blood was real.

The man tightened his grip, drew me closer. And with nothing now blocking the doors, they closed. The lift began to move.

And I was trapped inside with a dying man.

I panicked. The lift began to close in on me. I was aware suddenly of the graffiti scratched into the stainless steel walls, the smell of stale chips and something else, something sinister. It was blood. The lift seemed to be filled with the sweet smell of it. I tried to stand, but the man on the ground, weak as he seemed to be, was stronger than I was. His breath was coming in dying gasps. His fist tightened on my coat. His eyes, watery blue, were wide with alarm. Afraid to die, or afraid of something else? His mouth moved, but no sound came out.

'Let me go.' I said it softly. I was afraid too. Afraid to be here. What if whoever did this came back? What if the lift doors slid open and he was there? I could almost picture him, all in black, a balaclava hiding his face, holding his knife high, the steel glinting in the light. Ready to strike again. Ready to plunge that knife into me. I felt a cold sweat cover my body. 'Let me go,' I said again. But the man only pulled me closer to his face.

I couldn't make out his whispered words. Not at first. The man drew in his breath painfully and tried again. He wet his lips with his tongue and smeared more red blood across his teeth.

This can't be happening, I thought. This can't be real.

'Stop.' One word exhausted him. But he said it again. 'Stop.'

It seemed like agony for him to speak. What was I about to get? A death-bed confession?

'Four teeth.' My brain was racing. Four teeth. I almost giggled, hysteria setting in. Was he trying to tell me he only had four teeth?

There was a rattle in his throat and he said it again. 'Four teeth.'

Was that really what he said? A few painful seconds passed and the man spoke again. Spluttering out the next words. 'Heartbeat. Stop.'

There were more muttered words I couldn't make out. A desperate string of incoherent words. He shuddered, made one final dying attempt to make me understand. 'Four teeth. Heartbeat. Stop.'

And in that second that's what happened. His heartbeat stopped.

Death flushed across his face, draining the life from it. And I knew in that second that I had seen death before.

But where?

No time to think. The lift was creaking to a halt at the ground floor. The man's hand was still clasped tightly on my jacket. I had to touch those hands to pull them from me. No choice. As soon as the doors opened I had to be ready to run. I was shaking now with fear. Covered in blood myself. If I could I would have prised those doors open with my bare hands. My heart was pounding. If I was found here in this lift with a dead body, it would look as if I was the one who had killed him. But who'd believe that? I was just a boy. How could I be capable of murder?

The doors opened at last as if in slow motion. A girl was standing there. She wasn't looking at me, too busy studying her nails, chewing gum, hardly interested. At this time in the morning she had obviously been out at a late-night party, though she looked too young. Even with the black mask of her eyes and the white face, she looked young. Not much older than I was.

She stepped back to let me out of the lift and her eyes shifted to me, roamed over me, appraising me. Suddenly she saw the blood. The blood on my clothes, the blood on the floor, and then her eyes followed the trail of blood to the body, a scarlet streak of blood.

She stopped in mid-chew. Her eyes popped. She began to scream.

I couldn't move. Try as I might I couldn't move. I stood staring at the girl as she screamed and screamed. The sound pierced into my eardrums like a skewer.

'Please. Please.' I muttered the words, wanting her to be quiet. I stretched out my hands towards her. I only wanted to reassure her that I meant no harm, that I was no threat, that I had nothing to do with this. I was as innocent, as scared, as she was.

That wasn't the message she got. Her eyes opened wider. She stepped back, still screaming, as if she thought I was about to attack her. My hand brushed against her jacket and smeared blood on it too. 'Please,' I said again. I half expected her to crumple to the ground. She didn't. She lifted her handbag and swung it hard at me. It sent me hurtling back against the wall.

Only will power helped me keep my balance, and I stumbled away from her. Why wouldn't she stop screaming? Why wouldn't she listen?

I took another step away from her, backing towards the entrance to the flats. I didn't take my eyes off her, sure she was about to attack me again. For a second our eyes locked.

'Please . . . don't think I did this . . .' I tried again to talk to her, to explain, but my words were lost in her screams.

It was no use. No time to waste. I turned and ran. Any moment now, doors would be flung open, people would flood down the stairs on to the street, investigating those hellish screams. A police siren would be heard in the distance. Police would be swarming everywhere.

And I couldn't be caught. I couldn't risk waiting around to give any explanations. I didn't have any to give. There was a blackness in my mind, like the darkness looming inside a tunnel. I didn't know who I was, or where I came from. I didn't even know my name.

I ran into the night air, stopped for a second and looked up at the tower block. Already lights were being snapped on, floor by floor, curious tenants awakened by that girl's persistent screaming. In the flats across the street, someone was at their window, peering through Venetian blinds. I looked all around, at the houses, the boarded-up shops, the lonely car park.

I was terrified that someone might see me. I began to run.

Someone was watching him, though he didn't know it. Someone sitting in a car in that car park, engine off, lights off. The man they called 'the Wolf'. He had a clear view of the street, saw the boy stumble from the building. Afraid. A young boy, his hair dark, wearing clothes too big for him. The Wolf watched him stand, transfixed, not knowing what to do. Who was this boy? Because of him, the Wolf hadn't had time to finish the job. And he didn't like leaving anything unfinished. He had heard the boy coming, heard the door of the landing creak open. And the Wolf had run. The Wolf didn't like running. Decided he didn't like this boy. He watched as the boy's frightened eyes searched around the street. The figure in the car slid down further in the front seat. Just in case. But the boy saw nothing. Only an empty car parked inconspicuously among others in a lonely car park.

As he watched, the Wolf lifted his mobile phone. A number was punched in. A moment later a voice asked, 'Is it done?'

'Done,' the Wolf said.

'No problems?'

The hesitation said there was. 'Nothing much. I can handle it.'

'What problem?' The voice on the line was on the edge of anger, but then he always sounded on the edge of anger.

The Wolf was angry too. He had every right to be. 'Why was I told to do it here? This is not a good place.'

'It's done now,' was the answer. Then again: 'What problem?'

'A boy,' the Wolf said. 'A boy found him in the lift. One of the junkies who sleeps in there. I'm watching him now. He's terrified.'

'Who's the boy? Do we know him?'

'Not local. He's probably a junkie,' the Wolf said. 'Out of his face. No threat.'

The anger spilled through the phone like lava. 'No threat? That junkie found him. Was he already dead . . . or just dying?'

The Wolf sounded confident when he answered. He had every right to be. This was his job. He had killed many times before. 'I don't make mistakes. He was dead. He had to be dead.'

'Did he tell the boy anything? Did he?' The man on the line wasn't going to wait for an answer. 'Follow that boy. Don't let him out of your sight. Keep me in touch. We have to find out what he knows.'

The phone was clicked off just as the boy in the street took to his heels and ran. The car door opened and the Wolf sprinted after him.

6

I knew I should run and keep on running, but I had to see what was happening. I stopped for breath in a pathway between the tenement flats. It was overgrown with bushes, plastic bags trapped in them, snapping like flags caught in the wind. From here I couldn't be seen from any windows but still had a view of the entrance to the flats.

The girl was still screaming. What was it with her? Why didn't she shut up? She hadn't stopped since the lift doors had opened and she'd first seen me. Now there would be blood on her too. I remembered the way I had reached out to her to try to quieten her down, to re-assure her I meant no harm. There would be blood on her arm, on her clothes. Maybe that was why she was still screaming. The smell of blood was on me too. Blood all over me, soaking into my skin. I would have to get more clothes. But where? How? I could go nowhere like this, covered in blood.

The girl was being brought out of the flats, almost carried. A man with his arm around her seemed to be holding her up, leading her out into the open air. Her screams were suddenly louder, filling the night with their sound. People were spilling on to the streets now from the flats nearby. Windows were being thrown wide and curious neighbours were looking out, shouting, asking what the trouble was. The junkies and derelicts, who used the stairwells for somewhere to sleep, were spilling out too, running like rats from a sinking ship. Trying to get away before the police came.

And still the girl screamed.

Why didn't somebody slap her face? Wasn't that what

you were supposed to do if someone was hysterical? I would gladly have done that just to shut her up.

I could hear the wail of a police car in the distance. They would arrive soon, any moment now. Time for me to run. My eyes searched out the best route. Over the back gardens, leaping over hedges and walls. Out of sight. And then, in one of the gardens, I saw exactly what I needed. Some obliging mother had left her son's clothes hanging on the line. Jeans, a T-shirt, a sweater. Why, they were almost waving at me. Beckoning me over. *Come and get us!*

So I did. I sprinted into the garden, snapped the clothes from the line and with hardly a pause in my step I was off, into the shadows again.

PC Lewis Ferguson sat in the car with his partner, Guthrie. Of course, in this force, he was supposed to call him his 'neighbour'. That had disappointed Lewis. 'Partner' had a kind of NYPD ring to it. Lewis had only been on the force for a few weeks, a rookie, but he meant to make his mark. A detective, that's what he was meant to be. He could see it now. Rising in the force, achieving promotion after promotion, making a name for himself as a smart, sensitive, on-the-ball kind of guy. Maybe win a couple of medals on the way. That was his plan. His mother would be proud of him one day. At the moment all she seemed to do was complain about all the ironing she had to do for him and how hard it was to press a crease into his uniform trousers.

'A crease! I'll give them a crease all right! They'll be

able to cut their hair with the crease in your trousers.'

Ah, she was an old battleaxe, he thought, but lovable with it.

Suddenly, it seemed his day of glory might arrive sooner than he thought. The message on the car radio was clear. There had been an 'incident' at Wellpark Court.

Wellpark Court, just round the corner. It was on their beat. They never seemed to be away from the place. Junkies sleeping in the stairwells, leaving used needles on landings, dealing drugs. Tenants always complaining.

'Here we go again,' Guthrie said. An older man, he was marking time till his retirement. He planned to buy himself an apartment in Spain. Didn't want any trouble till then.

Lewis listened to the message on the radio. 'A body's been found. Looks like a stabbing.'

'Another stabbing,' Guthrie said drily. 'Maybe we should just move into Wellpark Court.' He sighed. 'I suppose we'd better go.'

'Should we not hurry?' Lewis made an attempt to sound casual.

His partner smiled at him. 'You'll be wanting to use the siren?'

Lewis tried to look as if the thought hadn't occurred to him. That he still didn't get a kick out of driving fast past the punters, blue light flashing, with the siren at full blast. But he couldn't keep the excitement out of his eyes. He was only a rookie after all.

Guthrie smiled. 'Go on then.'

It was no good. Common sense told me to run, to get as far away from there as possible, but the sound of the police siren made me stop in my stride again. I watched the car swerve round the corner. It seemed now that the street was alive with people, surging into the night. People in dressing gowns, people with coats thrown over their pyjamas. Old people, young people, their voices carrying through the still, icy night air.

Two policemen stepped from the car. The older one took charge immediately, holding the crowds back. I could see him talking into the personal radio on his collar. Then he headed inside the entrance to the flats. The younger one walked straight towards the girl, probably hoping he'd be able to shut her up. He was holding his hands out to her as if he was trying to calm her.

Better you than me, pal, I thought.

In a moment, she would tell her story, describe the boy she'd seen, and they would be after me. Those radios would call in reinforcements. I imagined them panning out, lines of police, battalions of them, searching for me.

Time for me to go.

Lewis calmly stepped towards the girl. He could handle a hysterical female. After all, he'd been living with his mother all his life. The girl was sitting on a wall near the entrance. A woman beside her had her arm round her shoulders.

It was nice to see the girl was being comforted, Lewis thought. The woman looked up as he approached. 'Thank God you're here. She's driving me potty. Can't get her to shut up.'

So much for tender loving care, Lewis thought. He knelt down in front of the girl, whipped out his note-book. 'OK, what's your name?' he said.

The girl looked at him. She screamed as if he was ready to attack her. The mascara on her big dark eyes had run with all her crying. She looked like a vampire. Or maybe she was one of those Goths and always looked like that. She screamed again in answer. Lewis looked round at the gathered crowd. 'Has anybody given her anything to calm her down?' he asked.

'A slap in the kisser,' some helpful soul suggested.

'Nothing violent, madam,' Lewis said. 'I meant a hot cup of tea or something.'

The mention of tea must have done the trick. The girl took one long gulp of air and shut up at last.

She was younger than he'd first thought. Lewis saw that now. Her dark hair stood out in spikes, her midriff was bare and she had a ring in her belly button. She must be freezing, he thought. It was an icy February night with a touch of snow in the air. 'Now what's your name?'

He tried to sound reassuring. The way he'd been taught during his training.

'Her name's Gaby McGurk. She lives on the fifteenth floor with her mother and her stepdad. He works on the rigs. She's a function waitress. You know, serves at weddings and funerals and that.' The old biddy who'd been comforting the girl, (if comforting was the right word), answered for her.

Lewis wrote it all down in his notebook.

'He's not my stepdad! He just lives with us,' Gaby McGurk informed him curtly.

'And what age are you?'

The same old biddy let out a loud guffaw of laughter. 'We've got a body in the lift here, covered in blood, and all the cops want to know is what age she is! What does that matter? We're all getting older by the minute while there's murderers runnin' loose.'

Lewis decided to ignore her.

Gaby McGurk grabbed his arm. 'Don't ask me to look at that body again. I couldn't look at it again.'

Lewis assured her that she wouldn't have to. Reassure the public. Just as he'd been taught at training college. 'Now tell me exactly what happened?' He held his notebook at the ready.

Gaby started slowly. 'I was just waiting for the lift, minding my own business.'

'You were out very late . . .' Lewis said.

Her face flushed. 'I was at my pal Zoe's house. We forgot the time.'

She somehow didn't look to Lewis as if she'd been sitting all night in her pal's house. But he said nothing.

'And then the door opened. And there it was, lying, covered in blood.' As soon as she remembered the body, the blood, she was off into overdrive. Even using shorthand, Lewis couldn't keep up with her. 'And he was there, this boy. He was a junkie. He was covered in blood. His eyes were wild. Wild. He lunged at me. He was going to kill me as well. I know he was.'

Lewis managed to get a word in edgeways. 'Did he have a knife in his hand?'

She hardly hesitated. 'He must have. Or else it was still stuck in the body. It would be covered in blood. He was covered in blood.' She looked down at her clothes, at the red streaks on her white stomach. She said flatly, 'Look. I'm covered in blood.'

In a moment Lewis could tell she would begin screaming again. He said softly, hoping the old biddy wouldn't hear him, 'Did you recognise the boy?'

'Never saw him before in my life,' Gaby replied at once. 'But they all sleep in these flats. All the junkies. It's not safe here.'

There was a roar of agreement.

'Would you recognise him again?' Lewis asked.

'Oh definitely,' Gaby answered. 'He had evil written

all over his face. EVIL.'

A woman suddenly raced from the flats. 'Gaby!' she yelled.

Gaby leapt to her feet. 'Mum, I found the body! It was horrible.'

'I know,' her mother said, grabbing her and hugging her. 'I've had to walk down fifteen flights of stairs. None of the lifts are working.' She glared at Lewis as if it was his fault. 'And me with bad legs.'

'I'm afraid the lift will be out of commission for a while. Forensics will have to come, and we're just waiting for CID.'

This delay in getting the lift back in working order brought another roar from the crowd. Lewis couldn't believe them. 'You don't want to travel up and down with a dead body, do you?' But by the looks of some of this crowd they wouldn't mind a bit.

Lewis turned back to Gaby. 'By the way, what age are you?'

'Fourteen,' Gaby said.

She was immediately contradicted by her mother. 'She's thirteen.' Her alarm had now turned to anger. 'You'll not be fourteen till next week. And I've been pacing that floor for hours waiting for you to come in. What's the idea of staying out till this time in the morning?'

Lewis strode off. When a mother gets like that, he knew from long experience of his own, it was better to stand well back.

14

The chase was on. I didn't know these streets, hadn't been in this town long enough to know the back alleys, the gardens, the lanes. I ran on, sure I was going round in circles, sure I would suddenly find myself back where I started, surrounded by police. Caught.

NO!

I stopped, breathless, pressed myself into an alcove in the wall. I was still clutching the clothes I had taken from the line, stiff and damp from the chill night air. Didn't matter. I needed to change. I tore the blood-soaked clothes from me. They had nothing of my past in them. Nothing to help me remember who I was, where I had come from and why I was running.

The damp clothes chilled me. But the smell of them was fresh. This mother used some kind of softener on her boy's clothes, designer clothes too: the jeans, the sweater, even the T-shirt. Whoever owned these was well taken care of. For a second I wished I could swap places with that boy. Be him. Sleep in a warm bed, in a house, with a mother who loved me.

I leant further into the alcove. Why couldn't that be?

My thoughts were jerked out of dreamland. A huge

15

dog leapt in front of me, barking wildly. I couldn't move. I was terrified. The dog was a Rottweiler, and in the dark alley all I could see of the black beast were its wild eyes, its razor-sharp teeth, and all I could hear was a sound that would soon be alerting the neighbours.

I just hoped it wasn't hungry.

I had to get away from there before windows were flung open, before heads appeared, curious heads searching out the cause of the commotion. But how? The Rottweiler was bouncing from side to side, making escape impossible. But I had to escape. I had to get away from it.

I tightened my grip on the bloodstained clothes.

The bloodstained clothes. Maybe it was the blood that was driving the dog into such a frenzy.

Well, he could have them. I threw them full force into the Rottweiler's face. It was taken by surprise. It yelped, blinded. With the clothes draped over its head, the dog was turned in an instant from something fierce into something comical. I almost laughed. Stupid dog! It was in a panic. Didn't know what was happening.

I couldn't waste a moment. I leapt over the dog as it twisted round, trying to grab the clothes with its teeth, but only managing to bind them tighter round its head. As I ran, I heard a thud and a whimper behind me. I think the Rottweiler had fallen down a flight of stairs.

I didn't stop running. Up the alley, across a garden, over a hedge. Creeping slowly along the ground past lighted windows. Racing like the wind when it was safe.

And all the while I was sure someone was after me. That there was someone close behind me, following my every move. At any moment a hand would reach out and grab me.

🏃

Nobody recognised the body in the lift. At least that was what they said. This area was notorious for no one helping the police with their enquiries. No one could say why the man was here, or who he was visiting. He didn't live here, that was the only sure thing they seemed to agree on.

All the police's questions were answered with the same blank stare. Or with eyes averted.

'They'll be scared,' Guthrie told him. 'Living up here in these flats would scare anybody. Added to that of course, they say they're haunted.'

Lewis had heard that too. That there was something weird lurking in the flats. There had been reports of strange noises in the night and all that. Since most of the reports had come from daft old ladies, or drunks, Lewis refused to take them seriously.

Lewis thought everybody up here was potty. This wasn't his part of town. The police never put young inexperienced policemen to patrol in their own areas, but he lived close enough to know the notorious reputation it had for drugs and violence. There were gang wars going on in the town too. The local paper reported on them every day. Gangsters from the big city fighting for territory. Goodness, it was like the Wild West. Here at Wellpark Court the trouble was caused by the junkies or the homeless sleeping rough on the stairwell for warmth. Dealers buying and selling drugs.

There were already mutterings of discontent from the crowd.

'This is what we've got to put up with. Every night there's some kind of trouble. And what do the cops do? Nothing!' A woman had stepped forward. (Why was it always a woman? Lewis wondered.) She looked as if she'd just got out of bed. Her grey hair was standing on end, a lilac dressing gown wrapped round her. 'I sleep with a baseball bat beside my bed. What have you got to say to that?!' She didn't wait for Lewis's answer. Didn't want one. '"You better not plan to use that, madam."' She did a fair impression of Sean Connery. A few of the people standing around actually smiled. '"Or you'll be the one in trouble."' Ha! I use my baseball bat on them and I'm the one ends up in jail. And then this happens. We have a murder! Murder!' She waved her hands towards the lift, the doors stuck open now, the body, bloody and still on the floor.

'And do you recognise the dead man, madam?'

She didn't even glance his way. 'Never seen him before in my life,' she said at once.

Lewis nodded. All mouth, he was thinking, but no heart to get involved.

It was as if she read his thoughts. 'That's your job,' she snapped at him. 'You find out who he is.' Then she turned to the other tenants. 'Mind you, he looks as if he couldn't find his backside without a map.'

This time they all laughed. Local comedienne obviously, Lewis thought. He was learning that as a policeman it was more difficult to deal with the little old ladies in this town than it was with all the thugs and petty criminals he came across. Give him a thug any time. They were less dangerous.

His partner rescued him.

'Right, PC Ferguson. Move these people away. CID are on their way.'

CID. Lewis dreamt of being CID one day. He drew himself up to his full height. Tried to look like a real cop, with some authority. 'OK, ladies and gentlemen, let's get back to your own houses. Nothing to see here.'

That was rubbish, of course. There was plenty to see here. A dead body in a lift? If he was one of them they would have to drag him away. But he was keen to show his partner that he could take charge. 'Back to your houses, please.'

The mouth – he saw now she hadn't put her teeth in – opened again. 'There's no any lifts workin'. I live on the twelfth floor. Are you going to carry me up there?'

Lewis kept on smiling. Carry you up, missus, and then throw you from the top floor, was what he felt like telling her. All he said was, 'Sorry about that, madam.'

'PC Ferguson, will you escort the young lady and her mother into the flats?' Guthrie said.

The young lady's dramatic sobs increased at that point. Her mother tightened her grip around her.

'Make way, please,' Lewis said. Opening a path between the crowds, he led Gaby and her mother into the flats.

Gaby drew in her breath as she passed the open lift. Her mother tried to shield her from the sight. So did Lewis. But Gaby couldn't resist a peek inside. She flinched once again at the sight of all that blood. And then Lewis clocked her eyes as she saw the dead man's face for the first time. She hadn't looked before. Lewis saw her eyes flash, saw her swallow. Then her eyes darted away. She cowered closer to her mother.

But in that second Lewis knew that Gaby McGurk had recognised the dead man.

I had to stop. My heart was ready to burst. Was I having a heart attack? Could you have a heart attack this young? I began to cough, tried not to. Couldn't risk making a noise. I could hear shouts in the distance, and police sirens. The world coming alive. The noises seemed all around me. Closing in. No matter how I ran, it was never far enough. They were close, getting closer. Just like in my dream.

For a second, a microsecond, I caught a glimpse of that dream – then it was whipped away like a feather in the wind.

Or was it a memory? I found it hard to tell the difference.

My legs ached with pain.

Maybe it would be better if I let them catch me. Then there would be no more running. They would find doctors who would delve into my mind, unlock my memories. Plenty of time to do it. If I was convicted of this murder I'd be locked away for a long time. At Her Majesty's Pleasure, wasn't that the phrase? Where had I heard that? Why look for the real killer when you have a handy homeless boy with no alibi and no memory? A boy who was found in the lift with the body, both of them covered in blood.

So, why couldn't I just step out of the shadows now, walk towards those flats, my arms raised in surrender? And it would all be over. I took one step, just one, and knew I could never give myself up. What instinct held me back? Some other memory, locked inside me, warning me. I had to stay free, stay on the run.

I took one deep breath and turned, ready to set off again.

I let out a yell as I collided against someone, running round the corner, barging right into me. We tumbled in a tangle together. In the darkness, I was sure it must be the police. Panic set in. I fought like a tiger trying to push the person off, punching and kicking wildly.

'Hey, what are you playin' at, pal?'

It wasn't the police. It was a young guy, hardly more than a teenager. His voice was a whine. He yelped and rolled off me. In the strip of light from the street I could just make out his pasty face, his greasy hair. 'You pure hurt me there, pal.' The boy sat up, rubbed at his head, at his arms.

I stood up, and the boy looked at me. 'You runnin' from the cops as well?' He didn't need an answer to that one. 'I was sleepin' in that high flat. No' doin' anybody any harm, by the way, and there's sirens and people kickin' at me and shoutin', "Murder!" There's a corpse in the lift, man. He's dead, by the way. And I thought to myself, hey, you are out of here, pal.'

'You were sleeping in the flats?' I swallowed. 'So was I.'

I hoped I didn't look too guilty. Like I was the some-one who had just found that corpse.

The boy got to his feet. 'We've got to get out of here, pal. Do you know anywhere?'

I shook my head. 'I don't come from here. I don't know anywhere.'

There were shouts and calls coming from the dark-ness. The police moving closer. Both of us stiffened, listened for a moment in silence. Suddenly, the boy grabbed at my arm. ''Mon, I know somewhere.'

Here I was, running again, like a frightened animal in the forest, but this forest was filled with tenements and flats and boarded-up shops. Pulled along in the dark of the night through streets and alleys by this weird boy with the whining voice, this boy who could be leading me anywhere.

The boy turned for a moment and the street lights picked out the spots on his face. 'We're nearly there, by the way.'

We turned one more corner, ran up a pitch-black lane, and suddenly in front of me lay a small lake. An upturned shopping trolley lay abandoned, partially sub-merged in the water. The far side of the lake disappeared into darkness.

It was quiet here at this lake, right in the middle of the town. Civilisation seemed to lurk somewhere at the bottom of that dark alley. It was quiet too. Only our footsteps broke the silence. The boy didn't stop run-ning. He grabbed at my sleeve to pull me on. A duck suddenly squawked on the water, and the moon appeared from behind some clouds. Now I could see swans nesting on a tiny island in the middle of the lake, curled up in feathery sleep. We kept running, heading towards a small stone-built building on the other side of the lake.

'Is that where we're going?' I asked breathlessly.

The boy didn't even answer me. He just turned and nodded. The moon had disappeared again by the time we both fell against the door.

'How do we get inside?' I looked at the windows. Breaking one would make too much noise, and the old-fashioned panes were too small to let anyone, even a boy like me, pass through.

'I've got magic fingers, pal.' He waved his fingers about mysteriously. His voice was a whine. I was beginning to think that too much of this voice would get on your nerves. 'I can pick the lock. Good at that, me. You keep a look out to make sure nobody's coming.'

I turned back and looked across the lake. My whole body was shaking. Houses on the other side of the lake lay in darkness. Only one or two had lights in their windows. These houses were too far away from the commotion in the flats to be disturbed. I looked round quickly as I heard the door being opened.

The boy grinned and shouted a triumphant, 'Tara!' as if he was on the stage. He beckoned me to step inside like a magician showing me a magic trick.

It was only one room, with just two small windows to the front. There were shelves to the back with tools and small model yachts lying on them, an ancient white sink in one corner. 'Is this some kind of boathouse?' I asked.

The boy closed the door quietly. 'Naw. It's an Italian restaurant. What do you think, pal? The model boats are a dead giveaway.' Then he laughed as if he'd said something really funny.

I didn't laugh. 'You've been here before?' The boy was on his knees now, scrabbling around with his hands, searching for something in the dark. He looked back at me and grinned when he found it. A plug. He pushed it into a socket and almost immediately the bars of an old-fashioned electric fire began to glow softly.

'That answer your question?' he said. 'It's a good place. Nobody comes here during the week. Just the weekends, when all these daft men come and sail their model boats out there.' He threw a dismissive hand towards the lake. 'And what's even better is, we can have a cup of tea.' He stood up and started rummaging on a shelf for tea bags, and mugs and sugar. He turned for a moment, holding out a jar of coffee whitener. 'Only got this if you take milk,' he said.

'Take it black.' I didn't care how it came. As long as it was hot. Something warm inside me was all I needed. I couldn't stop myself from shaking. I wanted to cry. I was giving myself a headache trying to hold back the tears. I couldn't cry in front of this stranger. Though he seemed friendly, and definitely dim-witted, he was still a stranger. And what good would tears do anyway? Getting away from this town was all that mattered. Tomorrow I would think about where to go and what to do.

'I'm Eddie, by the way. What's your name, pal?'

My name? How could I admit I didn't know. I searched round in my mind for an answer.

Eddie 'by the way' gawped at me. 'It's not exactly a multiple-choice question, pal. I only asked your name.'

And it came to me, I don't know where from. A name that wasn't a name. 'Ram,' I said. 'My name's Ram.'

Lewis didn't like the feeling of being squeezed out by the big boys, and as soon as the CID arrived he knew that is exactly what would happen. He wanted to make an impression before they came. He wanted to find out as much as he could – it would stand him in good stead when he became a detective. DI Lewis Ferguson. It had a good solid ring to it. He could see himself now. A mixture of Sherlock Holmes, Columbo and Sean Connery.

'I wonder what floor he was on when he was attacked?' he said to his partner. He was sure Guthrie hadn't thought of that. He went on to explain. 'The girl pressed for the lift, so it had to be on another floor. She heard it coming down. So where had it come from and what was the dead man doing there?'

Before he could continue, his partner said, 'Come on, Lewis. He was probably just another junkie sleeping rough here. A fight broke out between two of them, probably fighting over drugs.'

Lewis thought about the dead man. His clothes soaked in blood didn't look as if they belonged to any kind of junkie. The white shirt was bright white, just-out-of-a-washing-machine white. And his face was the face of an older man, not a teenage junkie. 'He doesn't look like a junkie,' he said. 'He's clean shaven, wearing a gold chain. You'd think another junkie might have grabbed that.'

'Might not have had time; the lift doors open and the girl's standing there. Had to run.'

Sensible, logical. Just didn't sound right to Lewis.

'He might have been the dealer,' his partner said, and Lewis had to admit that sounded more reasonable.

Guthrie smiled. 'You're quite the detective, Lewis.'

Lewis tried not to blush. It was his worst bad habit. Always had been. But he was a grown man now, almost twenty-two, and a policeman to boot. Real policemen shouldn't blush. He should be past the blushing stage.

He blushed anyway.

'One thing's for sure,' Guthrie said. 'He didn't live here. Nobody recognised him.'

And Lewis remembered Gaby McGurk and the look on her face when she saw the dead man. Yes, somebody recognised him.

'Can I just go up and have a look, sir?'

'You mean before the CID come?' Lewis didn't have to answer that one. Guthrie smiled again. 'Off you go, Sherlock. You've got to walk up the stairs, remember?'

'No bother to me, I'm as fit as a fiddle.'

He met up with the toothless terror on the ninth floor. She was sitting, wheezing for breath, puffing on a cigarette. 'Aw, here he comes, Inspector Clouseau,' she said as soon as she saw him. 'You come to carry me up the stairs?'

Lewis made a quick exit to examine the landing. 'I'm

on police business, madam.'

'Aye, police business,' she called after him. 'Looking for somebody to give you a cup of tea. That's your kind of police business.'

He ignored her. He was looking on each floor for signs of a struggle, for bloodstains, on the floors, on doors, on the walls. Anything suspicious. The junkies had gone, running off into the night as soon as the first police siren had been heard in the distance.

On the fifteenth floor he found what he was looking for. A smudged trail of blood on the ground leading into the lift. As if something, or someone, had been dragged inside.

Lewis stood for a moment, wondering what to do next. Could he have been visiting somebody here? He walked around the landing, looking at each name plate, and there it was. McGurk. Gaby McGurk lived on this floor. Was that a coincidence? he wondered, remembering her look when she saw the dead man.

No more time to think. His personal radio crackled. It was Guthrie. 'Come on down, Lewis. CID have arrived.'

A cold voice came over the mobile. The Boss. 'This better be in hand. I don't want any more cock-ups.'

The Wolf was confident, sure of himself. 'It is. That's a promise. It's all taken care of. I don't need any help.'

'I'll be the judge of that,' the Boss said. 'Do you know where he is?'

'I'm on to it, don't worry. The boy's as good as dead,'

29

the Wolf said.

There was a long pause. 'Make it look like an accident,' the Boss said. 'Don't want the cops looking into any more murders.'

Eddie wanted me to talk. He rabbited on, urging me to do the same. He wanted to know who I was, where I had come from. But I didn't want to talk. Finally, he gave up. 'Try and get a bit of sleep, pal. I'll keep watch.'

How I wished I could sleep but there was no real rest for me. If I drifted off all I had were dreams. Dreams of blood. Rivers of blood, great tower blocks with blood streaming from every window. And in the dreams I was running again, chased by faceless people, caught by disembodied hands and dragged into a courtroom. But it wasn't a courtroom, it was a lift. A judge was there sitting in a corner, all dressed up in red robes, pointing a finger at me. 'Guilty!' he was saying, shouting it. Screaming it. And suddenly I was surrounded by police. They filled the lift and they were grabbing at me, and the floor of the lift suddenly opened. Blackness yawned up at me, and I was falling, down, down, and yelling, 'It wasn't me!'

I jumped awake with Eddie hauling at my jacket, shaking me. 'Hey, shut up, wee man,' he said in a low growl. 'Somebody'll hear ye.'

I sat up quickly. 'Was I talking in my sleep?'

Eddie laughed. 'It wasnae me!' He held out his hands to the glow of the fire. 'What d'ye mean, it wasnae you?'

Should I confide in him, tell him about finding the

body? For a moment I wanted to talk about it. Wanted to let it all pour out. How long had it been since I had had someone to confide in, to talk to? How I wished I could remember. Even talking to this idiot, Eddie, might help.

Eddie pulled at my shirt again, flashed me an idiot grin. That decided me. It would be a sad day if he was all I could confide in. 'Come on, tell us? I think you're hiding something there, pal.'

'It was just a dream.' I lay back down, though sleep had gone from me now. 'It was just a dream.'

Eddie looked at me, waiting for me to say something else. Then he grinned stupidly. 'Aye, it wasnae me either, pal. That's what they all say, in't it? Just try not to make a noise from now on.'

I wanted to go back to sleep, but my mind was too full. As soon as I closed my eyes, I saw the dying man in the lift again, saw his frightened eyes. I had watched a man die tonight. I remembered the way the man had pulled me desperately closer. And those last muttered jumble of words. What was it he had said again? I couldn't think. Nothing important. The ravings of a dying man.

And the blood.

It was mostly the blood I couldn't forget, and the memory of it made me shake again. I tried desperately to get the image out of my mind.

I had thought when I arrived here – was it only yesterday? – that I might be able to hide out for a few days at least. Now it seemed I had to be on the run again.

Tomorrow I was getting shot of this town.

Gabriella McGurk woke up next morning to find herself a star. The phone in the house started ringing at seven o'clock. She tried to sleep through the call, but heard her mother muttering, then the phone being slammed down. She was still fuming with anger because Gaby had come in so late – what would you do with mothers? She'd found a body, for goodness' sake! She'd even seen the murderer! Yet all her mother could go on about was the fact that she'd come in too late.

Gaby turned over, ready to fall into a deep sleep once again. Her mother threw open the bedroom door. Gaby opened one eye to look at her. She was standing with the light from the hall behind her, her uncombed hair standing on end. She was the scariest-looking silhouette Gaby had ever seen.

'Right you! Up!' she yelled at Gaby.

Gaby glanced at the clock. It clicked on to exactly seven o'clock. She'd only got to bed at six, what with police asking questions and everything. And then she didn't get to sleep for ages. That wasn't enough for anyone. 'It's too early,' she moaned. 'I'm tired.'

'So am I,' her mother roared. 'And I've got work to go

to. I've got a funeral today.'

Gaby slid under the covers. Nothing was going to make her get up this early. Not today. If the police needed to talk to her they could just wait to ask her more questions. She'd told them all she knew anyway. She'd been traumatised finding that body. She'd probably need counselling, she decided. That should be good for a couple of weeks off school at least.

'If that was the cops phoning, tell them I'm too upset to talk.'

'It wasn't the police,' her mother said. 'It was a reporter from the *Globe*. He's coming over to talk to you.' Gaby was alert in an instant, sleep leaping from her. The *Globe* was the local paper. She'd always thought the name was a bit pretentious – it only served their small town. However, at the moment that didn't matter. She was going to be interviewed.

'And he's bringing a photographer,' her mother added.

The icing on the cake! Gaby leapt out of bed. 'A photographer? Look at my hair.' She caught sight of herself in the mirror. 'I'll have to wash it and . . . what am I going to wear?'

'Your school uniform maybe?' her mother suggested.

Gaby ignored that. 'What time are they coming?'

'They'll be here by eight o'clock. And they better be finished by the time I leave for work.'

Gaby let out a yell. 'Eight o'clock! I'll never be ready by then.'

Lewis's mother slapped more bacon and sausages on her son's plate. 'You're eating me out of house and home!' she said.

Lewis was looking forward to his day. He needed a good feed. He'd only had a couple of hours sleep yet he felt fresh and ready for anything. He'd told Guthrie about the blood on the fifteenth floor, and he had led him to one of the CID officers, DI Warren, and Lewis saw with some satisfaction that he was impressed, maybe even a little annoyed at his enterprise. He could almost read his thoughts: *He's a smart one, this boy. Here's one to watch. Be after my job soon.* Lewis could see his seat on the detective squad being dusted down for him already.

His mother, though she pretended she wasn't interested, was keen to know all the details.

'I can't tell you anything,' he reminded her. 'This is police business.'

'Is it true he was stabbed? Covered in blood and a young girl saw the killer running from the building? Gaby McGurk I think her name is.'

'Wait a minute, this only happened in the middle of the night. How do you know all this?'

'Jungle drums,' she said. 'You know what this town is like – bad news travels like diarrhoea.'

His mother had a wonderful turn of phrase at times, but no class.

'Do you want me to find out who the dead man is?' she asked.

Lewis had to laugh. 'I think the police can do that themselves, dear.'

'Somebody'll know him,' she went on, slapping another couple of eggs on his plate. 'They'll just not be talking to you about it.'

And Lewis remembered Gaby McGurk, and realised he hadn't told DI Warren about his suspicions there. But that was all they were, suspicions. What would be the point?

'You should let me go undercover,' she said, warming to the theme. 'I'd soon find out who he was and what he was doing there.' It seemed she had already figured out the whole thing.

'I don't suppose you could come up with the name and address of the killer while you're at it.'

'He'll be one of the junkies that sleep up there. It's about time the police did something about that. I wouldn't live up there for a pension.'

'And neither would they if you did live up there.' He finished the last of his breakfast and stood up. 'I don't know what we need the police for when we've got you.'

'Oh, we need them to give out parking tickets. Killers on the loose and what do the police do? Give out decent people fines for parking on a double-yellow line.' She was still smarting over the fine she'd got two days ago. She thought Lewis could have had it quashed for her. 'What's the point of having a son on the force if he can't pull strings for you?'

'Wait till I'm a detective, maw,' he told her. 'I'll get you your own parking space anywhere you want.'

He lifted his hat from the hall table. 'Right, where are my car keys?' he asked.

His mother laughed. 'Ha! Some detective you are.

How are you supposed to find a murderer, when you can't even find your car keys?'

And on this uplifting note Lewis left for the station.

'So, Miss McGurk, you saw the murderer?' The photographer, a young man with a faceful of spots, chose just that moment to take a photograph, when Gaby had her mouth open to speak. She just hoped that wasn't the one that went into the paper.

The photographer had the cheek to complain. 'If you could try to look serious, you know, as if you'd been through some kind of trauma. You're grinning away there as if you've just won the lottery.'

Gaby glared at him. She bared her teeth ready with an answer. And that's when he took another picture. She decided she didn't like him.

The reporter was another matter. He was kind of cute, she thought.

'I want to know how you felt the moment, the very instant that those doors opened,' the reporter encouraged her. Gaby didn't need that much encouragement.

Gaby closed her eyes, reliving the moment. 'He was bending over him, like this.' She hung over the floor and looked up, hoping for another photograph. Spotty was too busy fiddling with his lens. 'He was covered in blood. He looked right at me. I could see evil in his eyes. When you live in a high flat you can spot evil right away.'

Her mother, sitting at the table flicking through a magazine, tittered.

Gaby was pleased to note that the reporter was scribbling away like mad. She carried on. 'Then he jumped up and leapt at me. I knew I was going to be his next victim. I screamed, just like this.' Gaby let out an ear-scrunching scream. The reporter almost jumped back. 'I think that's what saved my life. He pushed past me and he ran.'

'Yeah, I think I would run if you screamed at me,' Spotty said. He was definitely beginning to annoy her.

'I'm telling you, he had evil written all over his face.'

The reporter stopped scribbling and looked at her. 'Really?'

'He should be easy to spot then,' the photographer said sarcastically.

Gaby had had enough of him. 'He did. You wait till they catch him. You'll see.'

'Evil written all over his face.' The reporter slapped his notebook shut. 'That will make a great headline.'

Lewis wasn't happy. First on the murder scene, and now he was relegated to behind the desk at the station. The full force of the law was searching for the boy seen running from the scene, and Lewis was standing behind a desk, trying to make sense of a story about an assaulted dog.

'You think someone did that deliberately, Mr Brown, assault your Rottweiler?' The man had his Rottweiler tucked under his arm. It still looked dazed.

'I found him unconscious at the bottom of a flight of

stairs. Somebody deliberately wrapped him in these!' He flung a plastic bag filled with clothes on the counter. 'They were wound round his head. The poor mutt couldn't see where he was going and fell down the stairs. Knocked himself out. That's cruelty to animals.'

Lewis tried not to laugh.

The man went on. 'I've had to take him to the vet. He can't stop shaking. Rottweilers are sensitive animals, you know.'

Lewis opened the bag. He took a deep breath. There was a shirt and trousers, and a thin jacket. All of them were covered with a dark red stain. Blood.

Lewis's reward for finding the bloodstained clothes was to be sent round doors in the neighbourhood, asking questions. An improvement from behind the desk, but not much. He wasn't even sent to Wellpark Court, where he would be sure to find out something, but round the walk-up apartments nearby.

The sergeant saw the disappointment in his face when he told him.

'Basic police work,' he told him. 'It's the way we find out everything.'

So while the CID took on all the exciting roles, he was left to ask questions. Had anyone seen anything suspicious? In this part of town, everyone was a potential suspect.

He walked round all morning, going from door to door. He was insulted regularly. Many of the people round here had no time for the police and made sure he knew it.

He was ridiculed.

'Ha, here comes PC Plod.'

This from a ten-year-old. He was a pretty fierce-looking ten-year-old or Lewis would definitely have cuffed him.

One old lady even had him in the house chasing her budgie to get him back in the cage.

'His name's Sweetie-Pie. He might come if you ask him nicely.'

'Nice' was a word Sweetie-Pie didn't seem to understand. But when Lewis threatened him with kitchen foil – 'If you don't get in that cage in ten seconds, you'll be wrapped and in that oven at Gas Mark 10!' – Sweetie-Pie was back in the cage before you could say 'roast budgie'.

But really, he thought, was this why he had joined the police force? Was this the way he was going to become a detective?

And then, just before he was ready to have a tea break, he knocked on the door that was going to change everything.

The woman who opened the door to him was built like a giant marshmallow. 'It's good of you to come so quick,' she said at once, and beckoned Lewis inside her spotless hallway. 'I thought something like this would be too trivial for the police to bother with, especially when there's a serial killer on the loose.'

'A serial killer? Who told you that?'

'That's what I heard. A string of murders from here to Land's End.'

'A bit of an exaggeration, madam,' Lewis said. How

did these stories spread? Then he remembered his mother. She was probably the one who started them.

In the living room Lewis turned to the lady. He was about to explain to her why he was here. He didn't get the chance. He should have known that with most women once they started talking they didn't even pause for breath.

'I never noticed till this morning,' she said. 'I looked out my window and then I remembered I'd left my washing out all night. I never do that. I always bring it in. I think it's so common to leave washing out all night, but I was watching a great film on the telly. A real weepie. I cried and I cried and it made me forget everything and then I looked out and there were my sheets and my pillowcases, and my . . .' She paused for breath and blushed. 'My smalls.'

Smalls? This woman must need knickers the size of a small African country.

'And then I saw them and they weren't there. My boy Jimmy's jeans and jumper. His best as well. Them designer ones, the only ones he'll wear when he goes to the disco. They had been snapped right off the line. Would you believe the cheek of that?'

The bloodstained clothes and the unconscious Rottweiler two streets away, and now, a boy's designer gear stolen from a nearby garden. Lewis had a feeling he knew exactly what their prime suspect was wearing now.

I brushed down the jeans. Eddie was watching me. 'Nice gear,' he said. 'You must have money to buy them.'

I held his gaze. 'I nicked them,' I said, hoping to impress him.

'When?' Eddie asked.

It was a time before I answered. 'Ages ago.'

'What are you acting so funny for? I'm trying to help you here.' Eddie's voice was harsh.

'I'm not acting funny. I'm scared. There was a murder last night.'

Eddie still stared at me. 'You never saw anything, did you?'

He didn't wait for my answer, wasn't really asking a question. It was a statement. 'You never saw anything.'

'It's still scary,' I said, and to prove it I held out my hand, palm down and it was trembling. 'See?' I said.

'I'm scared as well, wee man,' Eddie grinned. 'We'll help each other.' He looked out of the window. Cars were beginning to cruise down a distant street, morning life beginning. 'I'm going to run over to the shops, nick some rolls, eh?' He stood up, stared at me. 'You gonny run as soon as I'm out that door?'

I shook my head. 'Like the sound of the rolls.'

Eddie laughed again. 'You wait here, put on the kettle, we'll have a cuppa and a roll when I come back, sound good?'

In the clear morning air I could watch Eddie stumble off round the pathway towards the shops. Had I found a friend? He was daft, but he seemed genuinely to want to help me. Could I trust Eddie? Maybe it was time to trust somebody. I was so hungry I couldn't think straight. There was a mist rising over the lake and a family of swans sailing in a dignified line across the water. Peace

41

and tranquillity. Why couldn't my life have some peace and tranquillity? I was too hungry now to think. I'd wait for Eddie. Once I had some food inside me, I'd be able to decide what to do.

Someone else was watching through binoculars, trained on the small clubhouse on the lake. The Wolf. He saw the boy standing by the doorway, and tensed, waiting to see if he would run. That couldn't be allowed to happen. The police couldn't get him first. That would be too dangerous. But the boy at the door only stood watching. He hardly moved, his clothes were too big for him. He was small, and his thick dark hair looked matted. He looked scared too. Good. Let him stay scared, the Wolf thought. He wouldn't be scared for long anyway. His hours were numbered.

Gaby's mother wasn't finished with her. She was giving her a really hard time. She had ranted and raved since the reporter and his spotty colleague had left. 'You still haven't told me exactly where you were till four o'clock in the morning!'

Gaby had hoped her mother would have forgotten about that. Some hope. For a moment she thought about saying she had gone to Auntie Ellen's house on the fifth floor. Gaby had the key of the flat while her auntie was on holiday. It was her job to check on the mail and water her plants. Should she say she'd gone there, and fallen asleep watching her favourite soap . . . ? No, not worth it. Her mother had probably phoned there first, would know it was a blatant lie. With hardly a pause she answered, 'I was at my pal's house. Zoe's. We forgot the time. We were having such a laugh.' The lie came easily. She lied so often.

'Zoe. The wee one with the face like a donkey?'

'That's cruel. She's not that ugly. I'll get you her phone number. You can ask her yourself.'

Her mother snapped at her. 'Oh, if only your dad was here. Thank goodness he'll be back tonight.'

Why wouldn't her mother ever listen to her. 'He's not my dad!' She said it so often she sounded like a broken record. Big Dan was her mother's boyfriend. Though at her age Gaby thought her mother should be past boyfriends. Everything had changed when he moved in with them. Her mother was besotted with Dan. How Gaby wished it could be just the two of them again.

Her mother let out one of her exasperated sighs. 'You don't give him a chance, Gaby. All he wants is for us to be a family. He's really fond of you.' She was waiting for Gaby to agree with that. Gaby sucked in her cheeks and said nothing.

'Right! You're grounded, girl,' she said at last.

You better believe it, Gaby thought. Because she didn't want to go out, not now. Not if it meant that the boy, the one who had stabbed the man in the lift, might come back for her.

And there was something else worrying her. Not just the boy in the lift, but the man lying on the ground, the man who had died.

A man she recognised.

She had seen him only hours before – alive and well, and scared to death.

Eddie threw open the door of the clubhouse. His face was red with excitement. 'Everybody's talkin' about it. Talkin' about you, by the way. It has to be you. A boy your age, dark hair. They're saying you killed that guy. Stabbed him.'

I was on my feet, ready to run. Could I get past Eddie,

get to the door, escape? Or had Eddie brought a squad of police with him? Eddie was scrawny, but he was a lot taller than me. Murder, however, didn't seem to bother him. 'I don't care if you killed him. He probably deserved it.'

'I didn't kill anybody. I promise. I found him in the lift.'

Eddie looked as if he was struggling to understand what I was telling him. I hurried on. 'That's why I was so scared. Honest.'

Eddie didn't say anything for a moment, as if the duff computer that was his brain was trying to work things out. 'You would have been covered in blood, they said.'

I nodded my head. 'That's why I had to change my clothes. I stole these off a clothesline.'

Eddie seemed to find that funny. 'Good for you, wee man.' He threw two rolls at me. 'Buttered as well,' he said. 'I only steal the best.'

I caught the rolls, one in each hand. 'I've boiled the kettle.'

'Good boy,' Eddie said. He sat down and rubbed his hands together. 'Now, I want you tell me everything. All the gory details.'

And as we sat in front of the fire, warming our hands round the mugs of tea, and eating the rolls hungrily, I told Eddie everything. I didn't have to make anything up. The truth was gory enough, even for Eddie. Everything, except the fact I had no memory. That just seemed too unbelievable.

'And you were there in the lift with him when he died? That must have been dead scary.'

My voice trembled. 'It was. He was covered in blood, and his eyes were open and just staring at me.'

Eddie gasped suddenly. 'He was still alive? I'm just thinking. Did he tell you who did it? Did he tell who stabbed him?' His mouth fell open waiting for the answer.

'No, he didn't. He was too weak to talk.' And yet I still remembered the strength in the hand that pulled me close.

'Go on, you can tell me. I won't tell anybody.'

If I had known anything I would have told Eddie. I was so glad of someone to talk to, to tell. But there was nothing. 'The man was dying, Eddie. He was just rambling.'

Eddie's eyes went wide. 'Rambling. That means he was talking. What was he rambling about?'

I shrugged. It all seemed so pointless now. 'Something about his heartbeat stopping.'

That seemed to impress Eddie. 'Heartbeat? Wow!' He thought about it. 'Do you think he knew he was dying?'

The hole in the stomach might have been a giveaway, I almost said, but stopped myself. Maybe not the time for a joke.

'I think he did,' was all I said. 'But he definitely never told me who stabbed him.'

'That was everything he said?' Eddie sounded disappointed. He had probably wanted the man to gasp out his killer's name with his dying breath – maybe adding his address for good measure.

'I can see how you wanted to run. You had to get away from there. You're the chief suspect. Listen.' Eddie stood up. 'You've got to get out of this town. But you'd get caught in five minutes, the cops are everywhere. Look. I've got mates. Good mates. They can help us.'

The way he said 'us' made me feel better. As if we were in this together. I was no longer alone.

'Can you trust them?' I asked, and Eddie looked affronted.

'Can I trust them? They're my mates. Of course I can trust them.' He grinned. 'You wait here, pal. Big Eddie's going for the cavalry. We're going to get you out of this here town!'

He slapped me on the back and for the first time since I could remember, I was laughing too. I was going to be OK. Someone was going to help me.

I watched Eddie circle the lake, turning back once to wave at me. I waved back. Was this what it felt like to have a friend? Someone to trust. Even if it was only daft Eddie. I settled myself on the floor, leant back against the wall. I could sleep now. It was going to be OK. Eddie would come back, he would have people who could help me. People who knew this town, who could get me out of here. I felt as if I had been alone so long. So long. My eyes grew heavy as the heat from the fire warmed me. It was only in the final seconds I remembered the rest of the dying man's words. Words that still made no sense. *Heartbeat. Stop. Four teeth*. Like a telegram. *Four teeth*. In spite of everything it still made me laugh to think about it. I didn't understand them, neither would Eddie. But as soon as he came back I would tell him anyway. Eddie would get a kick out of that.

'So it would seem this young man took off the bloodied clothes he was wearing.' (Lewis didn't add he had caused grievous bodily harm to a Rottweiler in the process.) 'He stole a sweater and jeans from a line and he's now kitted out in designer gear. Sir.' Lewis almost forgot to add that final 'sir'.

Guthrie had taken him once again to see CID officer Warren. And he had listened to him, once again, stern and unsmiling. Did someone tell him that was the way you had to look if you were a detective? Lewis wasn't sure he could manage that. Warren stared at Lewis as if he didn't believe him. Lewis was every bit as tall as this man, yet he still felt as if he was looking up to him. He kept staring at Lewis for a long time, saying nothing. Finally, the hint of a smile came to his mouth. If you blinked you would have missed it. 'Good work. Ferguson, isn't it?'

Lewis tried not to blush. But it was impossible. How embarrassing was it for a grown man to blush? 'Just police work, sir. Routine police work.'

'It's you boys and your routine police work, the boys on the front line who plod on every day, you're the ones that are the eyes and ears of the community. We couldn't solve any crimes without you and your routine police work.'

All that didn't sound like a compliment to Lewis. He didn't like the sound of that 'plod on'. Was this guy taking the mickey? He'd show them who could plod on! Lewis decided then and there that he was going to solve this case. He'd show them all. He'd make a detective faster than anyone else in the force ever had before. And already he remembered he had a clue that none of the rest of them had.

Gaby McGurk.

She was hiding something. And he was going to find out what it was.

I slept. But in my dreams I was still running – never getting anywhere. Always afraid. I hated myself. Even in these dark dreams, I hated myself for being so afraid. Had I always been such a wimp? Or had something made me so afraid? The thing I couldn't remember? I wanted to stop, turn round and face whoever, whatever was after me. Yet I barely dared a glance. Because if I was caught it would be the end.

Sometimes, I didn't care – like now.

Couldn't I keep on sleeping? Waking up was never a relief anyway, only a continuation of the nightmare. If I didn't wake up I would never have to face the real world again.

I was warm in my dream and breathless. The running was making me cough. And the cough and the heat were waking me up. I rolled over, still coughing, and tried to open my eyes.

There was a fog all around me. The fog from the lake had seeped into the tiny clubhouse. The room was filled with it. I tried to stand up, but my lungs were choked with the fog and the heat and . . .

My eyes snapped open. Alert in an instant. Not fog. Smoke.

The clubhouse was on fire!

I could hardly stand up. My eyes smarted with the smoke. I couldn't stop coughing. I could see nothing. What was happening?

I threw myself on the floor to suck at whatever air was left down there, began to claw my way towards the door. The heat drove me back. I could see the flames now, licking round the door, round the window. I was trying desperately to think, not to panic. How could I get out of here? The door and the window were alive with fire. There were no other exits. I was trapped.

A moment ago, in my dream, I had wanted to stay asleep for ever. Now I knew I didn't want to die. Not like this.

Water. Water puts out fire. But all there was here was an old sink. No handy fire extinguisher. Just a sink.

And the blanket I'd been lying on.

My brain began to clear. I grabbed the blanket and pulled myself up to the sink The tap was stiff. I had to use both hands to turn it. The sudden surge of water sprayed my face, cooled me for a second. I plunged the blanket into the sink, let the water seep into it, soak it through. I had to stay conscious, but it was hard. Now I could hardly breathe. I was choking for breath.

The blanket weighed heavy as I dragged it from the sink. I could hardly lift it, but I had to. I draped it around me like a cloak, covered my head with it. The water soaked into me. I blinked to see where I was going, heading for the door, heading for the flames, burning orange flames. Heading for fresh air. Then I lowered the blanket over my head, and charged.

On a hill above the lake the Wolf watched. Binoculars were trained on the clubhouse as it was swallowed by fire. No one could survive that. Certainly not one solitary boy. Their problem was solved. A homeless boy would die in a fire started by vandals. End of story.

A tragedy soon forgotten.

Then *he* appeared, hidden by a blanket already smoking from the heat.

Outside, the boy threw the blanket off his shoulders. He looked around feverishly. Even from this distance there was terror in his eyes. Then he was off. Running into the trees, running towards the hills, gone in an instant.

The Wolf dropped the binoculars. Every muscle in his body tensed. This shouldn't be happening. He wasn't the kind who made mistakes. Yet the boy was still alive.

But not for long.

He began to follow him.

Lewis and his partner were on the scene before the fire brigade. But not before the usual suspects of nosy neighbours gathered round the burning building. He tried to move them back, use his authority. Most of them didn't want to go, pushed against him, craning their necks for a better view.

'Nothing to see here. On your way.' Here he was again, talking nonsense. There was plenty to see here. A fire, and everybody loves a fire.

'I saw somebody running out of here,' a woman said. 'He went thataway.' She pointed to the hills. Lewis stared at her. She'd obviously seen too many cowboy films. Thattaway, indeed. Then, another thought jumped on the back of the first. Was there anybody else trapped in there? But it was impossible now to get anywhere near the small clubhouse. If there was anyone else left in there . . . they would be dead.

The thought of a charred body, such a horrible end, chilled him. Now he noticed the wet blanket that lay on the ground. Someone with the knowledge and foresight to know how to save himself, how to escape.

'It would be vandals that started it,' the woman said.

A murmur of agreement went up from the crowd.

'Did you see any of them?' By their blank stares he knew they hadn't.

Everything was put down to vandalism. And they were probably right. The town was terrorised by boys with nothing better to do than torch empty properties. But it usually happened during the night, not during the day when traffic was about, when people were up.

But this property hadn't been empty. Had they known someone was inside, wanted them to die? Or was that an accident?

'A murder last night, and now this.' It was an old woman again. Lewis would rather face a whole band of terrorists than a handful of old women. If the Terminator had been up against an army of old women, with their teeth rattling, waving their Zimmers about like offensive weapons, he wouldn't have found it so easy to save the world.

This one was poking him in the chest. That was the other thing about old women. They had no respect for a uniform.

'You lot do nothing to protect the public. Bring back capital punishment. That's what they need.' And this was supposed to be the gentle sex! 'If we had capital punishment they wouldn't do it again in a hurry. You can bet your bottom dollar on that.'

They wouldn't be able to, Lewis was thinking. They'd be dead.

He tried to change the subject. 'This is the model-yacht clubhouse, isn't it?' He tried to avoid the old woman's eyes, hoping somebody sensible would answer him. No chance. The rest of them seemed quite happy to let this dottery old fool be their spokeswoman.

'Clubhouse! Ha! It's never used by them. The drug dealers use it, or boys and lassies for . . .' She hesitated. 'Well, you know what they're using it for.'

At last someone else spoke. 'Perfect spot for their drug dealing. Right in the middle of the estate, but secluded. Nobody can spot you there.'

'I'm glad it's burning,' the old woman said.

'Who owns it? Do you know?' This time he asked her. She probably knew the answer anyway. He had a feeling she knew everything.

'Barry McKay. Does he not own everything? He owns half the town. This'll be an insurance job.' She glanced around at her fan club. They all nodded in agreement. 'He'll have got some of his boys to torch this place, so he can collect on the insurance.'

'Make up your mind, madam,' Lewis said. 'Vandals or gangsters?'

'They're all the same. Barry McKay's got them all working for him. He's got everybody in his pocket. Including the cops.'

'You seem to have solved the crime, madam. Have you ever thought of joining the police force?' The sarcasm was lost on her. She rattled her teeth with her tongue.

'You wouldn't have a hose up your jumper?' Lewis said finally. 'You could put out the fire as well.'

I didn't stop running. I wanted to leave that burning building far behind me. I had dropped the smouldering blanket from my shoulders, but I couldn't leave behind the stench of the smoke and fire. Through woods and towards the hills I ran, not knowing where I was heading, not caring. Why had I ever come to this town? I had a foggy memory of arriving here, so vague it seemed like a dream. My first clear memory began with that gloomy stairwell, with the lift and the dying man. Was it because of the river I had come here? Maybe I had thought I could take a boat somewhere. Or was it the views over the hills that had drawn me here? I stopped for a moment, leaning my hands on my knees to get my breath back. Those hills seemed to be hemming me in now, trapping me in this town.

Who could have started that fire? Because it was deliberate. I knew that. The door, the windows, alive with flame. No escape. Targeting me? But why would anyone want to target me? I didn't know anyone in this town. Cancel that. I didn't know anyone – full stop. So there was no reason for anyone to kill me. Or was there? How could I know?

Could it have been Eddie? Had he come back with his junkie mates and decided it would be a laugh to set the clubhouse alight?

But Eddie had said he was going for help. No, the fire was either caused by boys with nothing better to do, or it was deliberately meant to harm me.

But who else but Eddie had known I was there? And why would anyone want to get rid of me?

No, I decided. It had to be just my bad luck to be in the wrong place at the wrong time.

The Wolf was after the boy, and he wouldn't lose him this time. Following discreetly so as not to alert him. The further away from the town he was, the better. He would finish him here, up on the hills. Up here a body could be hidden, and never be found. He should know. He'd hidden many a body here himself. It still had to look like an accident. A fatal accident.

Gaby was waiting at the shop for the local paper to be delivered. At least she hadn't had to go to school. She'd spent most of the day being interviewed by CID. Not as glamorous as it sounded. She felt that all she had done all day was answer questions, the same questions over and over. And they had treated her as if she was just some daft girl. As soon as she could she'd gone up to the newsagent's near the school to meet her mates.

Her friends at least treated her as if she was a celebrity. They met her at the shop, eager to hear all her news. Zoe was there, not quite so pleased to see her.

'You told your mum you were with me last night. She phoned me . . . and I had to lie about it.'

Gaby shrugged. 'That's what friends are for, Zoe.'

'So where did you go?'

Gaby thought about telling her, decided against it. Zoe could never keep her mouth shut. 'Doesn't matter. Nowhere important.'

She was saved from more grilling from Zoe by the papers arriving. Gaby grabbed at the top paper as soon as the pile was slapped down on the ground in front of her. 'Look, I'm on the front page. It's a terrible photo. I look awful in it.'

Her friends assured her it was a really good photograph. Gaby actually thought so too. She just wanted them to tell her.

'What do you think of the headline?' she asked.

EVIL WRITTEN ALL OVER HIS FACE

'Did you actually say that?' her friend Zoe asked.

'Well, of course I did. It wouldn't be in the paper if I hadn't said it, would it?'

Zoe shrugged. 'My dad says you can't believe anything you read in the papers.'

'Well, you can tell your dad this time he can. I did say that.'

'Do you think he was the killer, Gaby?'

Gaby had no doubts about it. 'Of course he was.' She suddenly remembered what the boy had said to her. 'He confessed. He said, "I did it." I forgot about that.'

Zoe looked as if she didn't believe her. As if Gaby always told lies.

Gaby carried on, trying her best not to get annoyed at Zoe. 'There was definitely evil in his eyes, blood all over him. You should have seen him. He tried to attack me, you know. He lunged at me with the knife.'

'You never mentioned a knife before!'

That really annoyed Gaby. Was Zoe trying to say she was making this all up? She tried to remember every detail of what happened that night. The lift doors opening, the boy standing there. He must have been holding a knife, because the knife hadn't been found. She tried to

57

picture a glint of steel, was convinced she could.

'Well, he *had* a knife,' she said. 'It was covered in blood.'

Other friends crowded round her, eager for the gruesome details. Gaby had suddenly become much more popular.

'Do you know what this means, Gaby?' Zoe said finally.

'Yeah,' Gaby was sure she did know. 'They'll probably want to interview me on television.' She saw a future stretch ahead of her, making such an impact that she was asked back, to be a newsreader, maybe, hosting her own television show, getting a big contract in America – the toast of New York. Oprah Winfrey, eat your heart out.

'No,' Zoe said flatly. 'This means you're the only one who can identify the killer and they've got your name and address on the front page. If this was a book and he was a serial killer, you'd be the next victim.'

Sometimes she couldn't believe Zoe! 'Thank you very much! You're a real comfort, Zoe.' Gaby tutted. The boy she had seen didn't look like a serial killer – he was too young. She pictured him again, covered in blood, reaching out to her. The memory of him made her feel sick. He wasn't a serial killer. And the thought slipped into her mind that maybe he wasn't a killer at all. Maybe it hadn't been evil she had seen in his eyes . . . but fear.

The thought slipped away as fast as it had come. It *was* evil she had seen. Had to be.

11

It would be dark soon. There was hardly any day here. Morning came late, and a few hours later, night fell. The February light was already being swallowed by the darkness. I had to find a place to shelter. A safe place. I rubbed at my arms to try to warm myself, but I couldn't stop the ice-cold air seeping through my clothes. There was no shelter here on these moors. I looked all around. I was heading towards a reservoir. Only one sign of civilisation – a burnt-out car lying on the bank. If I couldn't find anywhere else, that might just be where I ended up tonight. An icy mist was already hovering over the town, on the water. I would die of cold if I slept in the open. They would find my stiff, dead body curled up on the grass, half eaten by sheep.

No – sheep were vegetarians. It wouldn't be sheep who ate me, it would be wild animals.

A wolf.

Soon darkness would fall and with it a heavy frost, already sparkling on the stiff grass. Nowhere to hide. Why had I headed for the hills in the first place? Scary stuff here. Weird noises all around, hoots in the woods, rustling in the pine trees that surrounded me.

Over the hills and far away. Was that some old rhyme lodged somewhere in my memory, or had I just made it up?

I trudged along the road. Surely I would find somewhere to hide soon. A shepherd's hut maybe, even a bus shelter. Anywhere.

I heard a car in the distance, coming closer. But I'd been hearing a car all day, the same car, I was sure. As if it was cruising behind me, watching me. Whenever I would turn and look, there was nothing. It had to be my imagination, I kept thinking, and yet, a few moments later, I would hear it again. Coming after me. I listened now, saw its headlights beam across the darkening sky. No mistake this time. I leapt into the bushes. I would hide till it drove past.

But it didn't pass. Instead, at the brow of the hill it purred to a halt and waited. The lights stayed on. They seemed to be staring straight at me. As if the someone inside knew I was there. I backed further into the undergrowth. A dark figure stepped out of the car. A menacing silhouette against the darkening sky. I took another backwards step. A twig snapped under my feet. It was enough to give my position away. The figure straightened. It was as if he could see in the dark. His face turned to the spot where I was hiding. Who was this man? Now the figure began to move, to run, towards me. Coming after me. But why? How did he know I was here? Had he been following me all day? Since I had run from the boathouse? I began to run too. Looking for a hiding place, eager to be away from this dark figure looming out of the night. I glanced back once, saw nothing, but still knew he was after me. That was scarier than anything else, that I couldn't see where he was. My heart was about to burst. Gorse and nettles scratched at my skin. Still I ran. I snatched a look at the headlights still shining on the road, watching for the slightest movement between the trees. Who was after me, and why? No time to think, only to run.

I stopped for a second behind a bush. Held my breath. Listened. Heard nothing. No footsteps. No movement. Maybe he had given up. I had lost him. Slowly, silently I dared a look back at the car. Still it sat there. I turned back, ready to run again.

Lost him, I thought. Sure of it. I had lost him.

I didn't see it coming.

The fist, like a hammer, smashed into my face, pain, darkness exploding into light and then, nothing.

Why did Lewis have the feeling that everything he learned had some connection with the murder at the high flats? It was a coincidence, he kept telling himself, and yet he thought about the boy seen running from the fire, another boy running, and that seemed too much of a coincidence. Who had started the fire, and why?

He had tried to talk to Guthrie about them, but he brushed them aside. 'Oh, come on, Lewis. I know you want to get into CID, but don't make a mystery where there is none. A bunch of vandals torch a well-known hangout for junkies. One of them gets out by the skin of his teeth. Happens regularly in this town.'

Blame it on the junkies. Handy villains for everything. So out of their faces they can't remember if they are guilty or not. Well, maybe his partner was right, but Lewis was going to keep an open mind. Maybe once they located the boy who had been in the lift – Lewis refused to call him 'the killer' – there would be a simple explanation. There had been no money taken from the dead man, only his identity had been stolen. There was no wallet, no driving licence, nothing with a name on it. Had that been deliberate? Had the killer perhaps not wanted the police to find out who the victim was? The man's fingerprints were certainly not known to the police.

But someone had recognised him.

Gaby McGurk. He could still picture that flash of recognition when she looked at the body.

His mother came in from work then and Lewis's quiet time for reflection was over. She was holding the evening paper and pointed at the front page. 'Look at that!' she said. 'How stupid can you get? Plastering a wee lassie's name all over the front page, and her photo.'

Lewis snatched the paper from her.

EVIL WRITTEN ALL OVER HIS FACE

'Don't blame the reporter, mother. I've met this Gaby McGurk. You couldn't keep her quiet with anaesthetic. I'm surprised she didn't give them her telephone number as well.'

There was the picture too. Obviously before she had a chance to put on the full pack of war paint. She looked younger, more vulnerable. Underneath the photo was a caption.

Gaby McGurk traumatised by last night's events had been visiting friends.

Visiting friends, my auntie! Lewis thought. She'd been at a party, or a club. One of them was always being done for serving underage drinkers. And there had been a distinct smell of smoke off Gaby McGurk. She'd tried to disguise it with mints, but hey! Lewis had been there with the 'trying to hide the smell of smoke from his mother with mints'. It didn't work.

But when someone's just found a body it's hardly the

time to question them about whether they've been sneaking a smoke.

But now it was different. Maybe he should have a word with Gaby McGurk. Putting her name and photograph on the front page of the local paper laid her open to danger.

'I think that girl should have police protection,' his mother said.

Someone else was thinking the exact same thing. Gaby McGurk herself. She had begun to be afraid. The phone hadn't stopped ringing since she'd come back home. Aunts and cousins just learning the news from the papers, and angry that her mother, who most of them thought was one sandwich short of a picnic anyway, had allowed her name and photograph to appear.

'It's a pity your auntie Ellen's away on holiday. She would never had allowed it!'

Auntie Ellen was considered the sensible member of the family. Gaby was her favourite niece.

But mostly the calls came from cranks; at least she hoped it was cranks calling her, threatening to get her because they 'knew where she lived'.

Gaby had tried to talk to her mother when she came in from work but she wouldn't listen. Instead she had turned on her angrily. 'You are driving me potty, Gaby McGurk.' When she was angry her mother always called her by her full name. 'Staying out late, lying to me. I know you weren't at Zoe's, by the way. I don't know where you've been. And now this. I'm going to get on to that reporter in the morning. He should have known better.'

Her mother was in the bathroom when the next call came through. 'Get that, Gaby,' she called.

Gaby was afraid. She lifted the receiver as if it might bite her.

'You're dead,' the voice rasped. 'You are dead.'

She wanted to shout into the receiver. Scream at whoever was making these calls. But now she didn't want her mother to know about them. It was bad enough, but she'd never hear the end of it if she told her about these calls.

Instead she whispered, 'I've got my phone bugged.'

The voice laughed. 'Too late, I'm coming to get you. And I'm the Wolf.' She knew then it was a crank call. The Wolf didn't exist. He was a legend told to children in this town to frighten them. Like the bogey man. There was a muffled giggle. Lots of them. She pictured a bunch of boys crammed into a phone box having a right laugh at her. Another crank call. But what if next time it wasn't a crank, but the real thing?

13

My eyes snapped open. I was shivering with fear and cold. Trying to remember who I was, where I was and how I got here. There had been a car, its headlights shining on the road. The dark figure chasing me. Then, pain. A giant of a fist rushing towards me. My head still ached with the pain of that blow. Where was I? There was darkness all around me. Where had he put me? I reached up and my hand touched rusty steel. My fingers groped around, and all I could feel was steel. I was inside a steel box. And in that second I knew exactly where I was: in the burnt-out wreck that had been lying beside the reservoir. Trapped inside the boot. With both hands I tried to push it open, but old car or not, the lid wouldn't budge. I felt a roll as the car moved and for a second I thought maybe I was being towed somewhere. But the only place I was going was down.

Ice-cold water started to seep into the boot. I felt it licking at my back. That was when the panic set in. I think I stopped breathing. The car was sinking deep into the waters of the reservoir, and I was inside it! I struggled, trying desperately to bang on the boot. All the time the water was trickling in, too fast. This boot was going to be my coffin. I yelled for help. Screamed for it. Was anyone there? Anyone who would help me? Or was *he* still there? I imagined him standing, silhouetted against the twilight sun, watching the car sink beneath the surface.

By the time that sun set I would be dead. The water was rising fast, filling the car. I lay back, tried to kick at the door with as much strength as I had, but the lid of the boot stayed tight shut, locking me in. I tried to sit up, tried to get away from the water. Any moment now it would reach my chest, then my chin.

Death creeping up on me.

I was going to die alone here, deep in these cold, icy waters. And who would remember me? Me, who could remember nothing of my past. Who would search for me? No one. Years from now maybe a skeleton would be dragged up from the depths. A skeleton never identified. I'd be known as the body in the boot. A mystery never solved. No identification. Nothing.

I was nobody.

A calm came over me. The panic seemed to fade. Some vague memory told me that happened when you accepted death. I accepted it now. It was all I was meant for. I would never solve the puzzle of why someone wanted me dead, or even who that someone was. Never find out who killed the man in the lift. Never find out who I was. Or what I was running from. Why couldn't I cry? Or scream? There was no feeling in me at all.

I closed my eyes and waited for the water to cover my face.

From the hill the Wolf watched. This time there would be no mistakes. No figure leaping from the car, clawing his way through the moss and mud. Not this time. He lifted the binoculars and peered towards the car. No sound of any struggle. The struggle was over.

The water lapped gently over the hood of the car, as the last rays of the setting sun faded to black. The boot was the last to go under. It lay for a little time barely visible and then it was gone. The Wolf kept the binoculars trained on the spot for a few moments. Nothing. No bubbles of life. The water was calm and peaceful. A secret sunk for ever. Good.

The Boss would be pleased.

And so was he.

He had only been an ordinary boy after all.

In a city far away someone else had seen the headline in the paper. A dark man, sitting in front of a computer, searching newspaper files on the Internet. He was looking for just one kind of story. Any story about a boy, alone, unknown. A dark-haired boy of a certain age. He had searched a long time and found nothing.

It was late at night when he saw the story as he sat in the dark of his hotel room. He had left the blinds open and a full moon hung in the sky.

EVIL WRITTEN ALL OVER HIS FACE

The headline was nonsense of course, but it sold newspapers. The boy was only young. No one that young could be so evil, surely? Homeless? A drug addict? The police weren't sure. No one was sure. The search was on for him in this riverside town. They wanted to eliminate him from their enquiries. Could this be the boy he was searching for too? The description was unclear. The boy had been covered in blood, with wild dark hair. But the age was right, and the man wouldn't take any chances. He had wasted too much time in the past few weeks, following many wrong leads. This might just be another of those. It didn't seem hopeful. But he had to try. He switched off his computer and the room was plunged into moonlight darkness. He was going to find out.

It was as if there was a hand on my shoulder, a strong hand. Lifting me. Supporting me. And a voice in my ear. *You will not die this way. Fight.*

Leave me alone! I wanted to scream it. I was tired. So tired. Now I was easing myself into death. Let me be! How was I supposed to get myself out of this one? I was only a boy.

Fight for your life. It was like a whisper in my ear. Something deep inside me didn't want me to die. Wouldn't allow me to die.

Get yourself free. Get that boot open.

A surge went through me, like electricity. A pounding in my brain.

You are a boy with no memory, not even the memory of a name. But you are not going to die. I kept repeating that to myself again and again . . . You are not going to die.

Life roared back into me.

Take a step back, Mr Death. I'm not coming yet.

I was beginning to shake. Every muscle in my body came alive, every bone fighting for life. Blood pumped through me. The car was deep in the water now, but there was still some air here in the boot. I gasped at it. I would be free. I kept that thought in mind and nothing else. I would be free. I clawed at the rusty steel, rammed my feet against the boot. Once, twice, three times. Where did my strength come from? I don't know. I only know that suddenly the boot opened. I was out in a second. I ached with pain, in my head, through my body, but pain was nothing. It only proved I was still alive. I was going to live.

I hurled myself up towards the surface. The car slid down deeper into the depths of the reservoir. I could almost feel it dragging me down with it. But nothing was going to pull me down now. I had hardly any breath left in me. The moon quivered above the water. I headed straight for it. And broke through the surface with a roar of joy. Alive.

I threw myself on the mossy bank as the frosty moon looked down. My clothes – what was left of them – were soaking, weighing me down, freezing into icicles, chilling me to the very marrow of my bones. I couldn't stop my teeth chattering, or my body shaking. And it wasn't just the cold. I had been snatched from the very jaws of death. I had an uncanny feeling that something had happened to me down there as the car slid to the bottom of this lonely lake.

The past two days had been the most traumatic I could remember. Yet I could remember nothing before that.

Nothing! Why couldn't I remember! I beat my hands against my head as if I could push my past back in there, force it there. But my real memory only seemed to begin

71

when I came to this town. How unlucky can one boy get? First he finds a dying man, then just when he thinks he's found a friend, thinks he's safe at last, vandals set fire to his hideaway. And finally, someone chases him up here on the moors, traps him in an abandoned car and pushes him into the water.

I should be selling lucky white heather.

But all this had been deliberate. No accident.

Someone had tried to kill me. Had that same someone been responsible for the fire? Had to be. Too much of a coincidence to be an accident now. That man was after me. The man in the car, that huge dark figure silhouetted against the sky. I held my jaw, remembering the fist that had knocked me unconscious. A great beast of a man. I crouched further down in the bracken. Was he watching me now? No. If he had seen me burst out of the water he would be here already, to finish the job.

I waited an icy age before I got to my feet. I wrapped my arms around myself in a vain attempt to keep warm, then I walked towards the edge of the lake. The tyre tracks led into the water. There were footprints too, cut deep into the hard mossy soil. He had had to use all his strength to push the car into the water.

The thought of it made me shiver. He must really want me dead. Why was he after me? Why was this man trying to kill me? What had I ever done to him?

15

The day had been spent going round the doors, asking questions, not getting any answers. Real foot-slogging police work.

'Don't look down your nose at it, Lewis,' Guthrie had told him again. 'That's how crimes are really solved.'

It didn't seem that way to Lewis. People in this area didn't talk to the police. They told them nothing. They never helped with police enquiries. They kept their lips zipped, as they say. They didn't trust the police. Half of them had family in jail, and the other half, the ones who didn't, didn't grass. Anyway, why should anyone get involved in a drugs-related death? 'As long as they're only killing each other, who cares?' seemed to be the attitude. The police, it seemed to Lewis, had that attitude too. He felt there was a laziness in their enquiries. When he had suggested that no one goes around with nothing in their pockets – no keys, no wallet, no cards – Guthrie had repeated what everyone else seemed to think: the young killer, probably a drug addict, had stolen everything.

In fact, his partner had looked at him as if he was a bit thick for suggesting it.

He warned him against trying to be too clever. 'I know you want to be a detective, but nobody likes a smart ass.'

So Lewis didn't mention the fact that he was sure Gaby McGurk had recognised the dead man. She'd been interviewed all day and they were satisfied that she was only 'a daft wee lassie in the wrong place at the wrong time'.

Lewis thought she was a daft wee lassie as well, but she knew more than she was telling. And he was sure the dead man had been killed on her floor. Coincidence? According to his partner it had to be. 'They're one of the families who are never in trouble. Her mother works as a waitress, and her partner works on the rigs. No previous for any of them. Decent hardworking people. Everyone on that floor's been interviewed. No one knew the dead man. It has to be a coincidence.'

So it seemed the police and everyone else had decided the victim was an out-of-town drug dealer, no previous convictions, therefore unknown to the police, and his killer an out-of-his-face junkie who had stolen everything he could lay his hands on. If Lewis was going to prove anything different, he would have to find out for himself.

I was beginning to feel I was attached to this town with an elastic band. But where else could I head? I had to find dry clothes. I didn't want to survive all this and end up dying from double pneumonia. I needed dry clothes. I needed shelter. I had the best chance of finding both back in the town. There was none here on the moorland. I would die if I stayed here for the night, especially now. And I didn't want to die. I'd learned that as the car was sinking into the reservoir. I was determined to live. I didn't understand why. I had nothing. I could remember nothing. But I had to live and there had to be a reason for that.

I would find out one day.

As I ran, keeping off the single-track road, darting between trees, I thought about all that had happened. Someone had followed me from the flats last night, knowing I had found the dying man, afraid he might have told me something important. That same man had followed me and Eddie to the clubhouse, and as soon as he saw Eddie leave, that same someone had set fire to the place. That same man had to have followed me up to the hills, had to be the man in the car. The thought chilled me. I remembered the ruthlessness of the attack on me. A boy on his own, so dangerous to someone that they knocked me unconscious and locked me in a car, left me to die? But I was only a boy. I could have been killed anytime. Overpowered, murdered, just another victim. Or did my death have to look like an accident? In a fire. Underwater. Not trapped with tape or rope, just my own sweater. Yes, an accident, that seemed logical, But the question came again? Why?

It had to be something to do with the dead man, with the murder in the flats.

But what?

Or could it have been something else, something in the past I couldn't remember?

My mind was a whirlwind of thoughts, adding to the ache in the head I already had from the punch. It was too cold to think clearly.

And was I being watched now? The thought made me stop in my tracks.

Only a strip of moonlight illuminated the frosty road. I looked all around, but there was nothing. Midnight silence. I had to rest. An owl hooted in the woods, a lonely sound, but reassuring. I leant against a tree. Wanted to sleep, but there was a sudden roar of a car on the road and I was up in an instant and looking for somewhere to hide myself. I found my speed and launched myself into the bushes, rolled over and lay face down. The car appeared over the hill, racing towards me, the driver taking the sharp bends like a maniac. I could hear music too, pounding out of the open windows. There were roars and cheers as the car sped past me, stuffed full with boys, too many for one car, laughing and singing. Boy racers taking advantage of speed on the lonely road.

I put my face down on my arms, exhausted. I would rest for a moment, only a moment, then I would move on.

It was the last thought I remembered.

16

Dan was back. He sat in the armchair, watching television. Gaby's mother had told him about the murder while he waited for his favourite curry to be delivered. He could hardly miss the police presence. The incident van parked on the street, the black and yellow tape still across the lift. And she had told him about Gaby's involvement. He hadn't been pleased about that. 'Keep well back from the police,' he had told Gaby, 'and the press. We're a respectable family. Never had any trouble with the police.'

We're not a family, Gaby wanted to tell him. But she said nothing.

Gaby always said nothing when it came to Dan. He had only been in their lives for a few months and she still hadn't got used to his presence in her home. She was only glad he was here so little. Away so much on the rigs. Her mother was always on at her to confide in him. 'He's a good man, Gaby.' He was the kind of man she should be able to rely on. No one would mess with Dan. But she couldn't tell him where she was that night. That would only cause trouble for her. Could she tell him about the phone calls? He would only say how daft she'd been to let them print her name. What if she told him she had seen the dead man before? He'd already asked her all the details about coming home, what had happened when the lift doors opened and exactly what she'd seen then. Asked about the boy. She'd promised him she'd told him everything. He had seemed satisfied. She couldn't change her mind now. She watched him munching into his chicken vindaloo, his broad hairy hands curled round a can of beer. He turned to look at her, sensing her stare. 'What is it, Gaby?'

He was smiling, had been in a great mood since he'd come in. Pulling her giggling mother into an embarrassing clinch. Glad to be home, he said. Now would be the perfect moment to confide in him. Then her mother kissed him again and that decided her. She shook her head. 'Nothing, Dan.'

Her mother wanted her to call him dad. In her dreams.

Her mother giggled her way into the kitchen to fetch him another beer.

'You missed all the excitement.' Gaby told him. 'It must be dead boring working on those rigs.'

'It has its moments,' he said, and he turned back to the television.

SATURDAY

The freezing dawn woke me. I was stiff with cold. Worse than stiff. I heard my bones crack as I stood up. I had to get some shelter. Miles to walk into the town, and all the time I walked I tried to keep my mind off the numbing cold. But there was nothing to think about. I couldn't go back over old memories because I had none. Couldn't look forward to going home. I had no home. All I could think about was the pain in my jaw and the cold. At last, I reached the estate on the edge of the town. The houses still lay in early morning darkness. But something was open, a small newsagent shop. Its door lying ajar, sending a beam of light on to the pavement. A pile of last night's papers lay tied up outside, waiting for collection, and I couldn't miss the headline. I snatched the top one, read it in disbelief.

EVIL WRITTEN ALL OVER HIS FACE

She'd actually said that! That stupid girl, the screamer. I could gladly have murdered her right then. How could she see evil, when there had only been confusion and fear? She was a drama queen of course. Wanted attention. Well, she'd certainly get it now. I read on, read her name. Gaby McGurk. Gaby, that certainly suited her. She could gab. And her address too. She lived on the fifteenth floor of Wellpark Court. There was even a picture of her. I could see she was trying to look glamorous, pouting her lips, her eyes wide. She only managed to look stupid.

Wait a minute, she lived on the fifteenth floor. That was the floor where I had found the dying man. Could there be a connection? Or was that just a coincidence?

Don't believe in coincidences, a voice inside me whispered. There have been too many of them up to now.

I turned in alarm as the shopkeeper came out and dropped another neatly tied bundle on the pavement. He looked at me. 'You've been swimming?' he laughed.

'You're soaked through.' His accent was broad Scots though he was of Asian descent, Indian or Pakistani, I couldn't tell. I stood transfixed, waiting for the man to clock who I was. But he only stepped back into his shop and a moment later came out again, smiling. 'You want a cuppa tea, son? Thaw you out. You look like an ice sculpture there.'

I expected him to recognise me at once, the boy with 'evil written all over his face'. However, he only beckoned me inside his shop. The smell of freshly baked early morning rolls wafted towards me. I could feel hunger clawing at my stomach. And the warmth too. It wrapped itself around me. It was wonderful. The man saw my eyes dart towards the rolls. He smiled again. 'Hungry? You can have one with your tea.'

He handed me a steaming mug of tea and poured some milk in it. Then he lifted a couple of rolls from the board and began to butter them. 'I don't know why I have to open so early. Nobody's around yet,' he said. 'I usually have my tea on my own. Glad of the company.' His teeth were white against his brown skin. 'I'm Razool, by the way,' he went on. 'I've not seen you around here before. Know all the boys from this area. Bad and good. Got to in this business. The things I could tell you . . .'

He waited. I knew he was expecting some kind of comment. 'I'm not from round here,' I said at last.

'You've been out all night?' Razool asked. Then he said again, 'Swimming!'

I decided to tell him a little bit of the truth. 'I fell in the reservoir . . . the one up over the hill.'

Razool whistled. 'There's people died in there, you know.' (Tell me about it. I was almost one of them.) 'They say there are so many bodies in that lake you can stand waist deep in the middle on top of them all.' Then he laughed again.

I shivered, imagining myself there.

'They say the Wolf put them there.'

'The Wolf?'

Razool laughed. 'Doesn't exist. The bogey man. It's like one of those urban legends, you know?'

The Wolf. The very sound of his name sent the shivers through me again.

Razool saw the shiver, took it to be the cold. He handed me a roll. 'You can't sit about in those clothes.' He lifted a fleecy jacket from a hook behind the door. 'Here, shove this on. Somebody left it in here months ago. Never came back to claim it. Take off that T-shirt and put this on.' I did as he said and pulled on the fleece gratefully. It had been hanging all those months above a heater and it was toasting warm. Luxury.

'Mind it isn't the designer stuff you seem to be used to.' Razool examined the T-shirt I was wearing. 'Your mother is going to kill you when she sees the state you're in.' He laughed again as if the idea amused him.

It made me smile too, this alternative life Razool was creating for me. A caring mother who dressed me in designer gear.

'Your mates chucked you in, did they? Think it was funny, I suppose.'

I couldn't help grinning. Now I had mates. 'I'll get them back, don't you worry.'

The hot tea, the food gave a lift to my spirits.

'Boys! You're always up to something. See the school over there?' Razool nodded somewhere outside. 'Boys break in there all the time, trash the place. Why? What good does that do anyone? Last week they broke the security system.' Razool laughed as if he'd said something funny. 'Mind you, my customers are happy about that. At least now they don't get woken up by the alarm every night.'

Razool took another long sip of tea. 'I see there's been a murder here too.'

I began to choke on my roll. Spluttering crumbs all over the place.

Razool laughed and patted me on the back. 'Don't worry, you're perfectly safe here. I'm not the murderer. Anyway, I think the police know who done it. Just a young boy, about your age too. A junkie. They'll catch him, don't worry. I have every faith in the police.' He smiled again.

I knew I was staring, waiting for Razool to put two and two together and come up with me.

'My brother was telling me about it. I only work here Saturdays and Sundays. We have another shop in Glasgow. I work there the rest of the week.'

So that explained it. Razool hadn't been here in the town. Probably hadn't even read last night's paper, the one that said I had 'evil written all over my face'.

'When's your day off?' I just wanted to change the subject.

Razool laughed again. 'Day off? What's that? My mother is a slave driver. A day off makes you lazy, she says. She doesn't approve of lazy men, she says. Mothers. They would drive you round the bend at times. What about your mother, what's she like?'

My mother? I had to have a mother somewhere surely. Was she searching for me, worrying about me, trying desperately to find me? I tried to force my brain to remember. Create a picture of her face. But there was only a heavy curtain, blinds drawn over my past.

'What's she like?' Razool asked again.

I decided to go with the flow. Make up my own perfect mother. 'She's all right, my mum. She works really hard, in a shop in the town. A clothes shop. She loves clothes. Thinks she's still a bit of a chick.' Razool laughed at that. So did I. I could almost see this imaginary mother of mine. Bringing clothes home from her shop, trying them on, twirling in front of me. How I wished it was all true. 'She wants me to get a Saturday job delivering papers.'

'Well, don't ask for a job in this shop. My mother will drive you crazy.'

I wanted to stay there, in the safety, with Razool. But the first customer would be heading in soon. A customer who might just recognise me.

'Talking about my mother, I better be getting home. I've never stayed out all night.' I stood up. 'Thanks, Razool.' This had been a moment of kindness in these black days. I appreciated it.

Razool stood up too, handed me another roll. 'Here, that will keep you going till you get home.'

17

'This is ridiculous, the ironing I've got to do for you.' His mother didn't know how to keep quiet. Lewis turned up the volume on the remote. He was watching a film on Sky about a boy detective on the force in 1920s Los Angeles, astounding his superiors with the clues he was picking up and the pace of his investigation.

'Did you hear me, boy?' She threw a towel at him. It covered his head and reminded him of the Rottweiler.

He pulled it off, threw it back at her. 'I'm eternally grateful,' he said. 'And I promise not to put you into a home when you're old and grey.' He pretended to peer at her. 'Wait a minute, you're old and grey now. Or you would be if it wasn't for Born To Be Blonde hair dye!'

'I'll wallop you with your truncheon if you don't shut up.'

'I've been shut up till you came in. I'm trying to watch TV,' Lewis reminded her. He had just missed yet another brilliant clue found by the young detective. That young detective could be him. He was finding lots of clues. Except no one was listening to Lewis. Every time he passed a clue on to CID Warren, that was the last he heard about it. The bloodied clothes, the designer jeans yanked from a line, the body found on the fifteenth floor. No one had come forward to identify the dead man. He didn't have a criminal record, Who was he? And why had he been killed? It was early days yet, of course, but Lewis couldn't believe that it was just some drug-related death, even if everyone else did.

His mother hadn't finished. 'So my son and heir hasn't solved the mystery yet,' she said, spraying more steam on to his uniform trousers. 'I think you're talking to the wrong people.'

And Lewis remembered again, Gaby McGurk. If he could just get her to tell him where she'd seen the man in the lift, he would be one step forward, further forward than any of his colleagues.

I had to get out of this town, but how? I would have thumbed a lift but, after my description had been on the front page of the local paper, who would pick me up now and not recognise me? Then drive me straight to the nearest police station. If I could jump a truck I could hide inside. But which truck? The way my luck was going I would jump in one that was headed straight for the local jail. I squeezed myself into the doorway of a video shop and sat down, hunching my knees up to my chin. There had to be a way to get out of here. I couldn't try the hills again. I had been followed there before. I didn't think I was being followed now. Automatically, I glanced up and down the empty street.

And the thought struck me. Why should anyone be

following me? He thought I was dead. I pictured again the solitary dark figure on the moors, silhouetted against the sky. The Wolf? Was that who it had been? Maybe now I was safe from him. Surely I must be safe from him. He thought he had killed me, that I was deep down in the waters of the reservoir. Trapped in a car. I imagined fish swimming curiously in through the broken windows, could picture my white face, my hair floating all around me. I shook the image away. It was too scary.

But now, at least *he* wasn't after me. I smiled, couldn't help it. Saw the funny side of what I had just thought. He wasn't after me, but he was the only one. I still had half the police force in the country on my tail. But not the mysterious 'he'. And that man scared me more than the police. He thought I was dead. For the first time I had the advantage.

Good. I planned to keep it that way.

If only the dying man had told me the name of his killer I would have phoned the police, given them an anonymous tip off. Then the heat would be off me. But I had nothing to tell. Nothing.

What I needed was somewhere to hole up and hide. But where? I could see the big high school in the distance was deserted. No sign of life. It stood alone, surrounded by playing fields, secluded, remote. That must be the school Razool had told me about. The school that was always being vandalised. Inside that school it would be warm. There might be food in there, in the school canteen. It suddenly seemed like the best refuge in the world.

I got to my feet and looked all around. Dawn was just

breaking. A new day. I began to hurry towards the school.

In spite of what Razool had told me I was ready at any second for the screech of the alarm as soon as I climbed inside. Ready to hoof it out of there if the security system had been fixed. The school was an old dilapidated building, built on two storeys. There was a broken window on one of the rooms on the upper floor. I shimmied up a drain pipe and was on the ledge in a moment. I knocked away more of the glass with my elbow, waited a moment for someone to hear the sound. There was nothing. A moment later I was inside.

I found myself in the library. Above the bookshelves posters lined the walls. Posters advertising authors and books, posters urging you to read.

THIS IS A POSITIVE THINKING ZONE, one of the banners on the wall announced. I was all for that. Positive thinking. That was exactly what I needed at the moment. There were maps too. Mountains and deserts and oceans. I stood looking all around, alert for any sign of activity in the building – cleaners, the janitor – but there was only quiet. I tried to remember being in a school library like this. I must have gone to school somewhere. I could read. I couldn't remember any of the books, but hey, I was a boy, maybe I wasn't supposed to read. But I could recognise the places on these walls: a map of the British Isles, another of the Middle East, the contours of Australia. How could I remember that? Had I travelled to these places? Where had I learned about them? But nothing came. No matter how hard I concentrated, nothing came. Not even the sliver of a memory.

There was a walk-in cupboard. Long and narrow, it was almost as big as a room. It was unlocked too, stacked to the roof with books and papers, but unfortunately, nothing edible. I wandered back into the main library and fell into one of the seats. My body seemed to collapse with exhaustion. I hadn't realised how tired I was.

Initials were carved into the formica top of the table I was sitting at. 'RJ loves NW', 'SH was here'. Some of them were pretty rude. I opened a drawer and smiled. Some kind soul had left a Mars bar in here. I took it out, stripped the paper from it. As I munched into it I began to realise just how good a hideout this might be. There might be food. Had to be. In the school canteen, in the staffroom. Maybe even a change of clothes lying in a locker. And there would be warmth. For the first time in days the chill was leaving me. The school's central heating was thawing me out. Not just on the outside but the kind of heat that seeps into the bones. My spirits rose. Human beings, I decided, were wonderful. A little bit of food, and warmth, and hope bounces back up like buds in spring. Hallelujah! I was getting quite poetic in my old age. First things first – I would look for something to eat. Then I would find somewhere safe to sleep.

'He's definitely dead this time.' The Boss wasn't asking a question. He was demanding. Making a statement. Anyone else but the Wolf would be afraid. But the Wolf was used to people being afraid of him. The Boss knew that. He knew even he couldn't scare the Wolf.

'I saw him go under. He didn't come up again. He couldn't survive that. Nobody could.'

'You better be right about that, Wolf. I hope you're not losing your touch.'

The Wolf growled in anger. 'He's only a boy, a dead boy now. You can rely on me. You've always been able to rely on me.'

The Boss nodded. That had always been true. He hoped it was still true.

He wouldn't like to lose the Wolf. But if he had to replace him, he would. No one was indispensable. And there was someone eager to take over.

18

'They want me to do what?' Gaby McGurk's mouth was hanging open.

Lewis wished he hadn't been the one asked to do this. He couldn't understand why the CID even believed anything this girl said. The trouble with the CID was they weren't streetwise like him. They'd read the handbook, but didn't know a thing about real people. Lewis knew that Gaby had seen the boy everyone was looking for, but on no account would he believe she could describe him accurately. Evil all over his face, indeed. I don't think.

Sure the boy might have been on drugs, but he wasn't what Gaby was pretending he was, another Jack the Ripper.

She was standing in her living room, her face contorted in shock. 'You want me to do an artist's impression of him? I can't draw.'

Gaby McGurk was thick, he decided. 'We supply the artist, Gaby. You just describe the boy to him.'

Gaby put on her drama queen voice. 'I don't think I want to get involved in this. I'm the only witness. I want police protection!'

Lewis tried to make her feel better. 'That's what I'm here for. Myself and a WPC will accompany you to the station. How about that? Your mum can come too.'

'My mum! You've got to be joking. She's still raging because I spoke to the local paper.' She tried to look defiant. 'What if I refuse to go?'

'We could bring the artist to you.'

He could see that didn't appeal to her at all.

'Have you had any more phone calls?' he asked her.

She pouted her lips. She had reported the calls and now he could tell she was desperate to lie, to invent more, but she didn't. 'No,' she admitted at last. 'But I could get more if an Identikit picture goes in the paper.'

'It's an artist's impression,' he corrected her.

'Whatever,' she said. 'He'll still know it was me.'

'So . . . what about the man who was in the lift?' Lewis had quizzed her about this before. Now he asked it casually, hoping to catch her out.

Her answer came fast – too fast. 'Never saw him before in my life, I told you. I don't know why you keep asking me that.'

I couldn't have picked a better place to hide. Especially over a weekend. I walked the lonely corridors, trying each of the classroom doors in turn. The library had been left open but most of the other classrooms were locked up tight. All the time I tried to remember being in a school like this, but again there was nothing.

MR BRADY, a nameplate proclaimed. *HEAD-MASTER*.

Outside Mr Brady's office I found an outfit hanging on the coat stand. It was a black cloak with a separate hood and holes for eyes, and the face painted on it in stark white was that of a skeleton. I lifted the mask and stared at it. It reminded me of something. Something scary. I wouldn't like to see that on a dark night. Did it belong to Mr Brady? I imagined him striding about the school scaring the pupils. My headmaster is a monster? Or had it been confiscated from some devilish pupil? It brought a smile to my lips thinking about that.

The staffroom door was unlocked too. That surprised me, but I wasn't complaining. A big square room with comfy chairs and a low table in the middle. There was a sink and a fridge, and even a microwave. Jars of coffee and bags of tea were stacked in the cupboard. They all had labels on them.

Mrs Fisher's decaf. Don't touch.

Mr Brown's herbal teas. Hands Off.

Mr Hepburn's coffee. Help yourself.

I decided I liked Mr Hepburn. I helped myself. There were chocolate biscuits and a big tin of caramels, and as I sat in comfort, munching into them, I thought, Boy, teachers are good to themselves. Warming my hands round a mug of steaming hot tea I did an inspection of my new-found haven.

In the locker room next to the gym I found a pair of trainers almost my size. Mine were freezing and stiff. I kicked them off. How long ago now since I'd sunk into the lake? Seemed an age. I replaced them in the locker. It wouldn't be stealing. It was a fair exchange. I must have been a pretty honest guy once, I figured. Stealing the trainers just didn't seem right to me. There was even a pair of sports socks. Those I did take. The only thing I could replace them with was a couple of caramels. The boy's name was on the door. Akash. I wondered what Akash would make of finding his shoes gone and sweets in their place. There were tracksuit bottoms too hanging on the back of the door of the locker room. It seemed they belonged to no one in particular. I was almost ready to change into them when I opened the door into another room. Showers. I couldn't believe my luck. I could have a shower. A hot shower. The luxury of it made me yell with joy. Not caring who heard me. A shower, a change of clothes, hot food – because surely there must be something in the canteen I could heat in that microwave – and I would be ready for anything. I was beginning to think I was pretty good at this hiding lark.

A few hours ago I had almost given up on life. I'd been ready to die. Yet now my spirits rose for the first time since I could remember – and that wasn't very long. Things were going to be all right.

'So that's definitely him now?' The police artist sounded fed up. Lewis didn't blame him. Gaby McGurk had that effect on people. She'd been in the station for two hours trying to describe the boy 'with evil written all over his face.' Lewis was beginning to think she'd never seen him at all. She'd changed his nose three times. 'Too long', 'Too short', 'Too crooked'. His chin, with a dimple, without a dimple, weak, strong.

All that stayed the same was the hair, a wild black mane uncombed, unwashed. And the eyes. She was certain about the eyes. From the first it seemed the artist had got that right. Dark brown eyes that even in the artist's impression seemed to bore right through you.

'They were shiftier,' was the only other comment she had made about them.

Gaby studied the finished sketch for a while. It was a boy's face, Lewis was thinking, a young boy's face and to him the eyes didn't look evil at all. Just frightened and sad and confused. What had he been doing there on that stairwell that night? Where was his family? He didn't look like any drug addict he'd ever seen. His eyes, those eyes, if Gaby McGurk had got them right, were too bright, too alert.

Finally, Gaby looked up at Lewis. Her face was pale, as if she'd seen a ghost. 'That's him, honest. That is him to the life.'

Tonight was my first chance to sleep in a proper bed, in the medical room, left unlocked, and tucked at the end of a corridor not far from the library. A narrow little room with a single bed in it and tiny triangular toilet in the corner. There were clean sheets on the bed, and a duvet. I even found a book to read, lying on the desk in the school library. *The Diary of Anne Frank*. Sounded a bit too much like a girls' book to me, but I hadn't dared put on a light to choose any other. I found a torch in one of the drawers and, tucking myself under the duvet, I used that to read by.

I've died and gone to heaven, I thought as I lay in the bed. I was warm, my belly was full and I had a book to read. How ridiculous that must sound. School and heaven just didn't go together. But I felt safe here. For the first time in so long, I felt safe. No one knew where I was. No one even knew I was alive.

If only I could stay here for ever.

I pictured myself years from now, a young man with a long beard (I wouldn't risk shaving) emerging from my hideout. I could stay here till I was sixteen, whenever that might be. When I could step from the shadows, an adult. Beyond the law. And no one could harm me or force me to go back.

Go back where? And why did the thought of that frighten me so much? Why did I have to hide?

It will come to me, I told myself again. It has to. One day I will wake up and my past will be laid out before me like a map. I'll be able to follow my life back through all the twists and turns, through all the detours and find out who I am and where I came from. One day I will understand everything.

And to some, wasn't I dead already? Trapped in the icy waters of the reservoir, fish eating out my eyes.

The thought of that made me feel sick.

Why had the man on the moor wanted me dead?

It had to be because of the dying man in the lift. Heartbeat. Stop. Four teeth. It meant nothing. Unless 'Heartbeat' was the nickname of his murderer, a man with only four teeth. The thought of that – when I could dismiss from my mind the dying man's grey face, all that blood – made me smile.

I pushed the thought away and decided, no more Anne Frank. This story was too sad. They were all caught, betrayed. She died. I needed something to cheer myself up. I risked another journey to the library, bolder now, and with the torch I had found I chose another book. This one was more like it! A cracking story about a boy spy travelling the world, saving the planet, with all sorts of wonderful gadgets to help him.

If only real life could be as exciting as that.

Lewis had accompanied Gaby back to the flats and had been ambushed by a crowd of residents. Lynch mob might be a better description.

And they were all women.

His worst nightmare.

'Right, because of this murder you've managed to get rid of the junkies sleeping in here, now. Keep them out,' one of them ordered him.

Lewis managed a smile. He had been told his smile could charm snakes. It didn't charm any of these ladies.

Ladies, ha! There wasn't a lady among them. Boadicea would look like a wimp next to this bunch. 'We are doing our best, ladies. We are keeping a constant presence here. As you can see our incident van is in the vicinity.'

'Your best! We've seen your best. It's rubbish!'

Lewis looked around for help. Guthrie had kept well hidden in the car. And the policewoman had taken Gaby up in the lift.

'We are on the case, madam,' Lewis assured her, trying to push past them at the same time. They were like a brick wall barring his way.

'We want a secure entry system,' someone said.

'That's not our job. That's the council's area of responsibility.'

'The council's rubbish as well.' He began to wonder if there was anyone they trusted. 'Anyway, we had a secure entry system, and the junkies broke it. Keep the junkies away from here. That's what we need.'

There was a howl of agreement on this.

'We need police protection around here. The police

only stay for a few days and then they scarper. We need them here all the time. Bobbies on the beat. Not just now. For good.'

'I'll put that to my superiors, madam,' Lewis said.

'Would that be the cleaning lady?'

Lewis sighed. Not a shred of respect for a uniform.

'Is there anything else you would like me to organise?' He decided to be as sarcastic as they were.

'An exorcist.'

Now that did take him by surprise. 'An exorcist?'

'Aye, for them ghosts we've got.'

He expected her to be shouted down, instead they all began to agree with her. 'Oh aye, we've definitely got ghosts in these flats.'

Now he had heard everything. Lewis finally made his getaway. He had always thought the ghost stories were only believed by drunks. There must be something in the air up here, he was thinking, because they're all mad. Every last one of them. Ghosts indeed!

'Did you hear that?' Gaby held her breath, listening. The sound was like the wail of a wounded animal. It echoed eerily inside the lift shaft. 'It's the ghosts.'

The policewoman smiled. 'It's just the wind. There are no ghosts, Gaby.'

But she didn't live here. She didn't hear the noises that Gaby did, that they all did. It wasn't the wind.

She was glad to be out of the lift, but she still had her mother to face. Her mum was annoyed that she was back down to the police station yet again. And she gave the policewoman a right telling off. Really embarrassed Gaby.

'They would only have brought the artist up to the house,' Gaby tried to explain. 'I thought this way would be better.'

'We never have any bother with the police. Never. Neither has Dan, and now we've got them practically sleeping in the living room.'

Gaby sat back. 'It wasn't my fault I was there when the killer came charging out of the lift.'

Too late she remembered the truth. 'Actually, it was your fault,' her mother told her. 'If you'd come in at the right time, you wouldn't be in this predicament.'

Big Dan came into the kitchen just then. 'What's all this noise?' he asked. He looked at Gaby's mum. 'Are you on at the lassie again?' But he was smiling. Still in a great mood because he was home.

'Trust you to stick up for her,' she said fondly. She looked at Gaby. 'Dan won't say a word against you.'

'She's been through enough. That must have been a trauma for her, seeing all that. And that junkie, he could have got her as well.' Gaby was nodding, thankful for the support. Then Dan said softly, 'Hopefully, that'll be the last time the police want to see you. You've not got anything else to tell, have you?'

Time for confession? No. She shook her head. 'I'm done with the police. There's nothing else I can tell them.' And all the time running through her head was the picture of the dead man when she had last seen him, alive.

And scared.

99

It was the glass breaking that woke me, somewhere along the corridor from where I slept. I was always now on the edge of sleep, the slightest noise alerting me. I sat up in bed and listened. I could hear voices. The buzz of whispering voices, one, two, maybe three. Someone was in the school. I pulled the covers up to my chin. I could stay here, keep quiet, maybe slide the lock on this door and wait for them to go.

Who were they and what were they looking for?

Were they looking for me? Had someone spotted me climbing in here, phoned the police? No. This couldn't be the police. Not breaking glass. Not whispering.

Vandals then. The vandals Razool had told me about. Boys breaking in, hoping the alarm system was still broken, smashing up the classrooms, trashing the place.

Let them do what they want.

I heard a door banging along the corridor. They were in the library. They had climbed in the same way as I had. As long as they didn't find me, didn't bother me, they could do what they liked.

I slipped out of bed. I would lock the door then I would wedge a chair under the handle. Just in case they tried every single room in the school – like I had, trying the doors for the ones unlocked. This was the medical room. They might think there would be drugs in here. Some junkies would take any kind of drugs they could find – aspirin even – and sell it on as something more sinister.

And that was when I began to think. If these vandals trashed the school, stole anything, the police would be called in. I could picture it now. Police roaming around the corridors, searching for clues, taking fingerprints. Finding mine. Matching them with the fingerprints they had found in the lift that night. My fingerprints. I would be caught. I would be on the run again.

More whispering coming from the library. Or was that the wind? The eerie noises mixed and mingled in the silent corridors.

I stood straight. Determined. I wasn't going to let them spoil this for me. This was my place, my refuge. For the first time I felt safe. I wasn't going to let anyone take this from me. I had staked my claim here. It was mine. And they weren't going to take it from me.

There had to be a way to get rid of them. A way to make them run and not alert the police.

There had to. Maybe I could frighten them off. But how? How could a little guy like me frighten anybody? And then I remembered and I smiled. There might just be a way.

The three boys had moved into the big cupboard where the librarian kept stacks of books and papers. I could hear them rummaging about, hoping there might be some money in there too. I slid quietly into the library, tucked myself between the bookcases. I could hear their whispered voices discussing what they should do next. They didn't seem too sure. Their words were punctuated with giggles and swearing.

'I definitely want to trash old Hepburn's class. I hate him. I'm going to have a ball in there.' There was a viciousness in the boy's voice. Bitterness at some past wrong old Hepburn had done him.

Old Hepburn. 'Help yourself' Hepburn. I liked him. I couldn't let them trash his class.

'Don't be daft, Dev,' another boy spoke more softly. I could tell that Dev was the domineering one. The boss. 'We'd never get into the class anyway. Old Hepburn always locks his up.'

'We need the 156 key,' Dev said mysteriously. 'That would get us in anywhere.'

The 156 key, I supposed, must be some kind of master key that would unlock the doors of all the classrooms.

'Och, that's dross,' another whingeing voice broke in. There were three of them then. 'I want to trash somethin'. You should have lifted the key, Dev. You know some daft teacher always leaves it in the staffroom. 'Mon we'll get it.'

The staffroom! There was no way I was letting them get to that staffroom. There was no way I was letting them out of this library.

'If that key goes missing again I'll get the blame. I always get the blame.' This was Dev.

The other two boys laughed. 'That's because you're

always the one that nicks it.'

Dev didn't laugh. 'OK, I'll get the key, and we'll trash every class. Right?' There was a menacing pause. 'Burn them.'

The way he said that frightened me as I waited there in the shadows. There was so much hate in those words.

Now was the time for me to move. In between the bookcases I became a shadow, a silhouette. I rustled as I moved, the only sound I made. I heard one of the boys catch his breath. 'What was that?'

My bare feet made no noise on the floor, there was only that rustle, and then, my nails trailing along the spines of books.

'Somebody's out there.'

'I saw somebody.'

I knew they were watching. They had stepped to the door of the cupboard to see. Had caught a glimpse of something in the dark.

'The janny,' one of them whispered.

Dev shut him up. 'The janny would be in here, like a shot. Not out there.' Dev didn't sound as scared as the other two. 'And he'd have phoned the cops first.'

Then I stayed silent. I knew they were waiting for more noise. So, I stayed silent, didn't move. I had plenty of time.

'It was nothing,' Dev said at last. He could try and pretend he wasn't scared, but I could hear the relief in his voice. 'A mouse or something.'

I could see them standing in the shadowy doorway, alert, still listening. 'Yeah, nothin',' one of them agreed. They waited another few minutes, and then they moved back inside the cupboard.

'That dizzy librarian always leaves dosh lying about in here. I'm going to find it,' I heard Dev say.

I had all night. Wanted them to feel they had been mistaken. I wanted them to separate. After a while one of them came out and walked close to where I was hiding. He was pulling books from shelves, scattering them on the floor as he went. He stopped at the librarian's desk, looking for something to steal. I slid further behind a bookcase. I heard drawers being opened, papers being strewn over the floor.

'Hey, look. I've found a photo of the librarian's wee boy,' the boy called, laughing, but no one answered him. The other two, out of earshot in the cupboard. 'Boy, is he ugly! The dad must be from another planet. This looks like an alien.'

Silently (where did I learn to be so silent?) I moved towards him. I almost glided in the outfit I was wearing. The boy had his back to me, rifling through the drawers. Intent on finding something to steal. I stepped behind him. He heard nothing, not until I was so close I could almost reach out and touch him. Then he turned, alerted by the swish of my cloak. 'Is that you, Dev?' But the words died on his lips when he saw the figure in the shadows.

I watched his eyes go wide with terror. 'Tell me that's you, Dev. You takin' the mickey?'

In answer, I cocked my head to one side, like a bird. It was enough to send the boy stumbling back.

I took another step forwards. The boy looked around for somewhere to go, saw the open window. He was out like a bullet. I heard him shriek as he fell.

I stood at the window, looking down. The boy looked up, rubbing at his ankle. When he saw me, he shrank back. This was working better than I had hoped. Hearing movement behind me then, I slid behind one of the bookcases, watching, unseen, as the second boy came closer.

'What's with the noise, Sean?' It was the boy with the whingeing voice.

In the darkness only slivers of moonlight lit the room. I watched him through a gap in the books. He was skinny, wearing a hooded top and a baseball cap back to front.

He sniffed. 'Where are you, ya numnut?' He wasn't afraid. The strange noises he had heard earlier were forgotten. For now. He walked to the open window, looked out. His mate Sean was still there, lying on the ground rubbing his ankle.

And I stepped from the shadows and moved behind him.

Sean dared to look up. Saw his mate staring down at him.

'Get outta there quick, Bailey!' he shouted.

'What's wrong with you?' Bailey called. 'What are you doing there?'

He was about to answer, when behind Bailey the figure appeared. The figure in the black cloak, with the hooded skeleton mask. The figure in the *Scream* outfit. Bailey wasn't aware of anyone behind him.

On the ground, Sean couldn't speak. His breath was

coming in gasps of fear. This was like something out of a film. He held up his hand, pointed. He wanted to shout, 'Look behind you, Bailey!' Couldn't find his voice. His hand was waving at the window. The figure was moving closer behind his mate.

At last he could speak. 'Look . . .' was all he could manage, still pointing. Bailey turned round ever so slowly as realisation dawned on him, the realisation that something was behind him.

He screamed when he saw what it was. Staggered backwards towards the window. He wanted out. The figure lunged at him, and Bailey was tumbling out of the window with a scream of terror.

In the cupboard, Dev heard the scream from the library. Were his mates daft? Didn't they know they could alert someone? Even though the janitor lived on the far side of the school he might still hear all that yelling. What were they playing at? He dropped the books and came through into the library. It was quiet in here. Silent. No sign of his mates. He grunted. 'Bailey? Sean? Where the hell are you?'

Nothing. No answer. One of their daft games. Trying to scare him. As if. There was a sudden noise from behind one of the bookcases. He leapt there. 'Right, you!' But there was no one. There was nothing there, only books pulled out of shelves and hurled across the floor. Yet he felt there was something there. He shivered. 'I'm goin' to kill you two when I get ye.' They couldn't have got out of the library. Unless . . . he saw the open window. For the first time wondered if they had scarpered. He could never rely on those two. He crossed to it and looked out. There was no one out there. But they'd gone, he was sure of it now.

Again a noise behind him, a movement caught in the corner of his eye. He turned so fast he stumbled. 'Who's there? Is that you, Bailey?'

Something shifted in the darkness, some quick movement he couldn't quite catch. He moved forwards, angry now. 'Sean, this isnae funny. We haven't got time for this.'

He was breathing quick now, felt his mouth dry. Something moved again, something black, like a cloak. Dev moved back into the shadow of the room, now it was to his left. His eyes darted there, then suddenly to his right. The edge of a movement, a silent movement. Dev stepped back now towards the window. He called out once more. 'Who's there? Sean?' He waited for a moment, but there was no answer. 'Bailey?' His voice trembled as he said it, for now the movement was closer, coming closer. He could make out something between the shelves, something even darker than the shadows in the room, as if a shadow had come to life.

There was a sudden noise from the playground. 'Dev! Get outta there!'

He looked down, and there was Sean and Bailey. They looked petrified. 'Get outta there, Dev!'

Whatever was in here, it wasn't any of his mates.

Dev wasn't normally scared of anything. Not anything he could punch or kick. But what was this? Dev stepped back again. A flash of something. It was going to get him. His mind flicked back to the serial killer who was on the loose. He was here, in this school!

He was out of here!

Dev leapt on to the window sill, took one last look back, reluctant to run. It wasn't in him to run. The shadow moved again, one second and it would be on him, whatever it was. Dev leapt to safety. His mates were already stumbling out of the school gates. Dev landed on the ground, took one look back up at the window. It was dark in there, yet something moved. He hadn't imagined it. Something moved in the shadows. A shadow itself.

Dev got his feet and began to run.

I stood at the window and watched Dev run. He'd catch up with his mates. They'd wonder what was going on, but I had a feeling they wouldn't alert anyone that I was here. They were gone. I had planned to give them a little scare, enough to make them leave. I hadn't realised I would almost give all three of them a heart attack.

I pulled off the mask I had found outside Mr Brady's office with a flourish and smiled at it. The twisted skeleton face grinned back at me. I hadn't a clue why it had frightened them so much. I thought it looked kind of stupid. But I was just glad it had. 'Thanks, pal,' I said.

I looked round the library. Books on the floor, drawers pulled open and their contents everywhere. I was going to have some job clearing all this up, but it would have to be done and it would be worth it. No one must suspect there had been intruders in the school, no police called, and I could sleep easy.

SUNDAY

It was the church bells that woke me next morning, ringing out loud and clear from somewhere in the town. How long could I stay here? How long would this peace and quiet last? I got up from my bed and in the staffroom I made myself a cup of Mr Hepburn's coffee and, in the microwave, heated some waffles I'd found in the fridge. They were two days past their sell by date, but I was living dangerously. Those boys had been right, and I thanked them silently. I had found the master key, 156, in the pocket of a jacket hanging on the back of the staffroom door. Just as they had said. I wandered the corridors, my mug of coffee in my hand, and began to explore, revelling in the silence. With 156, the magic key, I could go from class to class.

It was an old school. Paint was peeling from the walls, and some of the panels on the ceilings were broken, or missing, revealing the loft space in the roof. There was no sign of a janitor. Maybe Sunday was his day off. How different it would have been if those boys had trashed the place.

Tomorrow, Monday, pupils would flood into the

school. My peace would be shattered, my hiding place found.

Or would it?

My eyes were drawn to the roof again, to the loft space up there. It must be big enough for a little guy like me to hide in. There must be some way I could get up there. Lying low by day, moving around by night. Just like Anne Frank and her family. They had hidden from the Nazis for years in the attic space of an office. Why couldn't I do that? The idea took hold of me. Why couldn't I?

I resolved to spend the day finding a place where I could get through into that loft. When I did, I would take some food up there, a blanket maybe, and something to drink – there was plenty still in the staffroom. I would have everything I needed – food, shelter, warmth. The essential aids to survival.

I was on a high when I found myself in the girls' cloakroom. Girls were messy, I decided. Clothes had been left strewn on benches, doors of lockers not quite shut. One caught my eye because of the name on the door. A name I recognised. Gaby McGurk. Her locker was cluttered with jotters and notebooks and one shoe. There was also a box of hair colour. She must be trying to change her image. She'd need a personality transplant in my opinion. So she was a pupil here. Just my luck. I saw that dream of holing up here shattering. If she saw me, with the old 'evil written over my face' (what a joke!), she'd be back at the police before you could say, 'drama queen'.

But then again – why should she see me? I'd be

110

hidden by day. She would never catch sight of me. If only I could make myself look different too. So different she wouldn't recognise me. I thought of my disguise from last night. The black cloak, the mask. Now it hung back where I'd found it, on a hook outside the head's office. Of course I couldn't go about dressed like that. It might make me a bit too conspicuous.

But the thought wouldn't go away.

A disguise.

Everyone was looking for a boy with wild black hair. I lifted the box of hair colour from the locker. Honeysuckle Blonde. Serve her right if I stole that.

I smiled. No one was looking for a boy with 'honey-suckle blonde' hair.

MONDAY

'OK, who stole it?' Gaby turned on the other girls in the cloakroom angrily.

'Who stole what?' The girl who asked was the toughest in the school. Big Mo, they called her – and she didn't like being called a thief.

Gaby swallowed her chewing gum. The last thing she wanted to do was offend Big Mo. 'I didn't mean you,' she said quickly. 'I just meant somebody else.' She was stammering. 'I left my blonde hair dye in here on Friday . . . and now it's gone.'

Too late she noticed that Big Mo had dyed her black hair blonde over the weekend. It stood out in angry spikes.

She advanced towards Gaby. 'You saying I stole it?'

Mo had her mates all around her, every one of them as big as Mo herself. Gaby took a step back.

'Now I remember. I put the dye in my bag. I took it home. Fancy me forgetting,' Gaby said, thinking fast.

Big Mo came close up against her. Too close. Gaby was expecting to be headbutted at any moment. Big Mo was famous for that. They said that was why her nose was squashed so flat into her face. Finally, however, Mo only shrugged. 'Lucky for you I'm in a good mood.' She laughed as she said it, as if it was something hilarious. So did her mates. Gaby giggled too, grateful that Big Mo had backed down.

Big Mo beckoned to her mates. ''Mon,' she said. 'The smell in this cloakroom's awful.'

Gaby didn't breathe till she'd gone. Then she shook her fist at the door. So Big Mo was pretending she hadn't stolen the dye. Just a coincidence she now had blonde hair . . . admittedly, the roots were still black. And Gaby was pretending to believe her. It was necessary to her survival to pretend that. But she knew different. She had left that dye in her locker on Friday, and now it was gone. And today Big Mo was a blonde. It didn't take rocket science to work out who took it. Of course Big Mo had taken it. Who else could it be?

'Heard any more about the murder?' Zoe had come up so silently behind her that Gaby jumped.

'I was at the police station on Saturday,' Gaby told her proudly, the heroine in this dark story. 'Doing an artist's impression of the killer. It'll be in tonight's paper.'

Zoe shook her head. 'Oh, Gaby, you're the only one who's seen him. I hope he doesn't come after you and kill you or anything.'

Gaby stared at her. 'Thank you for those words of comfort.'

Akash was running past them as they came out of the cloakroom. 'What's the hurry, Akash?' Gaby called after him.

He didn't even stop, only called back to her, 'Some so-and-so's stolen my PE kit – shoes and everything.'

113

'Well, look for a blonde,' she shouted after him, ''cause she stole my hair dye as well.'

I lay up in my hideout listening to the noises of a school on a Monday. Did I ever go to a school like this? I had found the perfect spot to get into the crawlspace in the ceiling – a loose panel in the boys' toilets, right above one of the cubicles. A foot on the pan, another on the toilet-roll holder and I was on the separating wall between the cubicles. From there, even I could reach the panel. Slide it across and jump in. I had stuffed everything I needed into a bag and dragged it up there with me. Now I was getting stuck into a tin of peaches I had taken from the canteen. The food, the sleep in a warm bed, the feeling of safety, were all making me feel bolder. Maybe I'd be crazy to run now. The police would be strung out around the town, looking for me, watching for me. I could almost picture a whole line of them cordoning off the town, searching through lorries and cars. Looking for me. The other man, the one I really feared, thought I was dead now. I was safe while he thought that. People didn't look for a dead man, did they? I should stay here, in this hide-out, till the heat was off.

Till the heat was off. The phrase came to me easily and I wondered where I had heard it.

What did it matter?

A thought burst in my brain. A daring thought, exciting. I couldn't resist it. I needed to know what was happening in the town. What if I could mill out of the school at the end of the day along with the other pupils?

One blond-haired schoolboy blending in with everyone else.

I could go into town, find out the latest news about the murder. Perhaps they had already arrested the real killer. Then I could come back – I knew now how to get into the school silently and secretly. Knew too the alarms weren't working. And I had the master key in my pocket.

I smiled to myself, ruffled my hair. 'Let's do it!'

'Do you think you'll get a Valentine?' Gaby asked Zoe. In her heart she knew Zoe wouldn't. Zoe wasn't the sweetest chocolate in the box. She had two eyes, a nose, a mouth, same as every other girl, but they seemed to be in the wrong places. She looked like one of those paintings by that Picasso guy. However, Zoe was a perfect friend for Gaby. When she was with Zoe, Gaby knew no boy would prefer her friend. They took one look at Zoe and their eyes automatically travelled to whoever was with her. Whoever it was had to be better looking than Zoe. Gaby wasn't being cruel. She didn't think she had a cruel bone in her body. She was just being honest. Zoe grinned. Her teeth were crooked too. 'I'd love to get one from Chas Munro. Do you think he'll send me one?'

Gaby smiled. She tried to look sincere. After all, poor Zoe couldn't help how she looked. 'I don't see why not. Just because he's the best lookin' boy in the school doesn't mean he hasn't noticed you.'

Chas Munro had noticed Zoe all right. Gaby had seen him once bump into her in the corridor and his eyes had almost popped out of his head. As if they were on stalks.

'Wow,' he had said. And poor Zoe had thought it was a compliment. She'd blushed and moved off, and had talked of nothing since, sure after the encounter that he would send her a Valentine. Gaby knew different. She'd seen the way he'd run off laughing with his mates. Laughing at poor old Zoe. Gaby had wanted to run after him and kick his even white teeth right down his throat. Nobody laughs at her friend.

'Maybe you'll get a Valentine too, Gaby.'

What a cheek, Gaby thought. As if she wouldn't get a Valentine. Gaby always did. At least two. One from a boy in the flats where she lived. He'd fancied her since she was nine. Unfortunately he was growing up to be one ugly looking guy. And she always got one from her latest boyfriend. This year, there was no latest boyfriend. No one had taken her fancy. Not really.

Zoe answered her own question. 'Of course you'll get a Valentine.' She said it as if to comfort Gaby, and that annoyed Gaby too. Then Zoe went back to dreaming about Chas. He was so good looking, and she'd just seen him coming out of the boys' toilets.

'Look at him, Gaby. Look at his lovely hair. I love his hair.'

Dev stood in the headmaster's office silently. 'It wasn't me, sir.'

He always got the blame for everything in this school and he was sick of it. Chief suspect every time anything went missing.

'It won't be the first time you've stolen the master key.'

'I didn't steal your soddin' key this time,' Dev shouted angrily.

The head roared at him. 'Don't you dare talk to me like that!'

But Dev knew his rights. 'Don't *you* dare talk to *me* like that. Accusing me with no proof. That's against my human rights.'

The headmaster could barely contain his anger. Dev knew he hated him, had hated his brother and sister before him too. 'We had better find that key, Dev. Because if anything happens in this school, you'll be the first one I'll question.'

Dev wanted to yell at him, 'There's somebody hiding in this school!' He knew there was. The someone who had frightened them off the other night, wearing a *Scream* outfit of all things, HIS *Scream* outfit! Brady had confiscated it just last week when Dev had run into the girls' changing rooms wearing it, and scared the life out of all those daft lassies.

And his mates had fallen for it! When they'd told him that, they'd had to hold on to Dev to stop him from racing back to the school and thumping whoever was in there.

'But, Dev,' they had whinged, 'he was pure scary in that *Scream* outfit!'

And he had yelled back at them, 'At least I thought it was a serial killer after us, not something from a blinkin' film!'

Someone had tried to make a fool out of him, and Dev didn't forgive that easily. But he wouldn't say a word to the headmaster. Revenge is so much sweeter when you mete it out yourself. He was going to come back, and he was going to give whoever was hiding in here a good thumping.

117

I lay in my special space above the boys' toilets, waiting and watching till every cubicle was empty, till the last boy had banged his way out. That last boy, I decided after watching him preening himself at the mirror for ten minutes, was a first-class nutter. He had taken ages over his hair, combing it, teasing down a lock over his forehead, trying to make it look as if it had fallen that way naturally. He took almost as long to check out his teeth. Then he had stepped back from the mirror to admire himself. 'You are gorgeous,' he had said.

I had to bite my lip to stop myself from letting out a giggle. But I waited till he'd gone, till I was sure he wouldn't step back in for one last loving look at himself, before I slid the loft panel across and dropped to the floor inside one of the cubicles. Now, I was safe. Anyone coming into the toilets would think I was just one of the pupils. I flushed the loo and stepped out.

I stood at the toilet door for a moment, nervous about taking this step. Maybe I should stay where I was. Safe and hidden. This was probably the stupidest thing I could do. But there was a boldness growing in me, and I had to know what was happening. If they'd caught the real killer I would be free to leave this town anytime I wanted.

The decision was taken from me anyway. The door was suddenly flung open, almost knocking me over. Two boys burst in. 'Watch it, pal,' one of them warned me, as if it was my fault.

I didn't even answer. I kept my head down and walked into the corridor. It was still crammed with pupils, running downstairs, crushing past each other, pushing against me. They were shouting, yelling, jumping in the air. They were going home.

I pulled up my hood and fell in beside them. No one gave me a second look. I might have been invisible. I headed with the crowd towards the exit doors.

Suddenly, someone grabbed me by the shoulder. I froze. I was swung round to face a spotty boy, head and shoulders taller than me. He glared at me for a second, then grinned. 'Sorry, pal. I thought you were Rab.' The spotty boy looked around him. Above the crowd he could see everything. He still kept his hand on my shoulder. 'Have you seen him?'

I found my voice at last. I was amazed at how cool I sounded. 'I'm always getting taken for Rab,' I said boldly. 'I think I saw him going into the toilets.'

Spotty face grinned again, let me go. 'Thanks, pal.'

I took a deep breath before I turned and walked on. But I was smiling, enjoying this. I stood taller. This was more fun that I had expected. As I came out into the fresh air I felt like jumping for joy too.

It was cold and there was a dark sky growling overhead. I walked in step with a crowd of boys, running with them, as if I was one of them, before moving in with another. Anyone watching from a window, from a distance, would never see I was a boy on my own. I looked like one of the crowd. I ran on past them, a boy running to catch the bus waiting on the corner, and mingled with the gang of boys surging aboard. Then I was off again, sprinting behind the bus to catch up with yet another group. No one even looked my way. I was just another boy, desperate to be away from school. I'm good at this, I thought, my confidence growing. Where do you hide a tree? In a forest. Where do you hide a boy? In a school full of boys.

I would head for the town centre. The one place I wanted to avoid was the high flats where I'd found the body. It would be cordoned off probably, with a strong police presence and an incident room somewhere close by.

In the town centre, I could get lost. I shoved my hands into my pockets and slowed my pace to a stroll. I walked past a baker's shop and the aroma of pastries and pies made me realise how hungry I was. Let's hope the teachers had left something tasty in the staffroom for tonight, I was thinking.

There was a newsagent next door to the bakery. My eye was caught by the board outside and the headline. *IS THIS THE FACE OF A KILLER?*

I stopped in mid-stride. My heart raced. Did this mean the police had caught him? That I was safe now? Safe to leave this town. I had to read that paper. I pulled open the door of the shop and went inside. Up one of the aisles and out of sight of the counter, there was a stand stacked with the day's newspapers. I moved casually towards it. The shop was almost empty. There was a woman paying her electricity bill at the counter and another studying birthday cards. I stopped and searched around for the local evening paper on the stand.

There it was.

The front page stunned me.

IS THIS THE FACE OF A KILLER?

The face of the killer they had been talking about was my own. The artist's impression that stared back at me from the front page was myself. A sketch that could only be me. My face to the life. Front page on every paper in the town. And I was in the town centre. I felt my knees go weak, my mouth go dry.

I lifted the paper from the stand. The artist's impression had been made with the assistance of Gaby McGurk.

I might have known. Her again, and she had caught my likeness to a T. My black hair, my eyes, even the dimple on my chin. Was mine really the face of evil? I was certainly staring back like someone demented, but evil?

At that second, I felt a hand on my shoulder. 'Right, son!'

24

Someone else, somewhere else, was also studying that artist's impression. Clicking into the newspaper's website, following the story of the boy on the run.

Just in case.

Not believing what he was seeing.

He'd been right to follow this story. Because this had to be the boy he was looking for. Had to be. Yet, how could it be?

Impossible but true.

This time it wasn't a blind alley. Those eyes, it was the eyes that gave him away. He couldn't be mistaken. Eyes that had seen too much. Now he knew where the boy was. This time he'd find him. He had to.

I was sure I was about to faint. I saw dots swim in front of my eyes. I was caught.

The man swung me round, stared at me. Then his eyes moved to the paper I was holding in my hand. To my picture. I swallowed hard. The front page seemed to leap towards me.

'Are you planning to buy that?' the man said. 'Because

this is not a library. You don't browse.'

I tried to answer him but I couldn't say a word. My mouth opened and shut. I must have looked like a fish.

The shopkeeper snatched the paper from my hands. 'Honest! Some of you boys have got the cheek of the devil.'

I couldn't believe it. The man had been looking at the mirror image of me in the paper and he hadn't recognised me. That was all I could think of. The words kept repeating themselves over and over in my head. 'He didn't recognise me.' Even with my face plastered all over the front page he couldn't see the resemblance.

I smiled. How could I help myself?

'You're lucky I don't get the cops on you,' the man nodded across to the counter and my heart almost stopped again. There was a young policeman, tall as an oak, standing at the counter waiting for a couple of sandwich rolls to be made up. He looked at me.

I couldn't look away. Try as I might my gaze was held by the policeman.

Then he winked at me. 'Hey, Mr Fisher, we're trying to get the kids to trust us, not terrify them.'

Mr Fisher laughed. 'I don't trust any of them. They come in here taking everything they can lay their hands on. You,' he prodded me with his finger, 'get outta my shop.'

My legs were like lead. I was sure any moment that the policeman would suss out who I was. Hand on the shoulder. 'I arrest you in the name of the law.'

'Sorry,' I muttered at last. 'Sorry,' I repeated it, sounding like some kind of idiot.

The policeman began forking out money for his rolls. If I didn't leave soon I would be going out the door with him. Mr Fisher was tidying his papers on the stand. Watching me suspiciously from the corner of his eye.

I legged it out of the door.

Mr Fisher shuffled back behind the counter. 'So, Lewis, how do you like being a policeman?'

'Love it,' Lewis said.

'You've been thrown right into the middle of everything with this murder. Any clues?'

'Don't ask me. I'm just a rookie. CID have taken over everything.' He tried not to sound too disgusted at the idea of that.

'Just wait till you're a detective, Lewis.' Mr Fisher had known Lewis since he was a boy, had known about his ambition for years.

'If only I could break this case, Mr Fisher, they would take notice of me. It would be a step in the right direction. It always happens in movies. Never seems to happen in real life.'

Mr Fisher wanted to help. 'The clue is probably right in front of our very noses, and we can't recognise it.'

'I would spot it. I know I would.' Lewis leant down to talk to Mr Fisher. Once, he remembered, Mr Fisher had seemed to him a tall and stately man. Now he realised just how small he was, a small man with a balding head. He could see the bald patch perfectly from this height. 'Listen, Mr Fisher, you keep your eyes and ears open for me. We both know the people here don't talk to the

124

cops. But the rumours go round in shops like yours, the truth. If you hear anything, let me know, will you?'

'Of course I will. If I hear anything I will let you know, pronto!' Mr Fisher promised. 'But first I'll check the stock in case that blond boy was shoplifting. He had a definite shifty look about him.'

Out in the street I ran for all I was worth. I wanted to put as much distance as possible between myself, Mr Fisher and the idiot policeman, before they realised just who I was. Yet, even as I ran, I was beginning to laugh. I had been in the shop with a cop. An artist's impression of me, and an accurate one, had been in plain sight, and I hadn't been recognised. I almost wished I could go back, just to tell him, just to see his face. What a plonker!

But I couldn't go back. The police were still after me. The thought sobered me immediately. I was still the prime suspect.

But at least I knew they wouldn't recognise me. Not in a disguise. Not with blond hair. Bet even daft old Gaby McGurk wouldn't recognise me. And now I had a safe place to hide. I'd stay there, I decided, for a while at least. No more trips to town, however.

I enjoyed the lonely walk to the river away from the shops and the car parks. Here by the riverfront there were only bars and nightclubs and restaurants. It was still too early for the nightclubs to open but some of the restaurants were already serving. I stopped at one of them, watched waiters laying plates of food on tables, pouring wine. The lamps were lit and inside it looked warm and inviting. What a luxury to have a meal made for you, to have it served up in front of you, piping hot. My mouth watered at the thought of it.

Beside the Italian restaurant, there was a seafood restaurant. Seafood A Go-Go. What a stupid name! Speciality of the house: mussels, crabs, haddock, langoustine.

There was a whole line of restaurants. The waterfront was obviously the entertainment centre of the town. And beside the restaurants, lay the nightclubs and discos.

SATURDAY NIGHT PARTY AT AL CAPONE'S
JOSHUA'S BAR
HEARTBEAT
RAVE ON –
Heartbeat?

I caught my breath. Heartbeat.

The man in the lift.

I was whisked back to those nightmare moments as the man had lain dying in a pool of his own blood.

'Heartbeat,' he had said. His dying word. *Heartbeat*.

Coincidence?

I stood for a while staring at the closed door of the nightclub. Heartbeat. It had to be a coincidence. What else could it be?

But, *another* coincidence?

Gaby's mother was at her again. 'If you dad hears any more about this he will go spare.' She threw the paper across the table at Gaby.

She wished her mother would stop referring to Dan as her dad. She'd never get used to him. Didn't want to. She wanted things back the way they used to be, just her and her mum.

Her mother knew exactly how she felt. 'You don't give him a chance, Gaby. I mean, he's good to you, isn't he?'

She couldn't fault that. Big Dan was good with the money. As if slipping her £20 would buy her loyalty.

'Lucky for you he's in such a good mood. He's had a big promotion. You might as well know that we might all be moving up to Aberdeen. What do you think of that?'

Gaby was on her feet. 'No! I don't want to go there. I like it here. My friends are all here. Zoe's here.'

'It'll be an adventure,' her mother said. 'You'll make other friends.'

This wasn't fair. First Dan comes into their lives, and now he was taking them away from everything she knew. She felt like crying, but she wasn't going to cry in front of her mother. She'd make an excuse to go down to Auntie Ellen's flat and have a good cry down there.

Her mother tutted loudly. She'd never understand, Gaby thought.

'Dan thinks the police have got a cheek on them involving a young girl like you.'

And of course, what Dan thinks had to be right! But what was she supposed to do when the police insisted she help them with this artist's impression? She couldn't very well say no to the police.

'That boy is long gone,' Gaby said. 'I don't know why they're even bothering about him. They'll never find him.'

Her mother sighed. 'Oh, Gaby, you'll be the death of me.'

Gaby was hardly listening. Like it or not, she was at the centre of this murder. Was it her fault she'd been at the wrong place at the wrong time? Every time she imagined the killer's face it grew more wild, more sinister, a drug-crazed murderer. Was it her fault she had been standing at the lift just as he was about to make his getaway?

Well, of course she had to admit that it was. If she'd been home when she was supposed to she would have been safe and in bed when it all happened. She wouldn't have seen the killer.

Or the dead man.

He hadn't been identified yet, and she couldn't understand that. Why hadn't anyone come forward?

Keep out of it. That was the rule around here. But what if she told that dishy young cop? He knew she'd recognised him. What if she told him and asked him to keep her name out of it? Told her where she had seen him? But then, of course, he would know where she had been that night, and that would cause no end of trouble.

Could she trust the police? Even Lewis Ferguson?

Every instinct told her no. Her mother didn't trust them. Neither did Big Dan.

Big Dan, a big gorilla of a man. Maybe if he was home right now, right this minute, she might confide in him. He always took her side, she had to admit that. He might this time too. He would protect her. But the moment would pass by the time he came home.

No. She'd just keep quiet about it. Let someone else tell the police about the dead man. After all, she couldn't have been the only one who saw him that night in Heartbeat.

I slipped back easily into the school. This time there were people in the building. I could hear the cleaners, their buckets rattling, their machines whirring, their voices echoing as they worked their way along the distant corridors.

I checked it was safe and heaved myself back up into the crawlspace above the boys' toilets. I was ravenous with hunger by now, but food would have to wait till the cleaners had gone and the school was empty.

Time to think.

Heartbeat. The dying man had said 'heartbeat'. You don't waste your dying breath on words that mean nothing. Had he meant that nightclub in the town? That

Heartbeat? But why? And why would he say 'four teeth'?

I would have to find out, and I wouldn't find out the truth in the papers. They had already branded me a murderer. You couldn't believe anything you read in the papers.

I wanted to find out the truth for myself.

I'd go back into town, I decided. Risky as it was, I would go. I'd go back to this Heartbeat, look for some kind of clue that would link the dead man to the night-club. I'd be safe enough. I was sure no one would recognise me now.

'You lot are a bunch of wimps.' Dev had been trying to get his mates to go back to the school. He was even angrier than he'd been last night, more determined to make someone pay for that anger. Smashing up the school had been enough for him then, but not now. Not after what had happened. He wanted to go back and get whoever it was who had scared them stupid. This had been just an ordinary guy, dressed up in a *Scream* outfit. He wanted to rip off the mask, see exactly who was behind it. He just couldn't convince his mates.

'Remember, Dev, there's a serial killer running about.'

'Come on, that wasn't the serial killer. It was someone from the school, someone who's got it in for me. That's how he stole the key. To make me look guilty.'

That was getting to Dev as much as anything else. He'd spent all morning in the head's office trying to convince him he hadn't stolen the key. Well, not this time anyway.

'Aw naw, Dev. I'm no' going back there.' Sean said it, and Bailey agreed with him.

Sometimes, Dev didn't know why he ran about with this couple of muppets. They were thick. 'Are you not angry that somebody tried to make a fool of ye?'

Bailey shook his head. 'He did make a fool of me and I don't care. I'm not going back.'

Sean backed him up. 'Aye, come on, we can trash something else. What about keying some cars, eh? That's always a laugh.'

But Dev was determined to go back in – not by himself though. Dev never did anything by himself. No. he'd find a way to get them to follow him – he always did.

26

TUESDAY

Gaby was quiet. She had been quiet since Zoe had met her at the school gates. This was so unusual that Zoe thought she was sick. 'Do you want to go and see the nurse? I'll take you.'

Gaby thought about that. She didn't feel sick, just worried. She didn't know what to do – and Gaby always knew what to do. But then, if she went with Zoe to the medical room the nurse might let her lie down – she might even let her go home. Sounded good either way.

She shrugged. 'OK.'

Zoe took her by the arm as if her friend was about to collapse at any moment. She shielded Gaby in case someone might knock her frail body over. 'Out of the way, please. Sick lady coming through.'

Gaby enjoyed the moment. She tried to look pale.

'All right, what's the problem here?' Mrs Molloy was the only qualified first-aider in the school. The pupils always called her the nurse. She eyed Gaby suspiciously. She knew Gaby and all her tricks. Every teacher in the school knew Gaby. 'You're saying you're sick?' She didn't sound like she believed it.

Gaby said softly, in her best invalid voice, 'I don't feel well at all.'

Zoe backed her up. 'Honest, she was nearly vomiting all over the corridor.'

Gaby looked at her. Zoe looked back. 'We had to stop twice on the way here.' She was so convincing, Gaby almost believed her.

Mrs Molloy held the door of the restroom open. 'Sit in there for a moment. I'll go and get something for you to take.'

Gaby sank slowly on to the bed, helped by Zoe. She kept the sick look on her face till the door closed and the girls were alone. 'Think she bought it?' she asked Zoe.

'What is wrong with you, Gaby?'

Gaby had to tell someone. It might as well be Zoe. 'Promise you won't say a word? Promise on your mother's life.'

Zoe held her hand over her heart seriously. 'I promise.' Then she said, her voice full of curiosity, 'What is it? Do you know where the boy who stabbed that man is? Have you seen him again?'

'I wish I did. I wouldn't be half as worried if he was caught.'

Zoe sat on the bed beside her, put an arm around her shoulders. 'Well then, what is it?'

Gaby looked around as if someone might be listening. 'I recognised the dead man in the lift, Zoe. I don't mean I knew him, but I'd seen him before. I thought they would have found out who he was by now. Someone would have identified him. But they haven't. They're calling him the mystery man and if anyone knows who he is they should come forward. And I recognised him.'

Zoe gasped. 'Tell the police,' she said. Zoe came from another area of the town, an area that wasn't so wary of the law. She didn't understand the way things worked where Gaby came from.

'I'm in enough trouble. I saw the murderer. I should have kept my big mouth shut about that.'

'But this is different,' Zoe said. 'This couldn't get you into any trouble.'

'I was going to tell that young cop – Ferguson, I think his name is. He's on our beat. He was there that night. He knew I'd seen him before. I couldn't hide it.'

Zoe couldn't understand her problem. 'Tell him then, and ask him not to reveal his sources. I saw them doing that on *CSI*. You could be his snitch.'

'I don't want to be his snitch,' Gaby said quickly, but the thought did appeal to her. 'Are they really allowed not to tell who told them?'

Zoe was sure of it.

Gaby bit at her knuckles, thinking hard. 'No,' she said finally. 'I don't want involved any more. My mum'll kill me if I go to the police again.'

'Where did you see him then?' Zoe asked eagerly.

Gaby looked around once more, sure there were ears somewhere, listening intently. 'Heartbeat,' she said. 'Same night he was killed. I saw him talking to one of the guys in there, and he looked scared, really scared. I think he knew somebody was after him.'

She made that bit up, as she made so much up, but he had looked frightened. She wished now she had listened in on that conversation, but at that moment she had been trying to hide from the bouncer. He was after her to throw her out for being under age.

Just then, Mrs Molloy came back in. She was carrying a small glass full of a thick yellow liquid. It looked revolting, like melted earwax.

She held it out to Gaby. 'Drink this down, Gaby. And you'll be fit to go back to your class in ten minutes.'

She was right about that. Gaby was back in class in ten minutes, but not before she had vomited the melted ear wax back up all over Mrs Molloy's shiny clean floor.

I had almost given myself away when I heard her say that word. Heartbeat. Lying in the loft space above the medical room, listening to the two girls talking. Gaby McGurk had seen the dead man there. It couldn't possibly be a coincidence now. But what did it mean?

In the staffroom Mrs Swankie, the English teacher, opened the fridge. 'Oh, for goodness' sake! Somebody's taken my roast chicken dinner. I left it here yesterday!' She looked round at her fellow teachers accusingly.

'Don't look at me,' one of them said huffily. 'I'm a vegetarian.'

'And my chocolate mousse dessert's gone too!' Mrs Swankie was really annoyed about that.

'Well, you did say you were going on a diet.'

She looked around them all again, saw guilt in every one of their faces. So that was why they had taken her food. Some smart alec thought she should lose weight.

I couldn't get what Gaby McGurk had said about
Heartbeat out of my mind. So at the end of the day, I
navigated my way through the loft space back to the exit
above the boys' toilets, and again, I slipped into the hub
of the school with ease. Jumping down inside the empty
cubicle, then out of the boys' toilets just like any other
pupil. No questions asked. I spotted Gaby McGurk hovering round the school gates, and kept as far away from
her as possible. She was too busy anyway with her flut-
ter of friends to notice me. I recognised someone else
too. The boy who'd broken into the school that night.
Dev. Did he never smile? His face was dark with anger
as he pushed his way through with his mates hurrying
behind him. For a second his eyes settled on me, stayed
there, and I felt my blood freeze into ice as I waited for
him to yell out 'It's him!', alerting the whole school. But
Dev's hostile gaze moved off after a few seconds. No
recognition. Nothing. I strode confidently down the
streets and alleyways to the waterfront, bold enough to
look people straight in the eye. I even stopped to help an
old man across the road. No one recognised me.

It occurred to me that Heartbeat would be closed. It
was too early in the day for a nightclub to be open, but
I still might find something. Some clue to let me know
what the dying man had been on about. There were
posters pasted on the walls outside advertising coming
events. A Queen tribute band was appearing soon, a
Valentine disco was coming up and a party night with
a sea theme: *Come dressed as a mermaid or a pirate*. The

poster encouraged people to make themselves look like idiots. I stood in a doorway across the street, watching for any strange goings on, for anything suspicious.

But there was nothing suspicious here. A beer lorry trundled round the corner and came to a halt at a side entrance. I glanced quickly right and left then crossed the street. The lorry was making a delivery and, as I approached, an iron hatch in the ground opened up for barrels of beer to be lowered into a cellar. I walked past nonchalantly, hands in my pockets, and as I passed I casually looked down, as any curious boy would. The lorry driver was calling down to someone in the cellar. I was as bold as brass, a boy with no reason to be afraid. I glanced into the beer cellar, slowing my pace so I could take a good long look. What did I expect to see?

There was someone in the cellar calling back up to the delivery men – a young man – and as I looked down, the boy in the cellar looked up and saw me too. My blood froze in my veins.

The man in the cellar was Eddie.

Eddie 'by the way'. The boy who had run with me from the tower block. The homeless boy who led me to the refuge in the boathouse. The boy who ran off to get his friends to help me. And never came back.

Eddie 'by the way' didn't look homeless now. Hair combed neatly, smart designer sweater, ordering men about like he was used to it.

I couldn't take my eyes off him, no matter how I tried. If I'd run then, he would never have known it was me. But I couldn't run. Eddie stared back at me, puzzled for a moment. Then his puzzled look turned in a few seconds to disbelief. Then to shock. He couldn't hide that shock. He looked as if he was staring into the face of a ghost.

And so I was a ghost. I was supposed to be dead. First in a fire, and then sucked down into the deep waters of a reservoir on the hills.

I was dead, and now I lived.

I had to get away from here before Eddie was able to stop me, to leap from the cellar and grab me. I stepped back. Eddie's face disappeared and the spell was broken. I turned and ran. I ran faster than I ever thought I could run. I ran towards the river, away from the school, sure a whole band of Eddies were after me. I had been afraid of one man, the man who had come after me, who had trapped me in a burnt-out car and tried to drown me. Now I realised that it wasn't just that one man, that man they called the Wolf, who was after me. Eddie had been part of it too. He hadn't run from the tower block at all. He had deliberately sought me out that night. But why? To find out what I knew. To find out what the man's final words were? And I had told him. Heartbeat. And that had been enough to sign my death warrant. I stopped for a second to catch my breath, glanced behind me.

The man's last words. Heartbeat.

Everything led to Heartbeat.

My sides ached with the pain of running. I doubled back on myself, took short cuts through back gardens, vaulted hedges, looking back constantly for signs of pursuit. I'm good at this, I thought as I ran. Running, hiding. I'm good at it, as if I've been used to being followed. Another puzzle, my past. My life was full of puzzles.

Had it been Eddie who'd set fire to the clubhouse, I wondered? Or the Wolf? I could have died in there. I was meant to die in there. My heart was like a stone, heavy with fear. Why were they after me? I had to get out of this town now, any way I could. Now they knew I was alive the man would be after me again. As I ran I worked out frantically what I would do. I'd go back to the school, grab whatever food I could and I would leave this place for ever. I'd hide in a lorry, or walk the railway track. I'd swim. Anything. But I had to get out of this town. Once I was out of here, I would be safe. This town would be the death of me.

How could I have been so stupid? I *had* been safe. They had thought I was dead. Why had I ever gone to Heartbeat? Too cocky, son! Too sure no one would recognise me. And because of that I had walked right into the spider's web.

I had lost the advantage.

They had thought I was at the bottom of the reservoir. Now they would be after me again. *He* would be after me again. The Wolf. This time he wouldn't give up till he got me.

I was afraid. No, afraid didn't even come near how I felt. I was terrified. Wished desperately to find someone to trust. But there was no one. I was alone.

Why didn't I have a home? Why didn't I have parents? It wasn't fair.

'He's alive,' Eddie said. He was shaking with nerves. He'd been unsure whether to follow the boy, try to catch him, drag him back, or run and tell the Boss. He decided telling the Boss was more important. 'He's dyed his hair blond.'

'You didn't follow him?'

'He was up on the street. By the time I jumped out of the cellar he was long gone. He's a right fast wee runner.'

'He knows too much,' the Boss said. 'He came to Heartbeat. He must know everything.'

'What are we going to do?'

'Get the Wolf here. He was supposed to have dealt with this.'

Eddie saw his chance. 'Let me handle it. The Wolf's

getting old. You've given him too many chances already. I could have got that wee rat in that clubhouse if you'd let me. It would have been all over by now.' He knew he could be better than the Wolf. All he needed was the opportunity to prove it.

The Boss ignored him. 'Get me the Wolf,' he said.

By the time I reached the school, the cleaners had gone. The lights were out and as I passed the janitor's house, with the living room curtains wide open, I could see him sitting comfortably in the living room, eating his dinner in front of the television.

All I wanted now was to be away. Already in my mind I was raiding the teacher's fridge, packing some warm clothes, even wondering if there was any money lying around I might take. I was too desperate to care if that was wrong. I had to get out of here. My teeth were chattering with the fear within me, remembering the terror of going down into that water. He would do that to me again, and worse.

He would be after me.

I had to get out of here.

I reached the broken window, grabbed hold of the drainpipe, and just as I was about to climb up on to the sill, a voice behind me whispered 'Gotcha.'

I turned slowly. My heart stopped beating. Every bone in my body quaked with fear. He had me.

'I knew we'd get you.' It was dark, too dark to see the faces but I recognised the voice. Dev. It was Dev. His voice was tight with anger. 'This is the one who tried to

frighten us. Eh, boys. What are we gonny do with him?'
He laughed but his friends didn't join in. I could make
them out now. The boys from the other night. Sean and
Bailey.

'I tell ye what we're gonny do,' Dev went on. 'We're
gonny thump the daylights out of you, pal. But first
you're gonny hand over that key you stole. I got the
blame for that, you know.'

He kicked out at me in his anger. Caught me on the
shins. I crumpled with pain.

One of the other boys laughed too – Sean – warming
to the idea of thumping someone. 'Can I have a go, Dev?'

Dev stepped back. 'Be my guest.'

Sean kicked at me too. Not with the same force, as if
he wasn't used to kicking. As if he was just trying to
impress his pal. The pain shot through my kneecap,
making me gasp. My eyes darted around looking for an
escape.

Dev saw what I was searching for. He grinned.
'Nowhere to go, wee man.'

But there had to be somewhere. I leapt forwards,
knocking Bailey, who was the littlest of them, off his feet,
and sprang through them across the playground. Dev
whooped with something like delight, relishing the chase,
knowing there was nowhere for me to hide. That they
would eventually catch me. They were at my heels like
hounds after a fox, laughing, shouting, 'You're for it now.'

I raced around a corner and saw at once I was trapped.
I had run inside a bike shelter. Cornered. There was
nowhere else for me to go. No way to escape. I stopped
and turned, backing deeper into the shadows of the shed,

hoping they might not see me. Foolish hope. Moments later, their silhouettes appeared against the night sky. They began advancing on me.

What had I done to deserve all this? I had no one to protect me, no one to turn to. I seemed to be afraid all the time, and I hated myself for it. These boys would get me, beat me up. I wouldn't be able to fight them off. And even if I did, someone else would find me. The big man . . . the man on the moors, the Wolf, and he was the one who really scared me.

It would be better if I was dead.

In that second I knew I couldn't go on. There were too many people against me. The police, the big man and now these boys. Fight off one, and the next one would step in to take his place.

I sank into the corner and hunched myself tight, my knees clamped together. I heard Dev call to his mates, 'I think he's surrendered, boys.'

'He's a bit of a wimp, in't he?' one of the others said. I think it was Sean.

'A bit of a wimp? He's a total wimp.' And Dev laughed again and so did the others.

They were right. That's what I was, a wimp. I didn't care what they called me. Didn't care what they did. Let them beat me, punch me, kick me. Nothing seemed to matter any more. I had no memory of my past and no one to care about my future. No one to help me. I was caught up in something I didn't understand.

I cowered further into the corner. They were coming closer. They wanted a fight. But there was no fight left in me.

28

Gaby saw the man before he saw her. She was sure of
that. He was hard not to notice. A tall dark man standing by the side of the road, staring up at the tower block.
He looked as if he was counting the floors, one by one,
right up to hers. Since the murder, Wellpark Court had
become something of a tourist attraction, but it was
mostly yobs and reporters who hung around. This man
was well dressed: a black suit, a tie, black hair slicked
back. He looked like a businessman. He definitely didn't
look as if he belonged here.

As if he felt her watching him, he drew his eyes away
from the building and looked at Gaby. She tried to hold
his gaze. What did she care if he stared at her? Maybe
he recognised her from the paper. But there was something about his eyes, coal black like buttons, that made
her look away quickly. He came towards her. She looked
quickly round her. With a police incident van on the
corner, she was safe enough out here, she thought, even
if he spoke to her.

'This is where the murder happened, isn't it?' he
asked her.

Gaby nodded. She had to stop herself from telling

him that she'd almost fallen over the body herself. It was such a good story. However, his next words made her realise he already knew that. 'You're the girl who saw the killer?'

'How did you know that?'

'Recognised you,' he said. 'Your photo was in all the papers. Do you really think he was the killer, the boy you saw?'

She hadn't expected him to say that. Gaby looked around again, checking the police van was still there. If she'd been alone this man would frighten her, she thought. Even here, in the middle of a busy street, he still frightened her.

He didn't wait for an answer. 'I saw the artist's impression too. He looks very young to be a hardened criminal.'

'They start young here,' she snapped the words out, trying to be cocky.

'I don't think he's a killer,' the man said. 'Not if he's the boy I'm looking for.'

Gaby took a step towards him. 'You know him? You're looking for him too? Then you've got to tell. You've got to.'

The man shook his head, and suddenly he looked vulnerable. 'I can't go to the police. I have to find him first. Only me.'

'Why?' Without realising it Gaby had again moved closer to him.

'Was this the boy you saw?' The man slipped a hand into his inside pocket and drew out a photograph. The boy in the snapshot was smiling, a happy grin on his face, his eyes bright. The last time Gaby had seen those eyes they had been filled with evil . . . hadn't they? But this was different, and yet it was the same boy.

Gaby tried to look as if she hadn't been sure she recognised him. 'Might be,' was all she said. Then, 'Who is he?'

The man's coal-black eyes filled with tears. 'My son.'

The boys were teasing me the way they would a trapped fox, jumping around, laughing, kicking at me. Baiting me to fight back. I brought my knees tight up to my chin, and folded my arms over my head.

That only made them angrier. 'This wee guy's a total coward,' Dev said, and the rest of them agreed. Dev pulled at my hooded top, trying to drag me forwards, but I stayed stiff and still, like stone, forcing myself not to move.

'Have you not got any fight in you at all?' Dev laughed, probably thinking how easy this was going to be. 'Maybe he doesn't know how to fight.'

It wasn't fair. I was always alone. Why couldn't someone come along and help me, even if it was only the janitor. Someone to help me, someone on my side, someone I could trust. Was that so much to ask? I pushed my mind into a place the boys couldn't follow. I wanted so much in that moment for someone to come and rescue me!

And I remembered the book I had read, about the boy spy. Why couldn't I suddenly produce some life-saving gadget? Or remember my SAS training? Or maybe suddenly discover I had some kind of magic powers? I could turn them into frogs or make myself invisible. Or leap tall buildings in a single bound. Then I could vault right over the school and be out of here. Or fly. Yes, if only I could fly. I imagined myself soaring like an eagle above their heads. Could almost picture their faces, astonished, angry that I had escaped. If only.

But that wasn't going to happen. This was real life. I didn't have any strange powers, I didn't have any magic tricks up my sleeve, or clever devices that would stun them till I made my getaway.

I had nothing. Only myself. My own wits.

No one to rely on. The boy with no memory. With no past.

But I'd done all right up to now.

With no one's help.

I had escaped a fire, survived drowning, lived unknown while the whole police force was on the look-out for me.

I didn't need anyone.

The thought surged into me like a tidal wave. I didn't need anyone. If I only had myself to rely on, then myself would have to be enough.

Was I going to let this bunch of lowlifes get the better of me? Was I going to let anyone?

In that second I knew I wasn't going down without a fight. A real fight.

A sliver of memory wound its way through my head. I'd had a glimpse of it before when I was sinking into the reservoir. This time it took hold, wouldn't let go. I *couldn't* go down without a fight. I had to survive. I

148

didn't know why. I just knew I had to. I began to shake, the blood seemed to roar through my veins. Everything in me, every bone seemed to come alive, quivered. I stood up. Why should I let them beat me up? It wasn't going to happen. I lifted my head and faced them. I wasn't going to be anybody's victim.

Dev laughed. He didn't know what was happening. Thought it was something he could handle. But I knew different. I ignored their jibes. Ignored them all. I felt a power inside me, a gathering storm.

I got to my feet, held out my hands, beckoned them forwards. 'Come and get me,' I said.

That took them by surprise. They stepped back. All except Dev.

He yelled in anger. 'I'm gonny give you a right kickin',' he shouted. Then he lifted his foot and aimed it at me. I grabbed Dev's foot, yanked it as high as I could, and Dev yelled with pain and shock as he was thrown backwards to the ground. I turned on the others.

'What is it wi' him? He looks weird.' Sean said it. He threw himself at me. In the same instant, I swung myself around, grabbed his leg and took the feet from him. He fell just as Bailey rushed towards me. I bent down, head-butted the boy in the stomach, taking the wind from him, sending him reeling backwards.

Sean was up again. He tried to grab at my legs. I leapt away from him, aimed a kick at his face, caught him a glancing blow. As he stumbled, I gripped his arm and swung him round towards Bailey. He was getting to his feet, ready to join in again. He didn't see Sean coming and they both went down in a heap. Dev was back on his feet now, advancing on me, darting this way and that. He leapt at my legs, trying to pull me off balance, but I was too quick for him. I was quick because I had more to lose than any of them. I jumped in the air and came down hard on Dev's hand. He screamed and rolled over. The other two leapt at me again. All I had to do was step aside at the last moment and they rammed into each other with such force they almost knocked themselves out.

Dev lay on the ground, clutching at his fingers. 'You've broke my hand. You've broke it.' Then he looked up at me. I was the only one left standing. 'Who are you?' he asked huskily. 'I'm gonny get the cops on you for this.'

The devil in me came out then. I couldn't resist it. 'I'm your worst nightmare,' I said. Then I was off, out of that bike shed, moving like the wind. Not sure where I was going. Only knowing I was never going to be anybody's victim again. Up to now, things had happened to me. From now on, I was going to make things happen.

'He's your son?' Gaby still couldn't get over what the man had just told her.

'I've been trying to find him for a long time,' he went on, his voice low. 'Searching through newspaper Internet stories that might just mention a boy, homeless, on the run. When I saw the artist's sketch in your local paper I was sure it must be him. Is that the same boy you saw?' Again he held out the photograph. He wanted it to be the same boy. He was almost pleading with her to say it was. Understandable, she thought. The man was searching for his son, wasn't he?

'I can't be sure,' Gaby said, for once trying to be honest, 'Same age I suppose, same black hair. But he was different like . . .' She tried to think how he was different. 'Well, he was covered in blood for a start.'

Did the man's face pale at the thought of that? She was sure it had. Maybe she shouldn't have mentioned the blood.

'But . . . it might be him?' he urged her.

Gaby shrugged. 'Might be, I suppose.' She was reluctant to say that it was. She didn't know why. 'Why did he run away?' she asked.

'His mother died,' the man said. 'He couldn't handle that. Neither could I. I suppose I neglected him. There were lots of fights. I did a lot of things wrong. I didn't realise how much until one day . . . he just went out and didn't come back.' He seemed genuinely upset. 'I've been searching for him ever since.'

Gaby hoped he wasn't going to cry.

'So you see why I can't go to the police. I want to find him first. I want to help him. He needs my help if he's in trouble. He's only a boy.'

She was studying his face, looking for a resemblance. She could see none, except for the dark hair and the black eyes. But then Gaby didn't look a bit like her mother. Everyone said she took after her dad. Maybe this boy looked more like his mother.

'You'd help him even if he . . . killed someone?'

'You can understand that, can't you? Maybe it was self-defence,' the man said. 'Maybe this man was trying to kill him. We can't know until I find him and we get this thing worked out. He must feel so alone, as if nobody cares. I have to find him.'

Gaby hadn't thought of self-defence. She had seen a boy coming out of the lift, desperate not to be found with a dead man. He had just killed him, it had seemed obvious to her. What else was she supposed to think?

'I don't know how you expect me to help,' Gaby said.

'You already have,' he answered her. 'I think it was my son you saw that night. I think he's still in this town. I have to find him.' He seemed determined. 'He's all alone. He needs someone. He needs me.' He looked at her and smiled. 'If you hear anything, will you let me

152

know? I'm staying here.' He handed her a card from one of the local hotels. 'I'm in room 114. The police might tell you something that even the papers don't know.'

Gaby took the card and hurried into Wellpark Court. She glanced back once to make sure he wasn't following her – but he had gone. Not a sight of him anywhere. As if he'd been sucked into the night air. It was only then she realised she hadn't even asked him his name.

I couldn't risk going back into the school now. Though there was food there, shelter and warmth. All that was over. Dev and his mates knew I'd been hiding there. Instead I ran back towards the town. It was a dark February night, an icy mist was rising above the houses. I stood in a bus shelter and tried to think. What was I going to do next? Less than an hour ago, I thought I had it all worked out. Getting out of the town away from all this, away from the big man who was trying to kill me – that was all I could think about. But something had happened to me back there in that bike shed. Maybe I was just sick of being a victim. No, it was more than that. It had been as if there had been a voice inside me, urging me on. A memory. I leant back against the Perspex wall of the bus shelter and smiled.

That had reassured me. A memory. My memory would come back eventually, I was sure of it now. And everything about my past would be clear.

But something else had changed too. I would survive. Had to. There was a reason why I must go on, and not give up. I didn't know yet what that reason was but I knew I would follow that instinct from now on, no matter what.

But survival didn't mean running away from things. I wouldn't run again, not until I was ready. Not until I had solved this mystery. I hadn't been responsible for that man's death and I was going to prove it. I was learning that they – whoever 'they' were – were afraid of what I knew. They were afraid of me. They had sent Eddie after me to find out what I knew, and then they had tried fire and water to get rid of me. But I was still here.

Heartbeat was the key. Heartbeat. The dying man's words. The place where Eddie worked. The last place Gaby McGurk had seen the dying man. I had to find out more about Heartbeat.

I needed somewhere to sleep tonight. And I realised I wasn't worried about that either. I'd find a place. I was alive and I intended to stay that way. Nothing was ever going to worry me again.

Dev, Sean and Bailey stood in the bike shed trying to get their breath back. Sean was cradling his head in his hands. 'I think I've got brain damage,' he said.

'First you've got to have a brain.' Dev had no sympathy with him, with either of them. He was too angry. His hand was too sore.

'I didn't know he was such a good fighter,' Bailey said. 'Did you see him coming right at us. It was as if he'd suddenly turned into Batman.'

There was more than surprise in his tone, there was awe, and that only made Dev angrier.

'Did you no' think so yourself, Dev?' Sean was trying to get round his big mate, but it didn't work.

'Batman, nothing. He was scared. That was all. Shut up! I'm trying to think,' he snapped. Dev was trying to think about a lot of things. The boy was smaller than him, he'd been sure he would be easily beaten. One minute cowering in the corner, the next leaping at them like a wild animal. Fighting them off, all three of them. Fighting like a devil. It was as if he had grown in height too. And those eyes of his, they had seemed to glow with a fire. It was the eyes Dev was thinking about most. He had seen those eyes before. He was certain of that. In those moments when that boy had stood facing them down in the dark, Dev was sure his eyes were familiar. As if he'd seen them somewhere recently. The boy had been sleeping rough, somewhere in the school. Living rough for how long? Homeless. On the run.

It came to him like a bolt of lightning. He punched the wall with his fist, then yelled with pain and cradled his hand against his chest.

Bailey jerked back, afraid the punch was meant for him. 'What is it, big guy?'

Dev's fury was gone. Even the pain didn't matter. He smiled. 'I've just figured out who that boy is.'

Now Gaby had two things to worry about. She'd recognised the dead man, and the killer's father had confided in her. Should she tell that good-looking cop about this? But what if the man was telling the truth? And why should he lie? she wondered. He wanted to find his son before the police did. That was natural, understandable. What should she do? She lay on her bed and tried to concentrate on her favourite soap. She could always find the answers to her problems in her soaps, but there hadn't been a storyline like this in any she could remember. She couldn't concentrate. It was impossible. She jumped up and stood at the window, looking down into the street. Down fifteen floors. She half expected to see the man standing there under a street lamp, his face illuminated, staring up at her – just like that scene in *The Exorcist*. Oh why did she have such an imagination? The man wasn't there, of course. He was long gone, back to his hotel. Waiting for a lead to take him to his son.

Her mother came barging into the room. She never knocked. Zoe's mother always knocked before she came into Zoe's room, but never Mrs McGurk.

'Do you not want any tea?' She'd called Gaby three times already. Gaby shook her head.

'Maybe later. I'm not hungry just now.'

'You're not on another one of your diets, are you?' Her mother sat down on her bed. 'Are you still worrying about that murder? You know your dad – Dan,' her mum corrected softly. 'You know he won't let anything happen to you. To either of us. You know that. You don't have to be frightened of anything. If there's something bothering you, I wish you would talk to Dan about it. I'm sure he would help.' She walked to the door. Their heart-to-heart over. Her mother only ever seemed to talk to her in sound bites. 'Well, I'm off to my yoga class. You be all right now?'

Always the same thing from her mother. Give Dan a chance. Let him be your dad. Always wanting to play happy families. If only she did have a dad, Gaby thought. Maybe she could confide in him.

There was money on the floor of the bus shelter. I spotted it in a corner under a crisp packet. Not much. One shiny coin. Not enough to buy me any food. Not enough to get me out of this town. Just enough to make a phone call. That was all. I could picture some old drunk fumbling with his change as he waited for the bus, stooping to pick up what had fallen from his hand, missing this one little coin.

If I could make a phone call, who would I call? I didn't know anyone in this town. I didn't know anyone anywhere. The only person whose name I even knew was

Gaby McGurk, and her address, Wellpark Court. That's who I would call, I decided.

Spur of the moment stuff. Gaby McGurk. I would find out her number and I would phone her. Tell her the truth. Tell her I wasn't a murderer. I'd stumbled on the body accidentally. That there was some kind of conspiracy going on in this town and it was centred at Heartbeat. Then she could tell the police, get her name in the paper again. That would keep her happy. The police would find out the truth, and I would be free. Free to do what? I wondered. Free to move on. Yes. I picked up the coin and palmed it. I had nothing to lose. I was going to phone Gaby McGurk.

Lewis saw the gang of boys rushing towards his car. Well, not exactly a gang, just three of them crashing down the street as if the devil was after them. He stepped out of the car. 'OK, boys, what's the problem?'

Dev was breathless but he wanted to be the one to tell him. 'We found that killer, boss. The one that stabbed the man in the lift. We've just seen him.'

Lewis looked round them, clocked the black eye and the lump the size of an egg on another boy's forehead. 'Did he do this?'

'He's a killer,' Dev said, as if that explained it. 'We tried to corner him, but he was vicious. He had a knife.' He had just thought up that bit and looked round at his mates, warning them to back him up.

They all jumped into the conversation enthusiastically. 'It was a really big knife,' Bailey said.

'It might even have been the murder weapon,' Sean added.

Dev thought they were going a bit over the top but he said nothing.

'We were trying to make a citizen's arrest.'

Lewis had a feeling this was far from the truth. He knew all about exaggeration. He had been a boy himself once, not so long ago.

'And where did you come across this . . .' He hesitated. 'This killer?'

'In our school. I sussed it out.' Dev said proudly. 'Things were going missing, the master key for the whole school. And I got the blame for it.'

Lewis nodded. This boy looked as if he would get the blame for just about everything.

'He's not there now, I take it?'

'No. He ran.' Bailey sounded disappointed.

'We scared him off.' Dev sneered.

Lewis looked again at the lumps, bumps and bruises and had a feeling it wasn't the other boy who'd been scared. He pulled his personal radio close to his mouth. He would call in for back-up and they could go to the school and check it out.

Here I was back where all this had begun. Wellpark Court. I stood at the corner behind the shops and watched the entrance. The last time I'd been here a man had just been murdered. The place had swarmed with police. The police were still here, probably a lot more than was evident to me. I saw a car with two men in it, looking as if they were waiting for someone. Plain clothes. I would put money on it, if I had any. An incident van was still parked up on the pavement. Why had I come back here? Because Gaby McGurk lived here. The girl who'd called me a killer.

I had found her number in a tattered old phone book that looked as if someone had peed on it. I felt my heart pounding as I waited for her to answer my call. and all of a sudden my mind went blank. What would I say to her?

Gaby was alone when the phone rang. Mum at yoga and Dan out at the pub. She lifted the receiver, expecting it to be Zoe. Gaby had phoned her earlier, left a message to call back as soon as possible. She was dying to tell her about the Dark Man who had spoken to her.

'Zoe?' she said at once, ready to launch into the story.

'Is that Gaby McGurk?'

She didn't recognise the voice – a boy. Someone from her school maybe. Someone who fancied her? It was after all, almost Valentine's day. Maybe it was someone asking for a date.

'I'm Gaby,' she said.

The boy on the other end let out a long sigh. 'I'm not a killer.'

Gaby couldn't say a word. She waited for him to speak again, but nothing came. Until he said once more, 'I'm not a killer.'

It was him. The receiver began to shake in her hand. It was him. He had her number.

'Are you still there?' He didn't wait for her answer. 'Listen to me! I'm not a killer and I've not got evil written all over my face. Where did you come up with that one?'

She found her voice at last. 'It was you!' she snapped at him. He was far away on the other end of a phone line. He couldn't hurt her. 'You were in the lift with him. You were covered in blood.'

'I found him in the lift. The doors shut and I was trapped in there with him.'

Did she believe that? What if she was the one who had stepped into the lift and found the dead man. Would she have been the chief suspect? 'Go to the police then. Tell them,' she snapped.

'You've got to be joking. They would never believe me. No one would believe me. Especially after what you said.'

161

She was trying to figure out his accent. Not from here, but where? He had a Scots burr in his voice, but there was something else, something she couldn't put her finger on. He was still speaking. 'Everybody's out to get me.'

'Everybody?' Gaby asked.

'The police, and somebody else. Somebody's trying to kill me. I don't understand what's going on. But this wasn't just an ordinary murder. It's some kind of conspiracy.'

'Rubbish!' Who was he trying to kid? A conspiracy. She wondered for a moment if she should tell him about the Dark Man. She didn't want to be talking to him at all. But she couldn't stop herself. 'I know somebody else who's after you.'

For a moment she thought he had dropped the phone, or they had been cut off, it took him so long to answer her. 'Somebody else?' he asked.

Dramatic moment. Gaby had watched too many soap operas not to make the most of it. 'Your dad,' she said at last.

I crashed down the receiver as soon as she said it. Felt my legs give way under me. My dad?

Something, some kind of memory, flashed into my head. Then, just as quickly, it was gone before I had a chance to snatch it, grasp it. My dad was looking for me. My dad was here in this town. Someone to help me at last. Someone who could answer all my questions. But where was he? What did he look like?

My *dad* – even the words were a comfort. As if a warm blanket had been thrown over my shoulders. I put the receiver back to my ear. Hoping against every hope that Gaby was still on the line. I should have asked her more, but the shock of those words had been too much.

She was gone. I punched the buttons angrily. I wanted her back, wanted to ask her more. How did she know? Had she seen him, spoken to him?

But I'd broken the connection. I pushed open the door of the call box and looked up at Gaby's window, willing her to come there, see me standing here. I didn't have any more money. So no more phone calls. But I wasn't going to leave it like this. I was going to have to talk to Gaby McGurk, face to face.

It was clear that someone had been sleeping at the school. The boys hadn't been lying. Well, not this time. With some other officers Lewis had gone to the school, searched the corridors, found the open vent in the boys' toilets and up there, in the loft space, they had found a blanket, some biscuits, a bottle of water. Evidence that someone had hidden here, by day anyway. There was a book too, taken from the school library. Was this the den of a killer? Lewis could only picture a frightened boy lying here, trying not to make a sound. But not a boy with 'evil written all over his face'. He picked up the book lying open on the floor. Not a boy who read *The Falcon's Malteser*. He'd loved that book too when he was a boy.

Lewis jumped down from the loft. The officer in

charge was waiting for him in the corridor. 'There has been somebody up there, sir,' Lewis said. 'But he was just a boy.'

The officer's face was grim. 'There is no such thing as "just a boy", PC Ferguson. If this is the same boy who fought off those three young thugs, he is someone to contend with. Don't underestimate him.'

He could have fought that lot off in desperation, Lewis was thinking – and was this another bit of information that would disappear into the air and never be mentioned again? As if it had gone into the Bermuda Triangle. If I wasn't such a trusting kind of guy, Lewis thought to himself, I'd say there was a conspiracy going on.

Gaby stood staring at the phone, waiting for it to ring again. It didn't. She wondered why not. He'd hung up as soon as she'd mentioned his dad. Didn't want to face him probably. Selfish so-and-so. She pictured the Dark Man again, almost in tears talking about his lost son. She crossed to the window and looked down into the street. People were milling about, women on their way to a night at bingo, couples going out on dates. A blond boy was watching other boys playing football in the street, in spite of the notices clearly marked *NO FOOTBALL*. Why didn't boys ever learn to read signs? she wondered. Did they think the police wouldn't bother about football if they had a murder to investigate? That wasn't the way it worked according to her mother. The police could spot an out-of-date road tax disc at a hundred yards, but serial killers on the loose roamed free.

Her eyes went back to the incident van. This was just the kind of incident they were looking for. 'Murderer calls only witness.'

The boy had said he was innocent. Why did he feel the need to tell her that? Innocent? No, she couldn't believe that. Hadn't he told her he did it? And she'd seen him with her own eyes, his clothes soaked in blood. He had lunged at her, hadn't he?

But what if what he'd said on the phone was true? Should she tell the police about the call? No. Big Dan had told her not to go near the police again, so had her mother. People up here didn't go near the incident van. No one wanted to be accused of helping the police with their enquiries.

She stood up straight. Made her decision. She wouldn't tell the police, but she would phone the boy's dad. She took out the card he had given her. Yes, that would be the right thing to do. Now she had another secret.

It would be madness to stay here with so many policemen in the vicinity, a police incident van nearby, yet I couldn't move.

I had to speak again to Gaby McGurk, but how? I couldn't go up to her door, I couldn't risk going to the school and I couldn't wait till tomorrow either. But I had to see her. I couldn't let those words go by without finding out more.

My dad.

Somewhere in the town, he was searching for me. The idea made my head swim. Maybe I wasn't alone any more.

Gaby was still staring at the card when the phone began to ring again. She jumped and the card leapt from her fingers. She stood staring at the phone, almost afraid to lift the receiver. What if it was HIM again? The boy? That would be the answer. She would tell him how to contact the man, his dad, she decided. She snapped up the phone just before it went into the answering machine, and held her breath.

'Gaby, is that you?'

The voice was Zoe's.

Disappointed, relieved, excited. She felt all those things. It was Zoe! 'Zoe! You'll never guess what's just happened. You'll never guess who's just phoned.'

She couldn't keep it to herself. She rattled out the story at machine-gun speed about the boy phoning, about the man who claimed to be his dad. She was even more breathless by the time she finished.

'You've got to tell the police.' That was always Zoe's suggestion. Why couldn't she understand just how hard that would be?

'My mother would kill me,' Gaby said.

'Well, I don't know whether you should phone this man. Do you trust a man who comes up to you in the street and tells you he's the father of a killer?'

'But you should have seen him, Zoe. He was dead upset.'

166

'I don't like it.'

'Are you goin' to meet me, Zoe? I need to talk to you about it before I decide.'

Zoe agreed at once. 'I'll get the 7.30 bus and meet you at the bus station.'

Gaby was glad to have someone to talk to. Someone to share the secret with. 'Great, Zoe. Thanks.'

She put down the receiver feeling a lot better. She would talk it over with Zoe. Maybe together they could go to the Dark Man and tell him about his son. Or even go to see that dishy PC Ferguson.

33

I almost missed her. She came hurrying out of the flats looking around as if she expected someone to be following her. Probably me. I darted into a doorway. It was dark and I became just one of the shadows. Her eyes passed me over. She began to hurry down the street. Where was she going looking so suspicious? To the police, to tell them I had called her? But she gave the incident van a wide berth as she passed it, as if she thought the long arm of the law would reach out and snatch her inside.

Or was she going to see my 'dad'? Perhaps if I just followed her she would lead me to this man. One look and my memories would surely come flooding back. My dad would clear all this up, with the police. He would take me home – to safety.

So why hadn't my dad contacted the police in the first place? Why talk to this Gaby first?

Maybe it was all a trap. As soon as I had phoned Gaby, she had immediately called the police. They knew I would follow Gaby McGurk and she would lead me straight into a police trap.

But then, how could they know I would phone

Gaby McGurk?

I was so busy thinking all this through that I almost bumped into her as she stopped at a shoe-shop window. I dropped to my knees, pretending to tie my laces, but I didn't have to worry about her spotting me. Her concentration was elsewhere. She was busy gasping at the array of coloured shoes on display. She wouldn't have noticed if a brick had fallen on her head. And was she talking to herself?

Yes, she was. Mouthing something that looked like – 'I've just got to have them.' Just my luck that the person I was relying on to help me was half daft. She finally dragged herself from the window and hurried on, checking her watch as she did.

She was meeting someone, I realised. And as she picked up speed, I knew she was scared she might be late.

Was she going to meet my dad? Had she called him as soon as she'd spoken to me? I found myself scared and excited at the prospect of seeing him – meeting him.

She stopped again for a moment. The road forked. The main street turned down towards the town centre. The other pathway was a dark alleyway that backed on to shops and a pub. She seemed undecided which route to take. But after a moment she turned into the alley.

I gave her a moment, then I quietly followed after her.

She was going to be late for Zoe. But then she was always late for Zoe. Zoe expected it. But tonight, she didn't want to be late. That was the only reason she'd taken this shortcut. It wasn't the kind of route she would normally choose. It was too dark, no brightly lit shop windows, no traffic. She glanced behind her again, sure someone was following her. She'd had that feeling since she left the flats. She'd feel better when she'd told the whole story to Zoe.

If she ever got the chance.

Her imagination relived scenes from films she'd seen. The beautiful heroine hurrying down a dark road, carrying important information about the killer. The killer is after her. Big knife. Blood. Beautiful heroine's blood. And she's left sprawled artistically on the grass. Eyes wide, hair spread out around her, beautiful still, but dead.

She'd seen so many films like that and had always been the first screaming out, 'Don't go that way, you idiot!'

And here she was, going that way! Was someone behind her? She caught her breath, sure she had seen a movement. She looked round just once. Nothing. No one. A car passed the alley up on the street and she felt more secure. She wasn't far from anything really. She could hear buses on the road. Hear music from the near-by pub. Too much imagination, Gaby, and she turned back with a sigh. Saw a face. And screamed.

Her scream was cut off as a hand was clamped over her mouth. All she could see was blond hair, spiked. A boy who looked as young as she was. It took some of the fear out of her. A boy! How dare he! She bit hard into his hand and this time it was he who screamed. He let her go and she took the chance to run. But he was faster

170

than she was, grabbing her by the shoulder and hauling her back.

'I just want to talk to you.' She didn't listen. Started screaming again when she heard the voice. Recognised it. The voice on the phone. The voice of a killer. This time his whole arm went round her mouth. 'Shut up! Shut up and listen.'

She tried to struggle, kicking at his shins. He was dragging her into a doorway. A knife-wielding maniac was dragging her into a doorway! No. This time she turned herself round and headbutted him. He let out a yell of pain, staggered back. As soon as he did she pushed him further so he fell against the wall, clutching at his head, and began to slide to the ground.

Gaby's head wasn't feeling much better than his, but she was ready to run. He grabbed at her ankle. 'Please.' The word came as a surprise. 'Please,' he said again, pleading with her. 'You have to tell me about my dad.'

Her common sense told her to run to get away. But she was never good on common sense. Something in his eyes, not evil – not this time. Pain. He had dyed his hair blond, but the eyes were the same. She tried to run, but she was held by those eyes. 'Please,' he said again. 'I didn't kill anybody. Honest.'

34

This girl, this Gaby, stood staring down at me. I hadn't expected her to put up such a fight. I was still seeing double from the headbutting. If she'd been a boy I would have headbutted her back. But I could hardly headbutt a girl, could I? And once again I thought I must be a decent boy, brought up well, when I couldn't hit a girl. But if she ran now, didn't listen to me, I'd never be able to catch her again. She'd go to the police, surely she would. 'Please,' I said again.

And this time she answered me in that cheeky voice of hers. 'Now why should I listen to you?'

I wanted to say the right thing, the thing that would make her stay and listen. But what was the right thing? 'My dad. You said you spoke to my dad.'

She took a step back from me as if she was afraid I'd reach out and grab her again. 'He says he's really worried about you. He wants to find you before the police do, so you can go to the police together, sort it out.'

'Do you trust him? What does he look like?'

Now she was intrigued. 'You don't know what your own father looks like?' Her lip curled in disbelief.

I decided to be honest. 'I have no memory. I can't remember who I am. Where I came from.' I had never told anyone before and now that I had someone to tell, it all came pouring out. As if a cork had been pulled from a bottle. I told her everything, from finding the body in the lift, to hiding in the clubhouse with Eddie, to the fire and the terror of the plunge in the car. Hiding in the school, the fight with Dev and his mates. Only a couple of hours ago. It seemed an age now.

'That would be Sammy Devlin. Dev, we call him. I think he's spawn of the devil if you ask me.' By now she had crouched down beside me, listening intently. 'And you scared him and his mates with a *Scream* outfit? His *Scream* outfit? That's mental.'

I didn't know what she meant. 'What's a scream outfit?' I asked her.

'You really have lost your memory, haven't you?'

'Do you know where my dad is?' My dad – the words sounded strange.

Gaby nodded. Told me.

I got to my feet. 'Let's go there. I have to see him.'

Gaby took another step back.

'I'm not going to kill you or anything,' I told her. 'I'm not a killer. Don't you believe me?'

She still wasn't sure. I could see that in her face. But she wasn't afraid of me either.

'Oh, come on then. I'll take you.' She turned to me as we stepped from the alley. 'But one false move, pal, and you are dead meat.'

Gaby strode in front of him. She kept glancing back just to make sure he wasn't coming after her with a knife. 'You see, you don't look so suspicious when you're walking with me.' Gaby found she couldn't stop talking. Nerves, probably, she told herself. She was usually really shy when it came to boys. She went on, 'They probably think you're my boyfriend.'

He pretended to be sick on the street. 'I think I'd rather be caught by the police,' he said.

What a cheek! 'That can be arranged. All I've got to do is scream.'

Actually, in the short time they'd been together Gaby had lost all her fear of Ram. (*Stupid name*, she thought.) He was just a boy. She had decided that even if he had killed the man in the lift – and she had no real reason to believe he hadn't – it was probably self-defence, or an accident. Added to that, she liked the mystery surrounding him. He had no memory. It was like an episode of her favourite soap.

She was leading him towards a big anonymous hotel by the river. Down here on the waterfront, away from the ugly built-up tower blocks, it was almost beautiful. There was a perfect view down a glassy black river with purple, snow-tipped hills on either side. It all looked so peaceful, she thought, it was hard to believe such a drama was happening in the middle of it.

In the car park, he pulled at her arm. 'You get him down here, outside the entrance. I just want to see him. Once I see him, I'll come over. But you've got to promise not to tell him I'm here. Promise!'

She yanked herself free of him. Giving her orders

174

indeed! 'I know what to do,' she said.

'Don't go to his room.' He looked genuinely worried about that.

'D'you think I'm daft?' she snarled at him. 'I can take care of myself. I'm not going to anybody's room. I'll get them to call his room from reception. Then I'll ask him to meet me outside, under the street light so you can have a good look. OK? I'm going to tell him you phoned me. Right?'

He looked nervous. Maybe, she thought, seeing this man – his dad – for the first time might be the trigger his memory needed. His past would come flooding back as soon as he saw his dad's face. And it would be all thanks to her. It gave her a glow to think about it. Gaby pointed to the bushes growing at the wall of the car park. 'Hide in there.'

He crouched down behind a massive rhododendron bush. Honestly, she thought, did he really think nobody could see him there? How he had ever managed to stay free without her help she would never know. She tutted. 'Try not to look so suspicious, eh?'

I watched her walk into the hotel. She tripped once over a cobble and almost fell. She must have heard my giggle, couldn't help it, and she looked back and glared at me. That look stopped me laughing instantly.

Why was I trusting her? She loved being in the middle of a murder, having her face splashed all over the front page of the papers. Maybe she would go in there and come out with a whole battalion of police. I'd be

175

trapped. I had only her word that she'd spoken to this man who claimed to be my father. Perhaps it was all a lie. A lie to catch me.

So why didn't I just run?

Because I wasn't going to run any more. I had finished with running. I had to see this man's face. The face of my father. I had to know.

'He's dyed his hair blond,' the Boss said, putting down the phone. 'And he's been sleeping rough in the high school.'

'Sure it's the same boy?' The Wolf was holding in his anger. He didn't want it to be the same boy. He wanted that boy dead.

'It's the same boy.' The Boss paused, letting the information sink in. 'If he's still here he must know something. Now he's seen Eddie he's connected what he knows with Heartbeat.'

'Maybe you should just forget the plan,' said Eddie.

The Boss turned on him and Eddie suddenly looked sheepish. 'Forget the plan? Never. No wee boy is going to make me change my plans. No. We're going ahead.'

Eddie changed tack. 'Well, let me get him then. I could finish him off. I know I could.'

The Boss ignored him. He glared at the Wolf. 'You go after the boy. Get him this time.'

The Wolf nodded.

'Find him. And this time when you kill him, make sure he's dead.'

The Boss left. The Wolf stood up to go. This was his

last chance. He had to get that boy. Not just for the Boss. No. For him. He was becoming obsessed with this boy. No one had ever got the better of him before. He couldn't let this boy escape his clutches. He had a reputation to keep up.

He looked at Eddie, at his pasty face, his skinny body. Yet, he had a tiger in his eyes. He knew how much Eddie wanted to replace him. To be him. But Eddie didn't have the bottle for it.

'You'll just have to wait, Eddie,' he said. And then he left. A man on a mission.

It seemed an age before Gaby came out of the hotel. She was alone. She didn't even glance my way, though she knew I was here, hiding in the bushes near the hotel. She was studying her nails, biting little bits on her pinkie, spitting them on the ground. She couldn't have looked more casual. And then, just when I thought nothing was happening the doors of the hotel slid open and a man emerged. He took long strides towards her. He was wearing a dark suit, and his blue shirt was open at the neck. His hair was dark, like mine. I couldn't see his features clearly, he was too far away. Did I look like this man? Did I walk like him? When he approached Gaby he stood with his back to me, talking to her. I still couldn't see his face. I'd never see his face if he stood like this. Gaby must have realised that too. She began circling round him casually so he had to turn to face her.

I saw his face at last.

His face.

A whirlwind rush from my past came at me like an express train. I knew that face from somewhere. Knew the dark features, the turn of his head. I saw a picture of him, shouting, then he was smiling. He was angry, warning me about something. Then laughing. I was laughing too. We were all laughing. But who were 'we'? The picture was so clear, I stumbled deeper into the bushes as if I'd been slapped. The face frightened me – but I couldn't remember why. Surely, my father's face shouldn't frighten me? I took another step backwards and almost stumbled over some stones. I had planned to approach this man when he was with Gaby, but I couldn't go nearer, I couldn't confront this man. It was too risky. I was too afraid of what the past might hold. I had to find out more.

He watched the girl from his hotel window as she hurried across the busy street and disappeared into the darkness. She had searched in the bushes as if she'd lost something, then stood around watching – for someone? Waiting for someone? But no one had come. A friend? Or the boy himself? Had he made more contact with her? And was it really the boy he was looking for? Impossible to believe, yet he had to try. The girl was the key. He had contacted her once, maybe he would again.

And the boy had no memory. That would account for a lot. If it was true. He was getting closer. He knew it. This time, he would find out the truth.

Gaby was raging with anger as she walked back up home. She'd done all this – and the boy had scarpered. She'd been waiting for him to rush from the bushes, throw himself into his father's arms. A wonderful reunion. She would have been a real heroine then, bringing father and son together. And what had happened? Zilch. Nothing. She had kept the man talking as long as she could, holding him there while she talked utter nonsense. Even the man seemed embarrassed. To make matters worse he then offered her a reward. She'd been mortified. 'No, I do not want a reward!'

'Sorry, I thought that was what you were waiting for,' he said.

'I'm just sorry I've got nothing else to tell you.' At that moment, she had been tempted to tell him his son was hiding in the bushes. *Go get him!*

But the Dark Man had patted her shoulder. 'Thanks for letting me know. At least I know he's still here . . . and he knows his dad is here too, waiting for him.'

But she'd been angry at him for leaving her like this. 'He doesn't know anything. He says he can't remember anything about his past. Can't remember you.'

The man looked stunned with the knowledge. 'No memory? How did that happen?'

She hadn't an answer. Couldn't think of one quickly enough. 'If he calls again I'll tell him where to find you,' she blurted out.

'No memory,' he'd said again, thinking about it. He looked so down as he walked back into the hotel. His shoulders slumped. He had to be telling the truth. He must be his dad. He had been so upset. She was going to give that boy a real telling-off. She hated people who upset their parents.

And then, he wasn't there! She had even searched through the bushes looking for him, getting herself scratched and her shoes dirtied. And he wasn't there. She stumbled back to the flats getting angrier by the minute. To make matters worse the rain came on. By the time she got home her hair would be all frizzy. And all because of that boy. She hated him.

I waited in the lane leading to Wellpark Court, staying well away from the incident van. I saw Gaby heading up the lane and pressed myself against the wall. I didn't want her to see me. As she passed me, I reached out and dragged her into the doorway beside me. Of course she immediately began to scream. What was it with her and the screaming? Once again I had to clamp my arm around her mouth. I made sure this time it was well protected from her teeth. 'Sssh! It's only me,' I whispered.

She hauled my arm down from her mouth. 'Where did you go? Your dad was nearly in tears. Look at my hair. I hate you.'

She rattled the words out angrily.

I stepped back, let her go. 'I couldn't go and talk to him. I didn't remember him. But I remembered something. He frightened me. His face frightened me. Why should my dad frighten me?'

'He said your mum died. You couldn't handle it. You were always fighting. Maybe that's why he frightened you. He said he was sorry about that.'

And now I had a mother? A mother who had died? 'Or he might not be my dad,' I said. 'He might be . . .' But I couldn't think who else he might be. Or any reason he might pretend to be my dad.

'Why would he come looking for you if he wasn't your dad? What reason would he have for saying he was?'

I couldn't answer any of those questions. 'Maybe I'm

182

worth a fortune, and he wants it. He might want to kidnap me.'

'Oh, you mean the white slave trade? I don't believe that. You know he said it was quite right we meet outside. He told me I shouldn't have come to the hotel by myself. He asked me if my parents knew where I was. I don't think white slavers do that kind of thing.'

'I need time to think,' I told her.

'Time's what you've not got, pal. The cops are looking for you everywhere.'

The sudden wail of a police siren in the distance seemed to reinforce that. Gaby looked at me. 'So where are you going to sleep tonight?'

'I'll find somewhere.' I said it defiantly. Hadn't I found somewhere every other night?

Gaby hesitated, she seemed to be mulling something over in her mind. Finally, she took a key from her pocket. 'I think I might know somewhere.'

'And where have you been, my girl?' Gaby's mother came racing down the hall as she came in the front door. Gaby, as always, had her answer ready. 'Been at Zoe's. Go on and phone her and she'll tell you.'

Her mother's mouth pinched in anger. Now if she only could see herself in a mirror doing that, Gaby thought, it added ten years to her face. Not that Gaby would ever tell her such a thing. 'Oh, I don't have to phone her. I can ask Zoe. She's been in the living room for the past half-hour waiting for you.'

And she threw open the living-room door and there was Zoe, her face like a thundercloud.

Zoe! Oh no. Gaby had totally forgotten she was supposed to be meeting her. Zoe's angry face became hurt. 'I don't believe you, Gaby! I came in on the bus and waited for ages. I thought something must be wrong. I couldn't even get you on your mobile. I thought, Gaby would never leave me standing. She's the one wanted to see me. She asked me to meet her. Well, thank you very much, Gaby!'

She stood up, ready to go. They didn't give Gaby time to say a word. Now her mother started on her again.

'Were you meeting a boy? I said that to Zoe. You use her to cover up going out with boys all the time. That's where you were the other night, wasn't it? Out with a boy! Boy crazy, that's you.'

'She wasn't with me the other night, Mrs McGurk. I can tell you exactly where she was.'

Now that was grassing in the first degree! 'Zoe!' Gaby yelled at her.

'Leave the lassie be. It's only gone nine o clock, she's hardly over her curfew, is she?' It was Big Dan, coming out of the kitchen, eating as usual. He was wiping his mouth with a paper napkin, just finished his tea. 'Leave her be,' he said again. He sounded annoyed. Gaby wasn't sure if it was with her, or her mother.

Of course that changed her mother's tune right away. 'Trust you, Dan. You've got a soft spot for that girl.' She smiled at him. Then she turned to Gaby. 'Am I not always telling you that? He lets you get away with murder.'

Even Gaby managed a grateful smile at Dan. Dan didn't smile back. He turned and went back into the kitchen. Zoe flounced past her. 'I think that's me and you finished, Gaby.' And she headed towards the front door.

'You better go after her.' Her mother gave Gaby a push down the hall. 'She's the only good friend you've got.'

Gaby hurried after Zoe. She caught her as she waited at the lift. 'I'm really sorry, Zoe.'

'I don't think!' Zoe said, turning her back on Gaby. Gaby tried to pull her round, but she was having none of it.

185

'I am. I just forgot.'

'You just forgot! You think that's makes things better? I'm so important that five minutes after you ask me to meet you, beg me to meet you, you just forget about me. That tells me a lot, Gaby. About just how little you value me as a friend.'

'But, Zoe!' But Zoe wouldn't let her get a word in now.

'You just use me all the time to cover up for you. You even copy my homework when you don't get yours done. And I let you! I'm the idiot. Well, that's it finished. Find yourself another idiot. You've used me once too often.'

She'd never heard Zoe talk like that. And it was so unfair. She'd never used Zoe. Had she? The lift arrived. Zoe stepped inside. Gaby stepped in beside her.

'I don't know where you're going. I don't need an escort. I can catch the bus home all by myself!'

But Gaby had come to a decision. She wanted to prove to Zoe that she really was her friend. That she trusted her. 'I'm going to take you to see what made me forget about you. Then you'll understand.' And she punched the button for the fifth floor.

I lay along the sofa enjoying a cup of tea. I had landed lucky again. I couldn't put a light on, or switch on the television, but I was warm. I was safe. For tonight at least. I was feeling pretty content. I liked my auntie Ellen's flat. I had decided to adopt her. She was mine. It was cluttered with furniture, like an antique shop, and her carpets made me dizzy with their swirls and their patterns. But for me it was heaven. I felt guilty even criticising it because tonight, thanks to Auntie Ellen, I would sleep safe and well, surely – and tomorrow, by the time I was fed and refreshed on a full stomach of food, (Gaby said Auntie Ellen had cartons of soup in her freezer I could heat in the microwave), I'd be able to think better.

Think about my dad.

If he was my dad.

But why should he lie?

Too much had happened over the past few days for me to trust anybody.

I was drifting into an exhausted sleep when I heard the key in the lock.

Gaby? Or Auntie Ellen back early from her holiday in

Benidorm? There was nowhere for me to hide, and I couldn't jump from a fifth-floor window. I darted into the kitchen, looked around for a cupboard to hide inside.

Then I heard the voices.

'What is this, Gaby? One of your tricks?'

'No, honest, Zoe. Wait till you meet him.'

I should have known here was another one I couldn't trust! Gaby the gab. She had brought someone to the house to see me. As if I was an exhibit in a zoo. If I was the kind who could thump girls, I would have done it then.

'There's nobody here,' the other girl, this Zoe, was saying.

Gaby tutted as if she was annoyed at me. At me! The cheek of her. She shouted into the kitchen. 'Just come out, Ram. I've told Zoe all about you. She's my mate. You can trust her.' Then she muttered to this Zoe. 'Don't ask me where he got a name like Ram from.'

That was it. There was no point in hiding. I burst out of the kitchen cupboard, not caring how much noise I made. The two girls were standing in the living room and they jumped back as if I had given them a fright. Good.

'I don't believe you!' I said. 'This is supposed to be top secret. I am public enemy number one, and you're bringing your mates here to gawp at me.'

Gaby put her arm round her friend. 'We can trust Zoe.'

'I thought he had wild black hair,' was all Zoe said.

'He dyed it. He was hiding in our school. Up in the

188

roof space. Can you believe that? And he dyed it in the toilets in our school.' She looked at me. 'Where did you get the hair colour from by the way?' Then her face dropped as realisation dawned. 'In my locker? You used my hair colour!' She turned to Zoe. 'That's who stole it!'

Zoe only laughed. 'And you nearly got thumped from Big Mo because you accused her!'

I gave up. I threw myself back on the sofa. They were talking about me as if I wasn't there.

'But he's a killer, Gaby.' Zoe stared at me as if I might at any minute turn into a homicidal maniac. 'You said he was.' Was she searching in my face for that evil? So I stared back at her boldly.

Gaby waved that away. 'Och, it must have been self-defence, or an accident. I mean, I headbutted him and nearly knocked him out.'

I was back on my feet again. 'I didn't kill anybody. That guy was dying when I found him.'

'But you confessed to Gaby,' Zoe said. '"I killed him," you said to her.'

Now I was totally shocked. 'I said . . . what?!'

Gaby tutted. 'Zoe! He never said that at all.'

'Of course I didn't!' I said.

'He said, "I did it."' Gaby turned to me. 'Didn't you?'

I almost collapsed. 'I never said any such thing! I said . . .' I tried to remember what I did say. 'I said, "Please don't think I did this."'

Gaby put a hand over her mouth and laughed. 'So you did. I remember now.'

'Goodness, you didn't half get that mixed up,' Zoe said. 'A bit like Chinese whispers.'

189

'Chinese whispers?' I asked. 'What's that?'

Gaby answered. 'Chinese whispers is where someone tells someone something and they hear it wrong and pass on something completely different. By the end, the story's nothing like how it started. We play it sometimes at school.'

'I can't believe you thought I'd confessed!' I yelled.

Gaby put a finger to her lips. 'SSh! This house is supposed to be empty. Anyway, I only told Zoe. Zoe's my best mate.' She grinned like an idiot at her 'best mate'.

'Why did you bring her here?' I asked. 'I don't want anybody knowing about me.'

'Because three heads are better than one,' Gaby said. 'And Zoe might not be much to look at, but she's really clever.' I watched Zoe's face fall. Gaby obviously thought she was giving her a compliment. 'I'll go make us a cup of tea and we'll work out how we can help you.' She wiggled into the kitchen.

'Is she always like this?' I asked Zoe.

Zoe nodded. 'She's just not always this nice.'

As we drank our tea the two girls made me feel like something of a celebrity, both of them hanging on my every word. 'Tell us every detail about yourself,' Gaby said.

'That'll only take two minutes. I don't know anything about myself.'

Zoe thought that was really exciting. 'There must be some way we can bring your memory back.'

'Maybe if we hit you on the head with something,' Gaby suggested. 'A sudden blow might do it.'

I moved away from her just in case she wanted to land

the sudden blow by surprise. 'I don't think that would work,' I told them. 'I've been punched, kicked, drowned and set on fire, and I still can't remember a thing.'

'Do you think you'd be able to remember my mobile number if I give it to you?'

She told me it once, and I repeated it right after her. 'Nothing wrong with my memory now,' I said.

'You phone me if you're desperate. But only if you're desperate,' she said. 'My auntie Ellen'll kill me if a mobile number comes up on her bill.'

'What if you need to contact me?' I asked her.

Zoe joined in eagerly. 'Use a code,' she said. 'I love codes. Gaby, you can phone here. Let it ring twice, hang up and ring again. Then Ram will know it's you.'

Gaby's face was like thunder. 'I was just about to suggest a code, just like that. That was my idea first.'

Zoe shrugged and I grinned at her. I don't think Gaby liked that either.

WEDNESDAY

Gaby felt better that she'd told Zoe. Now she didn't feel so alone. As she walked up to school next day it was good to know that Zoe would be waiting at the gate for her. She passed Dev. He was telling anyone who would listen about his adventure, making himself out to be some kind of a hero. Risking his life to bring a killer to justice.

'He overpowered me,' he was saying. 'He had a knife. Lucky my mates turned up. He ran for his life after that.'

Rubbish! She wanted to scream at him. All lies. What would his audience say if they knew the 'killer' was half Dev's size? And never had any knife. She longed to yell it at them, tell them she knew exactly where the killer was now, that she was harbouring him. It was awfully hard to have a secret like this and not be able to tell anyone about it. Gaby stood for a moment watching Dev, listening to his lies.

'Don't even think about it!' Zoe said to her as if she could read her mind. She seemed to come out of nowhere, grabbed her arm. 'You'd love to tell them, wouldn't you?'

Gaby pretended she was shocked. 'Me? No way. I

'know when to keep my mouth shut.' She stormed past Zoe, pulling free from her, a little annoyed by her attitude.

'Ram's relying on us to help him.' Zoe hurried after her.

'Oh. You want to help him now, do you?'

'After everything he told us, I don't believe he's a killer. Come on, get real, Gaby.'

'Don't you think we should tell his dad?' Gaby was remembering the sad eyes, the tears in the coal-black buttons.

'I agree with Ram. He might not be his dad. Ram has no memory. That man could be anybody. But I think you should tell the police about seeing the dead man in Heartbeat. You could give them an anonymous tip-off.'

'No. I've told you before, Zoe, I'm not getting involved.'

'You are involved,' Zoe reminded her. 'You're hiding the chief suspect in your auntie's house.' Then she giggled so much Gaby had to giggle too.

'Well, he can't stay at my auntie's for ever. She comes back from Benidorm next week.'

Zoe grinned at her friend. She shouldn't try a smile, Gaby thought, not meaning to be cruel. Gaby hadn't a cruel bone in the body. But a smile showed off Zoe's twisted teeth, not a pretty sight.

'I've been thinking about that,' Zoe said. 'It's all over the town now, thanks to Dev and his mates, that he's blond. Well, if he could dye it once, he can dye it again.' She slipped a box of hair colour out of her bag. Red. 'We could dye it for him. We could disguise him. I've got some of my brother's clothes in my rucksack.' She hauled out the collar of a blue shirt.

Gaby was getting annoyed. Ram had been her find. And suddenly, she felt Zoe was taking him over completely.

'We'll go straight to your auntie Ellen's tonight after school. Get him sorted.'

I slept like a baby the whole night. When I lay down in Auntie Ellen's single bed, I was out like a light. In the morning, I made myself coffee with some whitener instead of fresh milk, and I looked around for something to read while I ate my breakfast. I was completely at home!

Auntie Ellen had terrible taste in reading. Romance novels, and more romance novels. *The Man In the Maserati. Love Interest*.

Garbage. Every one of them. How could anyone read trash like that? There had to be something else. In a hall cupboard I found a whole stack of back issues of the local paper. Auntie Ellen was probably saving them for the recycling bin.

So I settled myself with my coffee and a couple of waffles I had toasted and I sat down to read.

It was a strange town, I decided as I read. From the lowest of society, such as murders in tower blocks, to the best – old ladies being awarded OBEs for services to the community. Some of the court cases were ridiculous: a drunk man had been charged with throwing his wife's dog at her. (The police had taken a while to decide whether to charge him with assault or cruelty to animals, the paper recorded.) Others were downright horrific: a young man was left for dead after being kicked, stabbed, bludgeoned by a crowd of teenage thugs. The community was trying to save the local hospital from closing, and there were marches and petitions and meetings. There were stories that appeared over and over in the paper. One of them was about the angry residents from Wellpark Court, pouring out their venom night after night about the addicts who used the stairwells as drug dens and somewhere to sleep. I had listened last night, and there hadn't seemed to be any sounds in the stairwell. It would seem the police at least had sorted out that problem. There were stories of ghosts here too, usually reported by drunks or daft old women. No one seemed to take them seriously. And there was world news. The bombing of a government building in London, that had just missed the prime minister. It was the work, so the public was assured, of a disgruntled civil servant and not terrorists. The civil servant had managed to blow himself up in the process. There were reports on the devastation caused by a major earthquake in Turkey. But earth-shattering world news was relegated to the inside pages. The world was not half as important as what happened in this small town.

The same names seemed to crop up too, the same families always in trouble. Petty criminals, thugs, drug barons. Gangsters moving into the town, trying to stake out their territory.

The best of towns, the worst of towns, I thought, and maybe that was just life.

And then I lifted another paper and the headline hit me like a brick.

MORE TROUBLE AT HEARTBEAT

And a photograph of the owner. Billy Taggart.

A riot broke out at local nightspot Heartbeat at the weekend. Police had to be called in and there were several arrests. Mr Billy Taggart, the owner, has been warned that if there is any more trouble Heartbeat could be closed down.

Two other establishments owned by Mr Taggart have recently been forced to close. His restaurant was reported to environmental health because of bad food hygiene and his snooker club was closed after police were given a tip-off that drugs were being sold there. Mr Taggart said today he was an honest businessman and there was a conspiracy against him.

I studied the photograph of this Billy Taggart. He had the look to me of a hard man. His nose had been broken in some fight. He had a snarl of a mouth. The photographer had caught him in an angry mood. Honest businessman, my foot. The man was obviously a gangster. He owned Heartbeat. Eddie worked for him. And the last words on the dying man's lips had been Heartbeat. Everything led back to this man, Billy Taggart. He was the one who wanted me dead. He must be. I still didn't know why, but I was going to find out.

Gaby and Zoe came bouncing in after school as they had said they would. 'It doesn't look a bit suspicious,' Gaby said. 'I always pop in to check my auntie's mail and water her plants.'

She hadn't been doing a very good job. Auntie Ellen's plants were drooping with thirst. 'Look at the mess you've made!' was the first thing she said as soon as she saw the newspapers strewn over the floor. She started picking them up. 'Typical boy.'

I was desperate to tell them my news. 'I think I know who's trying to kill me.'

You would think that someone trying to kill you was the most natural thing in the world. Gaby didn't bat an eyelid. 'Everybody's looking for you. The whole town, looking for a boy with blond hair. Dev and his mates went to the cops. Grassed on you.'

I ruffled my mop. 'I'll wear a cap. I'll even wear a wig. But I'm going into town. I know who's trying to kill me.'

They still didn't bat an eyelid.

'You don't have to wear a cap. I've come up with a better idea. Zoe helped.'

I could tell by the look on Zoe's face that the idea had

been hers in the first place. 'We're going to dye your hair again.'

I took a step back. 'Not on your nelly.'

'It's a good idea.'

'No, it is not a good idea. What do you think I am? A doll you can dress up? Your very own action man? I don't think so.'

Gaby threw the evening paper at me. 'Have a look at the headline.'

I caught the paper, opened it up at the front page.

SUSPECT STILL IN TOWN

Boys Fight Him Off at Local School

'So, there you are,' Gaby said. 'Just put yourself in our hands and you'll be fine.'

The Dark Man watched from the street. He sat in a car hidden by the lorries parked beside him. He could have been an ordinary man, waiting for someone, sitting casually reading his paper. But all the time he watched. He had seen the girl, Gaby, going in, her friend trailing behind her. Gaby positively bounced in. He had followed discreetly, but they hadn't gone up to the fifteenth floor. He had watched the buttons light up as the lift ascended, and it had stopped at several other floors, but not fifteen. Was she visiting someone on another floor? Did she know more than she was saying? He could wait.

Somehow he knew this was the right thing to do. If the boy had phoned her once, he might again. Or he might try to see her. Yes, he would wait and watch. There was still time.

I took one look at myself in the mirror and yelled, 'What colour is this supposed to be?' What had I let them do to me?

'It's red – "Alluring Red".' Zoe read from the label on the box. *'Excite your man with flaming red hair.'*

'I don't want to excite my man!' I was shouting. This was a nightmare.

'I think it's nice,' Zoe said.

'It looks as if my head's on fire.'

'Well, at least it's not blond. Everybody's looking for a blond.'

'Everybody will notice this. I'm not exactly going to blend into the background looking like this.'

Zoe grinned at me. 'Listen, with that hair and these clothes, you'll look just like every other boy in the town.' She held up the school uniform she had brought with her: navy blue blazer, blue shirt, dark trousers. ('They're my brother's. He's out of school now,' she explained.)

I took another look at the hair. Somehow I didn't think I'd pass unnoticed, with or without the uniform.

Afterwards they sat in the living room, watching me. I felt like an exhibit in a freak show.

'You really don't remember a thing?' It seemed to excite Zoe, the man without a memory. 'Where you came from, your name, nothing?'

Gaby joined in then. 'I think that's exciting. I've always wished I had been left on the doorstep. Find out I'm a beautiful princess. The heir to the throne.'

If Gaby had been left on a doorstep I'd bet she would

have been left on another doorstep after five minutes. It would have been like 'pass the parcel'.

'Just think, you could be anybody.' Zoe stared at me, studying me closely. 'You could be a foreign prince.'

'I think you look Egyptian,' Gaby said.

Egyptian! I looked at myself in the mirror, trying to push the red hair from my sight with both hands. My eyes were dark, my skin the sallow kind that takes a tan. But Egyptian? The girl was daft.

She hadn't finished with the Egyptian thing yet. 'Ram could be short for Rameses. He was a pharaoh. I'd love to be Egyptian,' Gaby went on dreamily. 'Like Cleopatra. She was irresistible to men.'

'He could be Italian.' Zoe was still looking at me closely. 'He's got an Italian look about him as well. Ram could be short for Ramon. Or is that Spanish?'

'Can't you get it through your thick heads, I made up the name.'

'Maybe not. It might have been lurking in your sub-conscious for a reason. It might be connected to your past. I saw that in a movie once.'

Gaby's face came so close to look at me, I could have headbutted her. It was very tempting. 'I think he looks more Irish,' she said. 'My mother told me a lot of the Irish are descended from the Spanish sailors ship-wrecked after the Armada.'

I was well impressed. I hadn't thought someone like Gaby could absorb that much knowledge. 'The Irish can look Spanish,' she said at last.

'Make up your mind,' I told them. 'Irish, Italian, Egyptian, Spanish. I thought you said I had a definite

Scottish burr in my voice?'

Now Gaby just looked annoyed at me. 'For goodness' sake, Ram. We live in a multicultural society. You could sound like Sean Connery and still have Egyptian blood gushing through your veins.'

'And in my veins is where I want to keep it.'

At last I had a chance to tell them about the paper. And this time I was going to make sure they listened. They hadn't paid attention to a word I'd said while they were dying my hair.

'I know who is trying to kill me; who's behind everything.' I held up the paper. 'Billy Taggart,' I said.

I waited for them to gasp with astonishment, tell me he was the worst villain in the town, that I was right to accuse him. Instead, they started to laugh as if I had just told them the funniest joke they had ever heard. I looked from Gaby to Zoe. 'What?' I asked.

'Billy Taggart?' Gaby said. 'Billy Taggart wouldn't hurt a fly.'

'I don't know what's so funny?' They couldn't stop laughing now, giggling in that annoying way girls do. 'I'm serious. The man in the lift said "Heartbeat" before he died. Gaby, you saw him in Heartbeat hours before he was killed. Eddie followed me, and he works in the place, and this Billy Taggart owns it. It all goes back to Heartbeat, and *him*.' I threw the paper at them. Let them see for themselves. 'All his places have been closed down. Trouble follows him around. He even looks like a gangster. He looks evil.'

Gaby snatched the paper. 'So do you, remember? Evil written all over your face!' She pointed further down the article. 'If you'd read on you'd have seen why trouble follows him around. Because this guy here,' she pointed to another tiny photograph further down the page, 'he hires his heavies to cause trouble for Billy. He's done it in every disco and restaurant Billy Taggart owned in the town.'

I took the paper from her again. 'What guy is this?' The other major player in the town, it seemed was Barry McKay. He always seemed to be unavailable for comment. And since the closure of the other places owned by Billy Taggart, it would seem he now owned everything. Everyone else had sold out to him. Apart from Billy Taggart and Heartbeat.

'Barry McKay is the biggest gangster in the country. He wants to take over the whole town. He runs protection rackets, makes shops pay "insurance" so he won't get his heavies to raid them. He deals drugs. It's his heavies that cause the trouble at Billy's discos. Then they get raided and closed down by the police. They say Barry McKay even has people killed.'

'By the Wolf,' Zoe said softly, as if this Wolf might just hear her.

My blood ran cold at the very mention of the name. The Wolf.

'He's some kind of mystery killer,' Gaby explained. 'Like the bogeyman. He doesn't exist. He's just a made-up story. An urban legend.'

Zoe didn't look so sure. 'I don't know. My dad says people have always talked about the Wolf.'

'I think he does exist,' I said it quietly. 'Someone's been after me. The same man. I think it was the Wolf.' The man who had tried to drown me, to burn me. The Wolf. 'So why hasn't this Barry McKay been arrested?' I wanted to know.

Gaby snorted. 'Because Barry McKay has got some of the cops in his pocket too. Everybody knows it. The decent police can never prove anything against him. So he gets away with it, every time. Billy Taggart has tried to open up places for people to go and enjoy themselves. Heartbeat is all he's got left.'

Zoe had to get her bit in too. 'There are no disco wars in this town, Ram. Billy Taggart is Poland, and Barry

McKay is Hitler. And Hitler wants to take over Poland.'

She was showing off, and I could see Gaby was getting annoyed at that.

'See this town,' Gaby said, trying to sound as clever as Zoe, 'it's as bad as Chicago in the 1920s and Barry McKay is Al Capone.'

'Who are these guys, Hitler and Al Capone?' I asked. 'More Glasgow gangsters?'

You would have thought I had told them a very funny joke, they both laughed so much.

'You really have lost your memory, haven't you?' Gaby said. 'Al Capone. The most famous gangster ever. Ruled Chicago in the 1920s. And Hitler, the world's most evil dictator.'

I decided then that Gaby wasn't as daft as she pretended she was.

I sat down. 'I thought I had it all sussed. Now I'm totally mixed up again.'

'Maybe not,' Gaby said. 'I think Heartbeat is the key. That was where I last saw the dead man.'

'And Eddie works there. But maybe it's Barry McKay who's his real boss.' The idea seemed logical to me.

'I think you should tell the police,' Zoe insisted. Both Gaby and I shook our heads.

'I'm not going to the police,' I said. 'Who's going to believe me?'

'And I'm not going to the police either, Zoe,' Gaby said with a long sigh, as if she was fed up saying it. 'My mum and big Dan would kill me.'

Forget about the police, I thought. I was going to Heartbeat to find out the truth myself.

The call came through when Lewis was at the station. He was handed the phone with a shrug. 'Won't say who it is.'

'PC Ferguson here,' he said.

The voice was muffled and breathless. 'I've got some information.'

'Who's speaking, please?'

There was a little catch in the breath. 'I can't tell you. This is anonymous. Right?'

It was a girl, though she was trying hard to disguise the voice. Was this a wind-up?

'Information about what?' he asked.

'The victim. The man that was stabbed in the lift. He was last seen in Heartbeat. There's something funny going on in Heartbeat. But it's not Billy Taggart's fault. I think you should check it out. Right.'

The phone was slammed down before he had a chance to ask anything. Had that been Gaby? She'd done a good job of disguising her voice if it was. Or had it been her pal? Didn't matter. Now he knew why she'd kept quiet. She'd been in a nightclub until three in the morning. Heartbeat. And she'd seen the dead man there. Heartbeat. They always had trouble there, especially lately.

He put the receiver down and found Guthrie at his elbow. 'Who was that?'

'I've just had a tip-off,' Lewis said, before he had a chance to think. 'It seems the victim was last seen in Heartbeat.'

Guthrie's eyebrows shot up. 'Heartbeat again, eh?

Come on, son, this is information you've got to give to Warren.'

Lewis was sorry now he had said it. Warren again. He would tell Warren and that would be the last he would hear of it. But what choice did he have?

Zoe put the phone down. She hoped she'd done the right thing. But Gaby would never tell, and Ram was so determined to go to Heartbeat and find out the truth. She was worried about them both. Now she had told the police, that nice policeman Gaby trusted. Zoe trusted the police. The police would investigate Heartbeat, and they would find out everything. Yes, she was sure she had done the right thing.

There was something funny going on. Lewis wished he could figure out what it was. He felt as if he was banging his head up against a brick wall. And it was beginning to bother him that no one was listening to him.

Now they'd practically offered him a job in CID.

He and Guthrie had gone to Warren with this latest information. He couldn't get that meeting out of his mind. Warren had listened patiently as he told him about the phone call. Then he had asked him. 'So who was it who phoned you?'

Lewis lied. 'Don't know, sir. The voice was obviously disguised.'

'Male or female?' Warren asked stonily.

Lewis had said it calmly. 'A boy, a teenager maybe.'

He didn't like lying to his superior, but saying it was a girl might lead the whole investigation back to Gaby. 'Definitely a boy.'

'Good work, PC Ferguson.'

Lewis decided to be bold. 'I could go down to Heartbeat, sir. Might be able to find things out.'

Warren smiled. 'No, Ferguson. This is our case. But

you've done well. I've been thinking about you a lot. You're just the kind of man we want in CID. Would you be interested?'

Would he be interested? It was his life's ambition!

'One day, sir, definitely. Keep me in mind, sir.'

Warren smiled. 'Oh, I was thinking, sooner, rather than later, Ferguson.'

Lewis was taken aback. He was only a rookie. Still on his probation period. There were rules that had to be followed before you could move to CID. Yet Warren seemed to be hinting that those rules could be broken. Did he mean he could move to CID whenever he wanted?

'Think about it,' Warren said. Then he added. 'But leave Heartbeat to us.'

'Do you think they're serious?' he had asked Guthrie later, and Guthrie had said.

'Yes, I do think they're serious. I know Warren. He doesn't say what he doesn't mean. He would find a way round the rules. I would jump at the chance if I was you.'

And Lewis surprised himself then. 'No, I don't think I want it, Guthrie,' he said.

Guthrie looked at him, genuinely surprised. 'You don't want to say no to Warren. What's wrong with you?'

Lewis was almost talking to himself. 'Why do I keep thinking there's something funny going on here? Maybe I should talk to someone else on CID rather than Warren.'

'What do you mean, Lewis?' Guthrie asked.

'I know it sounds daft, but I keep thinking there's

some kind of conspiracy going on.'

And Guthrie hadn't said anything after that, as if he agreed.

His mother couldn't hide her surprise either. 'You? A job in CID? You've just joined the force.'

For once, Lewis had to agree with her. 'I know, unbelievable, isn't it? They said I'm just the kind of bright young thing they need.'

That made his mother fall about laughing. 'I never thought I'd see the day you'd be called a bright young thing.'

'You're wonderful for my ego, Mother. Maybe it's not so weird.'

'Oh, come on, Lewis. You're only on the force. A rookie – and all of a sudden they're offering you a post in CID. Hercule Poirot you ain't. Sounds fishy to me.'

Sounded fishy to him too, though he hated admitting that to his mother. He had been offered the job of a detective. His life's ambition realised. No hassle. No struggle. Should it be this easy?

'But if it's not because I'm brilliant, why else would they offer me the job?' He was actually thinking aloud. But his mother answered him anyway.

'Maybe they want to keep you quiet about something.'

The shirt and trousers Zoe had brought for me were way too big. If I loosened the belt the trousers would fall to my ankles. Between that and the hair I felt stupid. And to make things worse Gaby thought I should lie low. For tonight at least. 'I can't have you running in and out of my auntie Ellen's house every night. The neighbours will notice. And you're making such a mess.' She picked up the towel I had dropped on the floor. It was splashed with purple stains from the dye. Goodness knew how she would explain that to Auntie Ellen.

Gaby giggled. 'Wait till tomorrow. It's my birthday. There's an underage disco on at Heartbeat.' She looked at Zoe. 'We'll all go together. You'll not look out of place then. You can do all the investigating you want.'

I supposed it was the sensible thing to do, so I forced myself to wait. And it wasn't easy.

No wonder people complained here. Addicts sleeping rough, needles left lying for children to find. The stabbing had been the last straw. I could see now why the police had looked no further for a murderer. Blame the junkies. I had thought last night that the police had managed to get rid of them sleeping on the stairs. Tonight, it seemed, they were back. As I lay on my bed I could hear noises, as if they were settling down for the night. I could hear them scratching on the walls, as an eerie wind whinnied through the lift shaft.

Or maybe it wasn't the junkies. Maybe it was those ghosts I was always hearing about. I could picture them floating up the stairs, oozing through the lifts, shifting like fog, heading my way.

I would be frightened sleeping out there.

Then I remembered that only a few days ago I had been sleeping out there. Grateful for the warmth.

Hypocrite.

Let them lie there, I thought. Let them sleep peacefully.

I lay on my back and tried to read my book with a spotlight trained on the words. *Mightier than the Sword*. I thought it might have a fight in it at least. No such luck. Another romance. But all the time I listened. Listening for any strange sound. The sound that might mean that someone was coming after me.

43

Lewis was in the car when the call came through. There was some trouble at Wellpark Court and he and Guthrie were told to look into it. Dead of night, Lewis thought, and still people were fighting, killing, dying. He got out of the car and looked up at the tower block. He'd gladly give this one a miss. 'I thought we were finished with trouble here.'

Guthrie seemed reluctant to go too. 'Yeah,' he said. 'Wish we didn't have to.'

Lewis looked at his partner. 'You stay in the car. I'll go.'

Guthrie shook his head. 'No. You start going up the stairs. I'll take the lift to the top and then go down.'

Lewis laughed. 'And meet in the middle. That is if we don't meet the trouble before that.'

That only seemed to make Guthrie nervous. Lewis tried to reassure him. 'Och, it'll only be some boys acting up probably. I'll protect you.' His partner's retirement was galloping closer. Lewis didn't want anything to happen to him now. That was the kind of thing that always happened in films. Old partner killed days before he's due to retire.

Guthrie stared at him for a time. 'You're a good lad, Lewis. A good lad.' Then he ran on ahead of him, and into the building.

Lewis took the stairs two at a time, listening for sounds up the stairwell, hearing nothing. The wind in the lift shaft, that was all. On the third floor he called Guthrie on his personal radio. 'Anything up there?'

It was a bit before Guthrie answered. 'Fourteenth floor and no trouble.'

Lewis clicked off his phone and stopped for a moment, sure he heard something in the stairs above him. But then there was nothing. Lewis sighed and began to climb the stairs.

Something woke me. The slam of a car door. I got up and stood at the window. There was a police car in the street. Were the police in the building, looking for me? What was I worried about? I was safe here, in Auntie Ellen's house. I padded softly into the hallway and listened at the door. Footsteps coming up the concrete stairs. But there was another noise too. Closer. Someone on the landing, breathing softly – waiting. Almost outside this door. I peered through Auntie Ellen's spyhole.

Someone was there, a man. At first I thought he was waiting for the lift. I could see the edge of a shoulder, an arm. And then he began to move stealthily towards the door that led from the landing into the stairwell.

But it was something else that, suddenly, made me shift back in fear. The flash of steel. That's what I'd seen. This man was waiting for whoever was coming up those stairs. Knife at the ready, ready to slice – to stab.

And I knew then I recognised the size of the man, the menace of him.

I was looking at the man who had tried to kill me.

I was looking at the Wolf.

The very thought of him made me shiver with fear.

Not my business, I told myself. I'm safe in here. He's not after me. Not this time. The Wolf doesn't even know I'm here.

I remembered the police car outside. Was it a policeman coming up those stairs? Didn't know what was waiting for him. Didn't have a clue. Another murder blamed on the junkies who slept here. Blamed on me. No. Stay inside, I told myself. Not your business. Still I looked. The figure loomed, big and dark. He was silent, pushing open the door from the landing on to the stairs without a sound. The footsteps were coming closer. A man who didn't know what was ahead of him. Didn't know the slash of a knife was waiting for him.

I stepped back. I wouldn't think about it. Look after number one. It's not your business!

Blinking lights! Lewis was thinking as he turned on to the fifth floor, and darkness. No wonder the residents complained. Lifts hardly ever working. Lights out on landings. He didn't like the dark. Not the kind of thing a big cop, even a rookie, could admit to. But when you could see what was coming, you could be prepared for it, and in the dark you could see nothing.

He wasn't prepared.

All he saw was the flash of steel. He stumbled back, caught his foot on the stairs. At the same time, the door from the landing flew open. A streak of light and Lewis saw a boy, a silhouette, with hair as red as sandstone. He leapt in from the landing, threw himself at the figure with the knife just as the blade caught at Lewis's throat. The man was thrown off kilter. So was Lewis, stumbling down the steps, clutching at his throat.

He could hear the struggle on the stairs above him, but all he could do was hold his throat and pray.

Was he dying?

No. Please. I don't want to die. I want to be a detective. I don't want to end my days in this dark stairwell. He tried to shout up to his partner, but his voice wouldn't come.

He tried to call into his personal radio, but it only crackled.

'Somebody help me.' Did he say it? Or just think it. 'Somebody help me.'

It was the boy again! The Wolf knew it as soon as the light caught his eyes. He could change the colour of his hair, but he couldn't disguise those eyes. Here again. The Wolf began to shake with the venom of his anger. Who was this boy? Was he a ghost, some kind of nemesis sent to get him? The boy clung to his back so tightly he couldn't get at him. The Wolf threw himself back against the wall, but still the boy clung on. The cop had rolled down the stairs. He'd got him, he was sure of it. But what if he hadn't? Another mistake. And it was all this boy's fault. He swung himself round and the boy finally lost his grip and tumbled off him. He slashed at his arm with the blade. The boy yelled and he knew he'd got him. He grabbed at him, but the boy fell back through the door, back into the landing, slammed the door closed against him. Darkness. He was engulfed in darkness. He had to get that boy. Hatred for that boy pumped through him like blood through his veins. Then he heard the low moan on the stairs below. The cop, not dead. He hadn't finished him. The boy had deflected the killing blow. It was the boy's fault. Everything was the boy's fault. There was no time to finish off the policeman. The boy filled his thoughts. Now he was this close he had to get him. He pushed his way into the landing. A drip of blood dotted the tiled floor and the Wolf snarled a smile. He had got him. Follow the blood and he would find the boy and finish him. There would be no more boy. All his problems had begun when that boy appeared. They would go as soon as he had gone. This time he meant to finish him off.

I was hurt. My arm nipped with pain, and blood was seeping into the blue shirt. No time for pain. I had to get away. The man, the Wolf, would come after me. I'd left Auntie Ellen's door on the latch, but her house was the last place I would go. I'd be trapped in there if he followed me. And he would. He wouldn't let me go this time. In that split second when I had seen his eyes, only his eyes, I had seen a hatred I couldn't understand. How many lives do you have, Ram? I was asking myself as I ran.

The Wolf had recognised me. Even in the dark with just a flash of light, the Wolf recognised me. And I knew that I had been looking into the face of the man who had tried to kill me, by fire, by water.

He'd failed. Well, he was going to fail again. I had no intention of dying. This wasn't the boy he had tried to burn, or the victim he had trapped in a sinking car. No. A lot of things had changed. This boy was going to survive.

I began to run up the stairs. Here, on this floor, it was brightly lit, yet it had been dark on the other stairwell. Was that deliberate? All planned? But why? Couldn't think about that now. Had to get away. I could hear the door below me pushed open and knew he was close behind me. I would never be able to outrun him. I raced up to the next floor, pushed the door into the landing. Where was I going to go next? Bang the doors, beg for help? Who would help me? Who would trust me? No one. As if in answer to my prayer, the lift doors lay open. Without even thinking I ran in and pressed the button to go up. Think what to do when I got there.

The doors were taking too long to close! I could hear the landing door crash open, hear his footsteps echoing round the corner towards the lift. Coming closer. At last the doors began to slide shut. Snapped closed just in time. I saw a shadow on the floor but he was too late. He punched on the doors as the lift began to rise. As if he didn't care who heard him. Getting me was more important. All he could think about. I could almost see him bounding up the stairs, ahead of the lift. Pressing for the lift on an upper floor, and the lift would stop and the doors would open . . . and the Wolf would be waiting there.

The Wolf.

And this time I would have nowhere to run.

Lewis tried to stand up. There was blood all over him. All he could think of was his mother and how she would moan about all that blood. She'd never get it out of his shirt. He was worried about Guthrie too. Had he been attacked first? Where was he? And who was that boy who had saved him? Lewis stumbled down the steps. He had to make it to the car. Get help. Whoever had attacked him was after the boy now. The boy needed help. Who was he? It was crouched in a corner of his mind who that boy was, like a tiger ready to spring. But he couldn't think about that now. Now it was taking all the strength he had to get himself out to the car.

I began to shake. The lift was coming to a shuddering halt. Someone had summoned it. And I knew who that someone was. Knew there was no escape from here. Why had I taken the lift? There was nowhere to run from here. Nowhere to hide. Stupid mistake. Well, it had been my mistake. I would just have to face it, try to dodge him as soon as the doors opened. Useless, but I wouldn't go down without a fight. I stood straight, braced myself, ready to barge against him as soon as those doors opened, maybe take him by surprise, knock him off his feet.

I was never going to be anybody's victim. Never again.

That's when it happened. I gasped as hands reached down, grasped me by the shoulders. I kicked and struggled as I was hauled up through the hatch on the roof of the lift.

He waited, knife at the ready as the doors opened, ready to lunge, to plunge it deep. He had him now.

And the boy wasn't there.

The doors opened and the lift was empty.

The Wolf stepped inside, looked all around. There was nowhere to go. He thumped at the walls, looked up and saw the hatch with its tiny air grille, rammed at it with his fists, but it was shut tight. Even he couldn't push it open. Anyway, it was too high for the boy to climb to. There was nothing in the lift to climb on. But where was he? Where had he gone? A drip of blood on the floor proved he had been here . . . but where was he now? Who was this boy?

The Wolf was afraid. A new feeling for him. But he was afraid he was losing what he had and it was the boy's fault. He'd had him, and lost him. Again. But how?

The lift must have stopped at another floor. The only answer.

He let out a curse as he ran out of the lift and down the stairs. He'd find the cop. At least he could finish him off. Get something right.

He pounded down those stairs, came to the landing

220

where he had left the policeman, and all that was lying on the stairs was blood. Drips of blood. And that made him quake with anger. The cop had gone. The cop wasn't dead either. The Wolf began to sway. It was all going wrong. Now the police would be calling for back-up. No time now to do anything. Had to slip away himself. He'd get the boy. Find out how he had got away from him. That boy filled his mind, his thoughts. He'd get him. Getting the boy would fix everything. Everything would be all right when that boy was dead. He would get him. And when he did, he'd make him sorry he was ever born.

I kicked. I struggled. I was ready to fight, to die fighting, sure the Wolf had got me. My eyes must have popped out of my head when I saw who had pulled me up. Two boys, older than me, but still teenagers. They had a firm grip on my shoulders as they laid me on the top of the lift. One of them placed a hand over my mouth to shut me up. The other slid the hatch back, screwed it shut tight. Then he turned to me and I saw that his face was grimy, but his teeth, white as ivory, seemed to brighten up the blackness. He put a finger to his lips to warn me to keep quiet. I nodded, and the hand was taken from my mouth. I could hear the lift doors open. Heard the Wolf step inside. The Wolf. I tried to make him out through the tiny grille on the hatch, but all I could see was the bulk of him. Then his fists rammed angrily on the hatch and the sound echoed through the lift shaft. I gasped, waiting for him to realise where I was, that there was nowhere else for me to go, but up here. But he didn't. There was a

221

silence, I heard him curse and then he was gone.

The boy with the ivory teeth waited a moment before he whispered, 'Jake Hope at your service.'

He introduced himself as if we were meeting at a fun-fair, or a pop concert. As if this was all entertainment. Jake Hope was wearing what looked like an army great-coat. It was khaki with buttons of brass. 'Lucky for you we were here.' He looked at my bloodstained shirt. 'We saw you through the grille; knew you were in trouble.' And he smiled.

I looked from him to the other boy. He was standing now, steadying himself with the cable of the lift.

'This is my friend, McBride,' Jake said.

I looked from one to the other. 'Who are you?' I asked.

Jake's smile was infectious. In spite of everything I smiled too. 'We're the ghosts,' he said.

Was he serious? 'You're the . . . what?'

McBride laughed. 'You must have heard of the ghosts? Well, you're looking at them. We're in here all the time. Riding the lifts.'

Even in the dark of the lift shaft I could see they didn't look like junkies. They were too alert, their eyes too bright. Who were they? 'Riding the lifts?' I didn't under-stand what they meant.

Jake stood up, nodded around him. Cables hung like the tentacles of monsters in the darkness. It was like being in an alien world here. There was a wind too, that whis-tled up through the chasm of the shaft.

'Nothing's more exciting,' Jake said. 'Up and down we go, jumping from the top of one to the top of another.'

That was the moment I realised, really noticed for the

first time, that I was sitting on top of a lift with a drop of eight floors below me. I edged into the middle, grabbed for the cable. Riding the lifts didn't sound exciting to me. It was too scary.

'You live here?'

Jake quietened me again, for it seemed to me that my voice bounced all round the walls and echoed down deep into the lift shaft. 'Do you live here?' I asked again, soft this time.

'Just when family life gets too much.' Jake poked a finger at McBride. 'And McBride here, his dad drinks – gets a bit handy with his fists. McBride goes off for a couple of nights till he sobers up.'

McBride bowed as if he was a dandy at a ball. 'We come here, for a bit of peace and quiet. For the adventure of it. Then we go back.'

'No one's ever found you?'

'Nope,' Jake said. 'At first we thought they might realise that someone was in the lift shafts. That the care-taker would find us. But he never did. And we know ways in and ways out that nobody else does.'

McBride sat down opposite me and took up the story. I felt as if we were round a campfire on a dark night listening to one of those urban legends Gaby had talked about. 'Then one dark night some old drunk heard the sounds of us.' He looked at Jake as if the memory was one they shared. 'Boy, did we give him a scare. Whispering through the grille on the lift, tapping on the roof. He started the rumour about there being ghosts in this place, and we just let it go on. Added to it whenever we could.'

'It's great fun being a ghost,' Jake said. 'Sure they're

223

even talking about exorcising us!'

That made them both grin.

'A policeman's been attacked. Stabbed,' I told them. 'The place'll be swarming with police soon. They'll search everywhere, even here. They'll find you.'

'Happened the night of the other stabbing. They didn't find us then.' Jake stared at me. 'You're the boy they're all looking for?'

I didn't answer. Didn't have to. My face gave me away.

'Did you see anything that night?' I asked.

But Jake shook his head. 'Saw nothing. That night we just ran with the junkies.'

'And now? What are you going to do now?'

Jake smiled. 'Now we run again. We know a way.'

The other lift, sitting above us on the eleventh floor, jerked into motion. Going down. Jake held his hand out to me, beckoned me. 'Come on,' he said. 'Ride the lifts with us. All the way down.'

I moved back. I understood now what riding the lifts meant, what he wanted me to do. Leap from the top of this lift to the other. Leap on to it as it sank past us. No way.

'Come on, boy. It's the only way down, unless you've got a parachute.'

I knew I couldn't do it. No. I stood up, unsteady on my feet, grasped tight on the cable. Jake reached for my hand.

I was shaking so hard now I knew I would fall if I tried it. I felt like a fool for being so afraid, but I couldn't help it. The lift was moving past us.

'There's a perfect time to jump, boy. It can't be too

high above you, and it can't be too low below you. Jump time, we call it.' He glanced up at the approaching lift. 'Jump time's coming.'

But I couldn't jump. Couldn't put the thought of that long drop out of my head.

'Watch me.' McBride leapt. He seemed to fly through the air. I stopped breathing, waiting for him to fall, to slip. Instead, he landed like an acrobat. Steady on his feet. So silently, without even a thud. His hand snatched at the cable and he steadied himself. 'Come on!' he urged me, beckoned me with his hands.

I wanted to please them. I'd known them only a few minutes and I wanted so much to please them, but I couldn't make that jump. I was like a block of stone. Jake finally gave in. Jump time passed. The other lift trundled too far below to make that leap. Jake called softly to McBride. 'I'll get him down on this one.' And McBride saluted and smiled.

Jake spun towards me and grinned. His long coat swung around him. All at once, the lift we stood on purred into life, beginning its journey down.

'There,' Jake said. 'We didn't have long to wait.'

'I'm sorry,' I said, clutching at the cable. 'I'm scared of heights.' I didn't mind admitting that fear. Not to him. I had proved to myself that no matter how scared I was, I faced up to things. But not this.

But Jake's smile never wavered. 'We'll get you out of here. Before the police come.'

He didn't ask if I was guilty. And I didn't ask how he would get me out. I trusted this Jake. And I had escaped the Wolf again.

46

Lewis had made it to the car. Fell inside. Managed at last to call for back-up. The real shock of what had just happened only getting through to him now. Someone had tried to kill him. Would have killed him if it hadn't been for that boy. Lewis could still see that someone, a huge silhouette in the dark, leaping at him, a knife flashing in his hand. And then the boy had saved him. Deflecting the blow that would have sliced through his jugular. They couldn't dismiss this. He wouldn't let them. If it hadn't been for that boy, he'd be dead by now, his life blood pumping out of him. Nothing could have saved him.

Someone had been waiting for him in the dark. Just for him. For Lewis Ferguson. But why would anyone want to kill him?

And what about Guthrie? Was he lying in a pool of his own blood on one of the upper floors? Lewis prayed he was all right. He was convinced now they had been lured there. A false call. He had a gut feeling about it.

Nothing would keep him quiet about it now.

Lewis lay back in the seat and waited for reinforcements.

Gaby sat up in her bed wondering what the commotion was. Noises on the stairs. There were always noises on the stairs, but over the past few nights, since the murder, there had been none. The police had managed to clear the place. Now the lifts were moving, feet were running. She jumped out of bed and hurried to the window. There was a police car sitting at the entrance, its blue light flashing. The police were here. But why?

Ram!

Her first thought was that they had found him, and in her auntie Ellen's house. She'd get killed for letting him stay there. Letting him sleep in the bed, eat the food. And what about Ram – would he implicate her? (*Implicate*, good word, she thought, hoping she would remember to use it in her essay.) She strained her eyes, expecting every moment to see Ram being dragged from the building, hands cuffed behind his back, maybe taking one last look – an accusing look up at her window. She stepped back just in case that happened and he saw her. Oh, why had she ever got involved with him? Why had she ever helped him?

And on the back of that thought she imagined how frightened Ram would be, listening to the footsteps pounding up the stairs, waiting to be caught, arrested, dragged off. He would believe she had betrayed him. Or that Zoe had? Yes – Zoe. Had she told someone? Gaby had had a feeling she'd been hiding something. It would be just like Zoe, she decided. Out of spite, phoning the police and telling them where they could find the boy they had been searching for. Her mind whirled from one speculation to another. She wished she had the nerve to go down to Auntie Ellen's and check that Ram was OK. But the thought of going down all those stairs, in the dead of night, was too scary. No. She couldn't do that.

She heard the front door opening. Her heart leapt. She went to her bedroom and pulled the door open. 'Is that you, Mum?'

There was no answer, but Dan appeared round the L shape of the hall. He put a finger to his lips. 'Don't want to waken your mum. Something's going on out there. Don't know what. Just stay inside. Better not get involved.'

Gaby closed the door and went back to bed. She hated to admit it, but for once she was glad he was here. There was something about him, something solid. No matter what was happening tonight in these flats, Dan wouldn't let anyone harm them in here.

Reinforcements arrived at the same time as Guthrie ran from the building. 'Where were you?' Lewis gasped out. 'I was worried.'

'Junkies on the thirteenth floor. Couldn't get you on the radio. What happened?'

He knelt down in front of Lewis and examined his neck. 'That could have been nasty.'

'Man tried to kill me. Boy saved me,' was all he could say.

Guthrie stood up. 'Naw. A couple of junkies fighting.

You got in the middle of it. In the dark, who would know?'

Maybe that was what had happened, Lewis thought. The older man waiting in the dark for the boy, waiting with a knife to steal drugs from him,. He mistakes Lewis for the boy, attacks him, and the boy jumps in and turns the tables on him. Sounded reasonable. Maybe Lewis hadn't been deliberately attacked. Maybe the boy hadn't saved him.

'Recognise any of them?' Guthrie asked.

Lewis remembered the flash of light, the brick-red hair and the sudden feeling that here was the boy the whole town was looking for. He almost said it. But at that moment more police were running towards his car. Another rookie who had come all through police training with him. Fabio. 'You OK, Lewis?' He saw the blood and his face paled. A rookie's worst nightmare.

Guthrie answered for him. 'A couple of junkies jumped him. Somebody in there's got a knife.' He patted Lewis's shoulder. 'You sit tight, buddy. There's an ambulance on its way.'

Lewis sat back again. His partner had it all sorted and explained. And he was probably right. It had all happened so fast it seemed like a dream now. He was making mysteries and conspiracies out of everything.

A couple of junkies had jumped him in the dark. That was it.

Suddenly, Lewis sat forward, his brain alert.

How had Guthrie known it was dark?

With my one strong hand I gripped the cable. I didn't take my eyes off Jake. I couldn't look down, I could only look at Jake. The lift plunged. It positively plunged to the ground and sent a wind roaring up through the shaft. I was amazed by the bravado of Jake. I was crouched on the top of the lift holding tight, almost wrapped round the cable, afraid to look anywhere but at Jake, and yet there he stood, his legs apart, his long coat billowing in that wind. He looked like some kind of pirate. 'What a feeling,' he said. 'It's great, isn't it?'

'It's terrifying,' I told him. And that only made him smile all the more.

Down we went, past the ground floor, until I was sure we must be heading straight down to hell. At last, the lift shuddered to a halt. We were in the basement.

'How come the caretaker's never caught you?' I asked him.

Jake shook his head. 'We know how to hide. We're too quick for him. And to tell the truth, he thinks there's ghosts too.'

And with that he drew his long fingers across the rippled steel on top of the lift. The sound echoed eerily up through the lift shaft. 'You can give old ladies an awful scare on the lifts, tapping on the roof, scraping your fingers on the steel. Whispering down the lift shaft.'

I had to laugh. 'That's cruel. You could give an old lady a heart attack.'

The ghosts. Here were their ghosts. If only they knew. Their fingers rippling across metal, their voices whispering in the dark.

'So, how do we get out of here?' I asked Jake as we jumped to the ground. Solid ground. It felt good.

'Show you,' he said.

The basement of the lift shaft was the gloomiest place I could imagine. The bowels of hell. Walls of concrete, a tunnel rising into darkness. I expected those cables to come to life any moment, move towards me, wrap themselves around my body. I wouldn't spend time in here for a fortune.

McBride was waiting for us. 'Come on,' he called softly. 'The cops will be here any time now.'

I couldn't think where they were going. There seemed nowhere to go in this pit. But I followed. I felt I could have followed Jake Hope anywhere. He stopped at what to me looked like a solid wall. Jake fell to the ground, pushed open a tiny hatch that blended into the wall. He looked back up at me and grinned. 'Our way out,' he said. He scrabbled out on his stomach while McBride and I waited. I was holding my breath – maybe even now police searchlights would spot us immediately we were outside. Alsatians already sniffing the ground to find us.

Jake's head appeared at the opening. 'All clear,' he

said. McBride pushed me down. 'You're next,' he said. This time I didn't hesitate. Crawling out into the icy night air. There was no one about. Not a window where we could be spotted. The hatch was hidden under overgrown bushes, blooming now with plastic bags and rubbish. A perfect spot to get in and out without anyone seeing. No one to see.

The air was clear. It was a frosty moon that hung in the sky. I shivered with the cold. Clamped my hand around my wounded arm.

Jake grabbed it and looked. 'You need stitches.'

I shook my head. 'No time.'

He looked at me for a long moment. 'You've got things to do, boy?' he asked.

I didn't say anything. I only nodded.

'Is that all you've got to wear?' Jake asked me.

The blue shirt, torn and bloodied now and those too-big trousers. I hadn't dressed for the cold. I had come out of Auntie Ellen's expecting to go back in again.

'I'll be fine.' But my teeth were chattering as much from nerves as from the cold.

Jake slid off his greatcoat and handed it to me. 'Take this,' he said. 'There's some money in the pockets. It's yours.'

'I can't,' I tried to protest, but I was taking it anyway, sliding my arms inside, pulling it tight around me. It was full of Jake's warmth. A *great* coat.

'It suits you.' He smiled. I liked this Jake. From the moment I'd met him, I'd liked him.

'Do you know where you're going?' Jake asked.

'I know exactly where I'm going,' I said. Meeting Jake

had given me a new lease of life. A new determination. I had beaten him again. I had beaten the Wolf! Got away from him again. I knew the man would never give up till he found me. Well, I wouldn't give up either.

'Take care of yourself, boy,' Jake said. And then he and McBride were gone. I watched them as they ran off and were swallowed into the night.

Maybe they were ghosts, I thought. They had come and gone so fast. But that was foolish thinking. I had Jake's coat. It warmed more than my body. It seemed to be filled with his devilish spirit. His daring was seeping through the cloth into my soul.

There was no time to lose. I had to be off too. I ran down the lanes and backyards, heading once again for the town. Heading for Heartbeat. I was going to solve this puzzle at last.

Gaby couldn't sleep. She watched the police activity from her window, saw the ambulance arrive and a policeman stretchered inside. Heard the calls from the street below – people wanting to know what was going on.

Another stabbing. When she heard that she leapt back into her bed and pulled the duvet right over her head. What had happened here tonight?!

She waited until she could hear her mother snoring in the next room, until she was sure they were both asleep, her and Dan. Nothing would rouse her mother, not even an earthquake. It had to be something to do with getting old. She punched her auntie's number into the phone, let it ring twice, then called again. Her signal to Ram that it was safe to answer.

And did he answer? No. He wasn't there! Her mind was a jumble. Finally, she decided to phone Zoe. She tapped her foot impatiently waiting for her to answer her mobile. When she did, Zoe's voice was heavy with sleep. 'What? That you, Gaby? What's the big idea ringing me at this time? It's the middle of the night.'

'Shut up for a minute, Zoe. Something happened

here. There's been another stabbing. Another stabbing and I've been hiding Jack the Ripper in my auntie's house. And he's gone. I've phoned the house and he's not answering. He must have legged it. It must have been Ram. I've been harbouring a killer. I was right the first time. He did have evil written all over his face.'

Zoe had woken up quick. 'No, he did not. There's got to be another explanation. I wonder where he went?'

'What am I going to say when the police come round asking questions?'

'Don't tell on him, Gaby.' Zoe's voice was almost a plea.

'It's all right for you. You don't live here. I'm not sure any more. I'm really scared, Zoe.'

'I'll see you tomorrow, Gaby. We'll talk about it tomorrow.'

After Zoe rang off, Gaby still couldn't sleep. She hadn't been lying. She was scared. If only there was someone she could tell all this to, someone she could trust and rely on.

She lay sleepless till dawn. A new day, and what a day. And it was her birthday.

THURSDAY

The Wolf could feel his anger growing with every minute. He couldn't tell Barry McKay he had failed again. That he hadn't finished off the cop, and he still hadn't finished off the boy. Was he losing it? No. He was as good, or as bad, as he had ever been. It was the boy. His hatred of him was growing like a cancer eating away at his body. The boy had caused him nothing but trouble since the beginning. If he could get rid of that boy life would get back on track. His reputation would be secure again.

He was filled with hate for him. A desire for vengeance. The boy. He was all the Wolf could think of now.

Lewis's mother had raced out to the hospital as soon as she was informed. She had actually embarrassed him, walloping doctors and nurses aside with her handbag.

'You should never have been a policeman,' she told him. 'You could have gone places in Tesco's.'

He didn't want to remind her he'd only been a part-time shelf packer.

But for all her histrionics and her jokes, he knew that was her way of covering up her genuine fear for him. Her eyes brimmed over with tears.

'I'm fine, Maw,' he quipped at her. 'Look, hardly a stitch.'

Three, in fact. The slash had just missed a main artery. He would be dead by now if it hadn't been for . . . for that boy. How a split second can change your life, Lewis thought. The boy leaping from nowhere, knocking the man off balance. If he hadn't appeared in that second he would be . . . Lewis chilled to the bone thinking about it. He would be dead.

'Who did it? Who did it? I'll kill them!' his mother had shouted, meaning every word. If she had got her hands on the man right at that moment he would have been dead meat.

But he didn't tell her who did it. He'd had time to think. A lot of time as he waited at the hospital, wondering whom he could trust. Not his partner. Not Guthrie. That hurt more than anything. But he was sure now that his partner had known the call was false. He remembered the way he'd looked at him when they'd first gone into the flats. 'You're a good boy,' he had said, almost as if he knew he wouldn't be seeing him again – alive. The man with the knife had aimed at his throat. So he knew he was a policeman, would be wearing a protective vest. Only his neck would be vulnerable. He had been waiting there, in the dark, to knife Lewis. And Guthrie had known it was dark. And it was his partner too who had insisted he go to Warren, that friend of his in CID. How far up did this conspiracy go? Because Lewis was sure now that it was a conspiracy.

So he went along with the idea that it had been two junkies fighting and he had unfortunately got in the middle of them. He didn't know who to trust, so he told no one.

At last he was allowed to go home. 'He's got the day off tomorrow, Mrs Ferguson. Boy deserves a rest.'

If the sergeant had expected thanks he didn't know his mother. 'A day off? It should be a week!' she had snapped back at him. 'And he should be getting a medal as well.'

He was quiet on the drive home. That wasn't like him and his mother kept glancing at him, as if she was sure he was about to have a relapse.

'Are you sure you're OK?' she kept asking. And he kept insisting that he was.

Heartbeat was closed when I got there. Doors locked, padlocks on.

THESE DOORS ARE ALARMED, the sign read. That made me smile. I had a vision of some very scared doors, like in a cartoon. But I wanted to stay close to this place. Didn't want to be far from here when it did open. I wanted to watch for Eddie. I looked around for somewhere close by to settle down for the rest of the night.

It was the smell that I noticed first. The smell of a Chinese takeaway. As I crossed the street the warmth hit me too. Who knows, there might even be an odd bowl of fried rice someone had thrown away, for me to tuck into. Was I that hungry? I didn't think so. I looked both ways as I crossed the empty street. The icy wind whipped some newspapers and litter along the pavement. Apart from that, all was quiet. The wind caught Jake's coat as I climbed the wall of the takeaway behind the Chinese, and slid into the darkness.

The flats were a hub of activity again. Police cars sitting all around the building, policeman knocking doors, asking questions.

'This is ridiculous!' Gaby's mother said for the hundredth time. She slapped down a bowl of cereal in front of Gaby. 'I could hardly get a wink of sleep.' That was a lie. Her mother had snored the night through, as she always did. Dan looked at Gaby and winked, partners in her lie. He was the one who looked as if he hadn't had a wink of sleep, just like Gaby.

Her mother's tone changed again. 'Happy Birthday, darlin',' she said, and handed Gaby a designer handbag, just like the one she'd seen in the shops and loved. Gaby leapt at it and screamed with delight, for a moment all her other troubles forgotten. 'Oh, it's gorgeous! Just what I wanted. How did you know?'

Her mother laughed. 'You've only been talking about it for a fortnight.'

'I'll use it tonight, when I go out with Zoe.'

Her mother asked her suspiciously, 'And where are you and Zoe going?'

'We're just going to the cafe.' It was a lie, but she'd

never tell her mother where she was going. She was always being warned to stay away from Heartbeat. 'Trouble follows that Billy Taggart about everywhere,' her mother would say. She'd never let her go there tonight. Even if it was her birthday.

But it was her birthday, and she was going to do what she wanted. She was going.

Dan fished in his pocket, opened his bulging wallet. He pulled out a wad of notes. 'Here, this'll buy you something to go with the bag.'

Her mother kissed the top of his head. 'You're too good to her, Dan.' She looked at Gaby. 'Now is that not a wonderful birthday present? What are you going to say?'

And it was generous. A huge wad pushed towards her, no questions asked. Gaby muttered a thanks. She even smiled. But why was it that just when she was beginning to warm to him, he did something like this. Dan thought everything could be bought with money. She was glad that just then her mobile began to ring. It was Zoe, singing 'Happy Birthday' off-key. Gaby got up from the table, holding the phone away her ear. She made a face at her mother. 'It's Zoe. Hear her? I don't think Kylie Minogue's got anything to worry about.'

'Mornin', Zoe,' her mother called and Zoe called back, 'Mornin', Mrs McGurk.'

Gaby wandered into her own room as casually as she could. As soon as she had closed the door her tone changed. 'Can you get to school early? I have to talk to you.'

'I'm here already,' Zoe said. 'I'm at your auntie's door. It's on the latch.'

Gaby almost shrieked. 'It's been on the latch all night? Oh my heavens. Anybody could have got in there. I'll kill him when I get him. Is he in?'

'I'm not going in by myself to find out. Anybody could be in there. Come down as soon as you can. We have to look for some clues.'

Zoe was waiting impatiently at her auntie Ellen's door. 'I didn't think I was going to get in the building. The police are all over the place, asking questions.'

Gaby pushed open the door, stepped inside warily, as if someone might jump out at her any moment. Zoe followed her.

'There's nobody here,' Gaby said after going into every room. 'And look at the mess he made,' she complained. Ram had obviously been lying on top of the bed reading, papers strewn about on the floor. A mug of tea, half finished on the bedside table. 'I'm going to get killed.' She set about picking up papers, tidying the bed.

Zoe stood thinking. 'What happened here last night?' she said.

'A couple of junkies jumped a policeman. One of them was very young. There's talk he was the same boy I saw. Ram!'

'It couldn't have been Ram, Gaby. He wanted away from trouble. He was safe in this house. What would make him leave it in the middle of the night?'

Gaby had a simple answer. 'Because he's evil. Killing comes naturally to him. I was right about him the first time.'

'Oh, come on, there was nothing evil about him.' Zoe picked up the blazer, lying across a chair. 'Look at this. He goes out into an icy February night with just a shirt on. He doesn't take this. He didn't take anything. I think he meant to come back. Maybe he saw something, saw someone about to attack the policeman. He was attacked on this floor. Ram went out to help. Then he had to run. He might be hurt, Gaby. He might be in danger.'

Gaby thought Zoe was living in a dream world. Ram rushing out to help a policeman? 'Well, he can stay in danger. He's not my problem any more.'

Zoe looked out of the window. The street seemed to be swarming with policemen. 'Where is he, Gaby? And what made him leave this house last night?'

I woke up shivering with the cold. The smell of curry wafted all around me. This early in the morning it did- n't make me hungry, it only made me feel sick. I had been spoiled at Auntie Ellen's with her hot soup and her baking. I could hear dishes rattling in the Chinese kitchen and so could a cat, leaping over the wall almost on to my shoulder. It turned to face me as if it thought I would take the rotting food in the bin from its mouth, as if it was ready to fight me for it. I stared back. The cat's tail whisked like the flick of a whip. Her eyes never left mine. I liked the cat. Nothing bothered cats. In my next life I would be a cat, I decided. Then I smiled to myself. Maybe I was a cat now. Nine lives. Well, I certainly had more than one. How many times could you die? I looked back at the cat and winked. The cat peered at me through half-closed eyes. Staying out all night, answering to no one. Yes, I was a cat.

A door was being unlocked. The cat stiffened, knowing what was coming. I bet she was here every morning ready to eat last-night's leftovers. I shot to my feet. Time for me to be off. The cat leapt at my sudden movement. I grabbed the wall with both hands and hauled myself over into the street.

It was still dark. The town was quiet as death in the early morning. A lorry delivering milk roared by on the main road and I squeezed myself into a doorway till it passed. The string of restaurants and nightclubs lay closed and empty along the waterfront road. I checked that there was no one about and I was off, past Joshua's Bar, past Seafood A Go-Go and all the other places. There was only one I was interested in. I stopped in front of Heartbeat.

Here it was, the key to everything, and I still didn't know what.

I strolled around the corner, checking out the windows and doors, looked at all the signs advertising coming events.

Queen Tribute Band: Saturday Night
Coming Soon: A Cowboy Special

And tonight, the under-16s' Valentine disco. The one Gaby and Zoe were planning for all three of us to come to. There was a banner plastered across the sign:

St Valentine's Day. 14th February.
TONIGHT

My own heartbeat skipped.

Heartbeat. The fourteenth of February.

Chinese whispers.

Words getting mixed up as they were passed along.

The dying man hadn't said 'four teeth'. How could I have ever thought he did?

He had said 'fourteenth'.

Heartbeat. Fourteenth.

Now all I had to do was figure out what I was supposed to stop.

She'd been so looking forward to her birthday and the Valentine disco at night, and who had spoiled it? Ram. Mr No Name. Mr No Memory. The boy she'd only ever tried to help out of the goodness of her heart. The boy who once again was right in the middle of a stabbing. If anyone found out she had helped him, she'd be in real trouble. And now he was missing. Well, she hoped she'd never see him again. He was all she could think about. And to make matters worse, if that was possible, here it was, St Valentine's Day, and she hadn't got a Valentine. Not one! She'd ripped open all her cards enthusiastically – and all she'd had were 'Happy Birthday's from aunties and cousins and friends. But not one Valentine. It was mega embarrassing.

'I didn't get one either, Gaby,' Zoe kept telling her, as if that was supposed to make her feel better.

'You never get one, Zoe. You don't expect to get one. This is the first year I haven't got one.'

Life was very unfair, Gaby decided. Of course, she knew who to blame for all this bad luck. Ram. Trouble followed him around like a bad smell. Well, if he got in touch with her again, she was going to the police about him.

'I kind of liked him,' Zoe said dreamily.

Gaby smirked at her. 'Of course we can trust your judgement, Zoe. You're the girl who thought Darth Vader was a goodie. No.' She said it with finality. 'Ram was a wrong'un, as they say. I was right first time about him. He had evil written all over him.'

I needed somewhere safe to wait and watch the comings and goings at Heartbeat. Somewhere I couldn't be seen. There was a car repair shop across the road on the opposite corner with nooks and crannies to hide in and a full view of the front and side door of the nightclub. I wedged myself between piles of boxes and cars and settled down to watch.

The silver BMW purred almost silently to a halt about an hour later. There was still darkness in the sky, but it was tinged with orange streaks. Morning coming. A man stepped out of the car, looked around, and I saw his face. Billy Taggart, and he still looked like a hard man to me. He had a bunch of keys in his hand and I could hear them jangling. Gaby had said he was a good guy, trying to bring decent entertainment to the town. I might not have listened to Gaby, but Zoe was a different matter. I trusted her judgement. And she said the same about Billy Taggart.

For a moment I thought about running from my hiding place, crossing the road and telling him about my suspicions. Tell him about Eddie. Tell him something was going to happen at Heartbeat tonight.

But what? And what if he didn't believe me? He might recognise me, hand me over to the police. I slid further into the shadows. Anyway, the girls might both be wrong. This Billy might indeed be behind everything that had happened to me. I'd be walking right into a trap. Eddie worked for Billy Taggart. He worked in Heartbeat. No. I couldn't take the chance of confiding in Billy Taggart.

He came out of the club after only a few minutes. He came out, got in his car and began to reverse it into the car park at the back of the club. I clocked that he had left the front door open. He'd be going back in soon. But for now, he was out of sight, and I wasn't going to waste the chance to have a look inside Heartbeat. There might be something there that would help me. I looked up and down the street, raced across, took the stairs two at a time, and slipped inside.

Lewis was having a lie in. Trying to anyway. Yet there was so much crowding into his mind, suspicions he couldn't put aside any longer. The only thing he had ever dreamt of being was a policeman – ever since he was a wee boy and used to watch Inspector Clouseau on TV. He was proud to be a policeman. He didn't want to think badly of any of them. Didn't want to believe that there were any bad apples, any corrupt cops, but he knew that was what he was thinking. He suspected the CID officer, Warren, who had taken all his information, but hadn't acted on it. Now, he even suspected his partner, Guthrie. Everything fitted in. Lewis being offered a

CID post, a 'here's a reward if you keep quiet' kind of post. But he had turned it down. So they had to keep him quiet some other way, luring him back to Wellpark Court on the pretext of an 'incident'. Only there was no incident, just someone waiting in the dark of the fifth floor with a knife.

That meant that when he left his partner to climb the stairs Guthrie knew it would be the last time he would ever see Lewis. He was sending him to his death. Could his partner really do that?

He had gone to Warren about the phone call. To tell him that the dead man had been last seen in Heartbeat. And that had seemed to sign his death warrant. Why had that information been so important.

Heartbeat.

What was it about Heartbeat?

I walked around Heartbeat, looking for a place to hide, listening all the time for a sign of Billy Taggart returning. Glasses sparkled on a steel rack above the highly polished dark wood of the bar. A ball of crystal hung on the ceiling, already catching light from the streetlamps outside. When I heard the outer door open I hurried behind the bar and crouched down, tucked out of sight under the sink beneath the counter. I could see Billy Taggart in the reflection from a mirror above the bar. He walked straight to the bar and began searching around for something. His keys. I could spot them dangling on the edge, almost ready to topple into the sink. If that happened he'd come round to this side of the bar and I would be caught. I gritted my teeth, reached up and ever so gently pushed the keys towards Billy Taggart's searching fingers. He grasped them with a satisfied sigh. His footsteps headed for the door and after a moment I heard the door swinging shut and the lock turning.

I was alone. I waited in my hiding place a while longer, until I heard the purr of the car engine as he drove off. Only then did I emerge from behind the bar and look around. I had landed lucky again. There was Coke in one fridge, and pies and rolls and sandwiches in another. There was a microwave. I could have breakfast, and I did.

I sat in a booth like a valued customer, drinking from the Coke, eating the hot pie. I savoured the last bit and wiped the table clean with my sleeve. No point drawing attention to the fact I'd been here. The toilets were spotlessly clean. It was a pleasure to use them. Then I explored all through the building – behind the bar, in the offices – looking for something. Something suspicious.

One of the doors led down to the cellar, the cellar where I'd first seen Eddie, barking orders at men delivering barrels of beer. And I could still see the look on his face when he'd caught sight of me. There were plenty of kegs still here, and boxes tight packed with bottles and cans. I didn't even know what I was looking for, but I was determined to wait here at Heartbeat and find out.

First though, I decided that I would phone Gaby. The mobile number she had given me leapt straight into my mind. How could I remember a once-told number, and nothing of my past?

It would come back, I told myself again. One day I would wake up and it would all be there, every second of it. Maybe I would regret remembering. Maybe I had pushed the past out because the memories were too painful.

There was a phone in the cellar. I lifted it and dialled Gaby's number, hoping she hadn't switched it off.

'Is that your phone, Gaby McGurk?' Mrs Wilson screamed at her while the rest of the class sniggered.

'Sorry, miss.' Gaby fumbled in her bag. She was always in trouble for not switching off her phone. 'It's probably somebody phoning to wish me a happy birthday. It's my birthday today.' She thought she would play the sympathy card. It didn't work with Mrs Wilson.

'Put it off. NOW!'

Gaby found it, pretended she hadn't so she could check out the number.

'I said, NOW!'

Gaby mimicked panic. 'I can't find it, miss.'

Mrs Wilson was advancing up the aisle, her face blood-red with anger. Gaby had only a second to glance at the number and see she didn't recognise it. She switched it off just seconds before Mrs Wilson snapped a book down on the desk, missing Gaby's fingers by inches.

I put the phone back on the cradle. I could try again later I thought, remembering Gaby would probably be in school now. I wanted to let her know where I was, and that I wasn't the one who had stabbed the policeman.

I might have a long wait in this cellar, so I decided to go back to the toilet again. Too much Coke, I thought. It was as I came out of the toilet that I saw something was different. Something had changed in here. At first I didn't know what, until I saw another set of keys laid on the bar. A set of keys that hadn't been there before. I backed into the toilet, my eyes darting this way and that. But I was already too late. One minute I was watching the keys on the bar, and the next, something cracked against my skull.

Lewis had been given a day off and he intended to use it wisely. He felt fine, hadn't lost much blood. After thinking he was dying alone in that grotty stairwell in Wellpark Court, he'd only had three stitches.

His mother still thought he should have a week off and deserved a medal. The old trout, he thought fondly. She wouldn't even have let him go out had he told her, but she was working herself, and he would be back before she even knew it. She was already looking for other jobs for her son. 'If you still want to wear a uniform they need a lollipop man at the school.'

Lewis got in his car and went for a drive, sure he was being followed. Looking for a conspiracy everywhere. He was becoming paranoid, he told himself. He drove around for a long time, down the coast, past the marinas with their yachts and schooners berthed for the winter, past the power station and the ferry terminals. But he knew there was only one place he really wanted to be. He wanted to go to Heartbeat.

In the playground at break Gaby rummaged through her

252

bag for her phone. She checked the number again. A local number, but one she didn't recognise. 'Why don't you phone it?' Zoe said. 'Find out who made the call.'

'I was just going to do that,' Gaby replied testily. She never liked it when Zoe thought of things before she did.

She dialled and waited. The temperature had risen and the icy roads had thawed. A smir of rain had begun to fall. The surface of the playground grew shiny and wet. Maybe it was a Valentine, Gaby was thinking. Some good-looking boy in the town calling to apologise for not sending her one, but assuring her of his undying love anyway.

The phone was answered. Gaby was about to ask who she was speaking to when she realised she'd clicked into an answering machine.

'Hello, you have come through to Heartbeat. The town's favourite nightspot. I'm sorry no one is here to take your call at the moment. Please call again later.'

Gaby clicked off her phone. Stared at Zoe. 'It was Heartbeat's number.'

Zoe gasped. 'Who would phone you from there?'

But they both knew the answer to that. 'Ram,' Gaby said. 'He was determined to go there. Maybe he found something out. That's why he phoned me.'

The bell was ringing, summoning them back into classes. Gaby was thinking hard. It had to be Ram who had phoned her. Phoned her from inside Heartbeat. The question was, was he still there?

I came to with a pounding head. My arms were tied to a post behind me. It took me a minute to remember where

253

I was and what had happened.

I was in a tiny room off the cellar. There were no windows, but the door was ajar and I could hear movement and see light. Daylight. The hatch on to the street was open and something was being delivered, probably more kegs of beer. I tried to shout, to call for help, and only then I realised my mouth was bound with tape too. I couldn't make a sound. And help was surely only in that other room. I struggled but I was trussed tightly. The barrels were being rolled into the cellar only feet away from me, and I couldn't move a muscle to help myself.

I banged my head off the post behind me, but it made no real sound. Nothing to alert anyone that there was a boy here, badly in need of rescuing. This time I had been caught, and how could I get away now? I felt myself begin to shake. Was it the Wolf? Had he come for me? Got me at last?

I heard voices calling, but couldn't make out whose, and finally the hatch was closed. First one flap, then the other and the cellar was plunged into darkness.

Footsteps came towards me, soft footsteps, and I held my breath. If it was the man who was following me – if it was the Wolf – I knew I was dead already. There had been hatred in those eyes of his. Even in the dark I could see it. He wouldn't waste time now.

If I could remember who I was supposed to pray to, I would have prayed then.

The footsteps came closer. Stepped into the cellar, and a dim light was switched on.

It was Eddie. Only simple old Eddie who had fooled me into believing he was like me, sleeping rough and homeless. It was Eddie who came into the cellar.

I blinked to get used to the light, and he stood in front of me, grinning like an idiot.

He slammed the door shut behind him. 'Oh, woken up, have we?' he said. His voice still whined, but there was a confidence in it now.

I couldn't speak. He whipped the tape from my mouth so roughly it stung.

'No point shouting or anything, son. Nobody here, and nobody would hear you anyway.' Eddie crouched in front of me and I struggled and shook myself to be free of these ropes. An inch closer and I could have headbutted him. He still smiled. Not Jake's smile that was all friendliness, but something sinister.

'You'll not get free of them. I learned how to tie ropes in the Boy Scouts. Not quite what they had in mind, eh? So what do you think of old Eddie? Fooled you completely, eh? Good actor, ain't I? I was always in the school shows, you know. Playing the baddie.' He was enjoying this. 'Wolf wasn't happy I got involved that night. Said he didn't need any help. But I was the one that found out what you knew. Heartbeat. And once you told me that, pal . . . you were a dead man. Or you were supposed to be.' Was it nerves or excitement that made him talk so much? He still hadn't finished. 'You were totally taken in, telling me everything. Poor wee homeless Eddie.' He spat on the ground. 'I don't think! Well, this time I've got you, not the Wolf. Me. And I'm going to show the Boss that I can finish the job the Wolf couldn't manage.'

The Wolf. It *had* been the Wolf all along. Not a legend. The bogeyman was real.

Eddie stood up and began strutting about the cellar. 'See, I'm gonny be a big man, right-hand man to the Boss, the one he can rely on. The Wolf's getting past it. You've proved that. And I'm gonny take over. I'm gonny prove I'm the man, by killing you, pal.'

He said it as if killing me was the easiest thing in the world.

'Well, the Wolf couldn't do it, could he?' I said. 'What makes you think you can?'

'Killing you is going to be a doddle, pal. The Wolf's past his sell-by date. None of this would have happened if he'd finished that guy last week.' Eddie was obviously in a talkative mood. I had a feeling no one ever usually listened to him. 'Wee guy comes here that night, shaking in his shoes, desperate to tell Billy Taggart what's going to happen at Heartbeat on the fourteenth. He knows everything. He's one of the delivery men, like, decides he canny go through with it. But Billy's no' here, only his good buddy, Eddie. Me!' He poked at his chest. 'So the wee guy spills his guts to me.' He began to laugh. Looked at me as if he was expecting me to laugh too. 'You've got to see the funny side of that, surely? Thought he was talking to one of the good guys. So I kidded on that I was phoning Billy to tell him, but it was the Boss I was phoning.' Eddie's smile disappeared. Annoyance seemed to set in. 'I could have handled that wee guy myself. But no! "Let the Wolf handle it," I was told. That should have been the end of that. Then you came along.'

'Always like to be of service,' I said.

'But I'm going to finish you off now. Do you want to know how I'm gonny do it?'

'What now?' I asked. 'A blow-by-blow account of my impending death? Come on, Eddie. You know what's going to happen. I'm going to escape, I'm going to save the day. We both know that.'

I was bold. He wasn't the Wolf and I wasn't afraid of him.

But I was getting to Eddie. 'You'll not get away this time. See that delivery that just came in? Bet you thought it was beer?'

'Send one over,' I said. 'Make sure it's cold.'

'You think you're so funny. You'll not be laughing later. It wasn't beer. It was all part of the plan to bring down Taggart. The Boss's plan.' Eddie jumped down to my face. 'Ever hear of acetylene? That's what's in the cylinders that have just been delivered. And tonight, at the Valentine disco there's going to be a fire. But not just any fire. Know what happens when acetylene gets really hot? 'He mimicked a massive explosion with his arms. 'BOOM! Not just Heartbeat, but all the other nightclubs and restaurants next door. The competition. Good plan, eh? And simple. And effective. If it doesn't look like an accident, Billy Taggart still gets the blame. End of Billy Taggart. End of you. And you'll be able to watch it all happen, boy. In fact, you'll be the first to go. A front-row seat. And it'll be all thanks to Eddie.'

He strutted round the cellar like an idiot and if I hadn't been so blinking shocked I would have laughed at him.

Because suddenly everything fell into place. Heartbeat. Stop. Fourteenth. This was what the man had wanted to stop. This was why he had died. To stop a bloodbath at an under-age disco in Heartbeat. I had come close to stopping it, but close just wasn't good enough.

Gaby headed for Heartbeat as soon as school was over. Zoe took the bus home, and without telling her where she was going, Gaby walked into the town. She hadn't a clue what she was going to do when she got there, but she thought she might find Ram hiding around the place. Hadn't she told him they would go there tonight? Together. He might just be lying in wait, hoping she would come. Why did she care? She could get herself into such a lot of trouble for this. But he had phoned her and she wanted to find out why.

Darkness was falling already in the February afternoon. Heartbeat was closed. The shutters were open on the windows, but the main doors were barred. She stood for a moment looking about her, then walked round the corner. She stamped her feet to keep them warm on the iron hatch of the cellar. A sudden movement caught her eye as a blind on one of the windows opened a fraction. Someone was there, watching her. She walked round again to the front doors.

Just as she was about to knock, she heard the locks being drawn and the door was opened. 'Can I help you?'

Gaby tried to look innocent. 'Just wondering when

the disco starts tonight.'

The pasty-faced youth pointed to the posters. 'Do they not teach you to read in your school?' There on the poster, clearly stated: 7 p.m. till 11 p.m.

Gaby giggled. 'Didn't notice.' She was trying to stay calm, not say a word. But she knew who he was. The pasty face, the whining voice. This was the boy, Eddie, who had tricked Ram.

This was also the same boy she had seen talking to the dead man that night at Heartbeat. Now she only wanted away from him. Wanted to get away.

'You're coming tonight then?' he asked her.

She nodded. Too enthusiastically. 'Yeah, wouldn't miss it.'

'Let's hope it goes with a bang,' he said, and then he laughed and closed the door.

Gaby ran. She ran till Heartbeat was out of sight. She had to tell someone, but who?

'Had a visitor there,' Eddie said, coming back into the room. He had taped my mouth again, and this time he didn't rip it off. I had tried everything to free myself, hoping to remember perhaps, in the locked-up memory of mine, that I had been an escape artist. I obviously hadn't. I couldn't budge. 'You'll never guess who it was?'

Eddie liked to talk. Talk too much. He would never make it with the big boys, even I knew that. You couldn't trust anyone who talked as much as Eddie.

'It was that Gaby McGurk. The famous Gaby McGurk.'

Good old Gaby, I thought. She had come, but she wouldn't know I was still here. What could she do?

'Coming to the disco tonight,' Eddie went on. 'And is she in for a surprise.'

He didn't suspect her, and why should he? Eddie knew nothing of how Gaby had hidden me. That was in our favour. If only she could figure out that I was still here, trapped in the cellar. If only she could find help and bring it here.

Soon they would start arriving for the disco, for a night of fun and dancing, and Eddie would start his fire and go, leaving me trapped in here. And no one would know that this was no ordinary fire – terrifying enough – but something worse. Gaby, I hated to admit it, was my only chance of survival at the moment.

Yet there might be someone else.

My dad.

The idea came without me even thinking about it. Gaby could go to him. Tell him everything, bring him here to help. My dad. Maybe this was why he'd been brought here – to save me, to save the town. Gaby, I kept thinking, willing her to do it – go to my dad.

Gaby was thinking the same thing. Sitting in her kitchen, worrying herself sick about what to do.

I should go to his dad. That poor man. I could call him and tell him, 'I think your son's in Heartbeat. He phoned me from there, and the man who tricked him is there now, and I have such a bad feeling about it.'

Tell his dad. His dad would come to the rescue. They

260

would be reunited, Ram's memory would come back, and it would all be thanks to Gaby. They would be eternally grateful. Maybe Ram had pots of money. Maybe he *was* an Arabian prince, with palaces in the desert. She would get a reward.

Her dream faded with reality.

Then again, Ram didn't trust this man. He was frightened of him. Maybe going to him would be the worst thing she could do. Ram wouldn't want her to go to him.

The police? No, she wouldn't trust the police. There was one she did trust. PC Ferguson. Yes, she liked him, trusted him. But he had been the one who'd been stabbed last night. She'd heard he was at death's door. In a coma. Never be able to speak again. She hoped he was OK. So, she couldn't go to him either. But she wanted someone to help her. Someone to trust.

Just then, Big Dan came in the front door. He poked his head into the kitchen where she was sitting. 'Hi, your mum not in yet?'

Gaby shook her head. And he went off into the living room.

Big Dan, a gorilla of a man. Muscles from working on the rigs. Always wanting her to trust him, to rely on him.

It was as if God had answered her prayers. Big Dan would help her. He would know what to do. No one would tangle with Dan. She was going to tell Big Dan everything.

I heard the beginnings of music in the bar upstairs. Soon teenagers would be arriving, looking forward to an evening of dancing and laughter. How could anyone want to spoil this? Eddie was cocky with success. Sure everything was going to go right for him. Why shouldn't he? How could anything go wrong now? But something had been going wrong, ever since I had found the dying man in the lift. I had made it all go wrong. I could make it all go wrong again. Tonight. If I could just think of a way.

'You mean this boy, this fugitive, was here in this building, in Auntie Ellen's house, all the time?'

She had told Dan everything, expecting him to be angry at her. She hadn't expected him to be amused.

He seemed to find the whole thing hilarious. 'The whole police force is after him, and God knows who else, and all the time he's right under their noses. With the help of Gaby McGurk. You really are something.'

Gaby smiled too. 'What could I do? I had to help him. You won't tell my mum, will you?'

Big Dan didn't let her down. 'Not unless I have to,' he said. 'So you think he's still in this Heartbeat, do you?'

'I don't know,' she said. 'But I recognised Eddie.' She had also told him about being in Heartbeat, seeing the dead man talking to Eddie. And he'd laughed about that as well. 'No one knows who this dead man is, and little Gaby has known everything all the time.' He stood up. 'We'll have to go there.'

'On our own?'

'Don't want to tell the police, do we? Wouldn't trust them.'

He was right, of course. No point in alerting the police, yet.

'I think I can handle this Eddie,' Dan said, and Gaby was sure he could too. A big brute of a man like Big Dan could wrap Eddie in a stranglehold no bother at all.

'Right, no time like the present,' he said. 'Let's go and see if we can rescue this boyfriend of yours.'

'What'll we tell Mum?'

'Sure she's always wanting us to be friends. I'll leave her a note saying we're off on a birthday shopping spree. She'll be delighted.'

Zoe had been phoning Gaby for the past half hour. No answer. She'd even tried her mobile and it was switched off. But finally Mrs McGurk answered the phone, breathless, just in from work. 'Oh, hello, Zoe. Are you looking for my Gaby?'

'We're supposed to be going to the cafe tonight, for her birthday, and I don't know what time to meet her.'

'Can't you get her on the mobile?'

Zoe told her it had been switched off. She waited for Mrs McGurk to complain. She never trusted Gaby with her mobile switched off. Instead she laughed. 'She'll not want to be disturbed while she's out shopping.'

Now that annoyed Zoe. Out shopping, without asking her along, and with who? She didn't have to ask. Mrs McGurk told her. 'Her and her dad. He's taken her out shopping for her birthday. I dare say she'll phone you later, Zoe.'

Out shopping with Dan? That took Zoe by surprise. After school, all Gaby could talk about was going to Heartbeat that night. Hurrying home to get ready for the Valentine disco! Expecting Ram to be somewhere there, just waiting for them. And now, she had forgotten all about him, and about her. Just because of a shopping spree. That was Gaby all over. She had no commitment to anything. She'd always said she hated Big Dan, he was trying to buy her friendship, even her love. But, offered a treat and she would put all that aside. Well, she'd have something to say about that tonight, when they met at Heartbeat.

The Dark Man watched the girl, Gaby, emerge from Wellpark Court. She was with a man, her dad, he assumed. Her little face looked pinched and worried, but he was smiling, as if trying to reassure her about something. Their car was parked near the entrance and they both got inside and drove off. He wondered about following them. Decided against it. The girl would come back.

Eddie couldn't resist a kick every time he passed me. Had I seen men like him before? For I was sure he reminded me of someone. Maybe of many people. Men who tried to be tough and hard, but were stupid. He was keeping me here without telling his boss, until he knew it was all over, and then he would have one over this man he called 'the Wolf'. Would Gaby come back? Would she bring my dad? I hoped she would. I waited in the dark as the music thumped in the room above me, expecting any minute that she would come barging in like some avenging angel. I even managed a smile. Gaby as an avenging angel – somehow just didn't seem right.

Every time he came down to the cellar, Eddie would come over and bait me. 'I bet you thought you were so clever, pal. Escaping from the fire. How did you get away in the water? That really scunnered the Wolf. Thought he had finished you for ever, and here you are. Back again! Oh, you are really getting on his wick.'

'Maybe I've got special powers,' I wanted to say, if he would only take the tape from my mouth. But I followed him with my eyes, those eyes that had evil in them and hoped he might see that too. I think they did disturb him, for after a while he left me alone. 'Things to see to up in the bar,' he said.

Where would he start the fire? Down here? Let it spread. I sniffed for smoke but could smell none. Not yet. But soon.

'What are you going to do, Dan?'

Big Dan had parked his car in the street behind the nightclub and Gaby was anxious to get there, to find out what was happening.

She answered the question herself. 'You could confront this Eddie. Threaten him with grievous bodily harm. I bet he would tell you anything.' She imagined him grabbing the skinny Eddie by the throat, throttling him until he was almost dead. Yes, that should do it.

Dan was saying nothing and it was taking all her efforts to keep up with him. He stopped at the side entrance to Heartbeat, at the iron hatch, embellished with the brewer's marks, that led into the cellar. It was dark here in the alley, with only a distant street lamp giving them any light at all. Already the music was blaring from the loudspeakers, a few early birds standing about inside.

'I think we should go in through the cellar. We don't want to alert anybody.'

Gaby didn't fancy this way at all, but Dan was down on his knees and slipping his thick, strong fingers through the iron rings on the hatch. She expected them to be locked, or too heavy for one man to lift. But Big

Dan was strong. She watched his jaw stiffen with the effort. The veins stood out on his neck as if they were about to explode. But inch by inch the hatch rose.

'You're doing it,' she said. She was almost proud of him, proud of herself for asking him to help. It would make her mother so happy too. They were doing something together. Something that would bond them for ever. Maybe at last they were going to be a family. With one final grunt he pulled the hatch upright and Gaby looked around making sure no one had seen them. But the alley was empty. Dan put his hands round her waist, lifted her, and dropped her gently on to the floor of the cellar.

'Are you sure this is a good idea?' she whispered as he jumped down beside her. 'I know I said I didn't want the police involved, but this might be dangerous.'

Dan didn't answer her. He put a finger to his lips to tell her to be quiet, and in the darkness she could hardly make out his face. The cellar was ice cold, and had shadowy corners where anyone could hide. Gaby took a step closer to Dan. Suddenly, she didn't know what she was doing here.

Then she heard a movement, somewhere close. Dan looked at her. He heard it too. They both stopped dead.

'Ram, is that you?' Gaby called softly.

The movement again. The sound coming from behind a door. Rats? She would lose the plot if it was rats. She clutched at Dan's arm. 'Ram, tell me that's you?'

I had heard the hatch being lifted and someone dropping on to the floor, light feet, followed a second later by a heavier thud. Two people. More trouble for me, or salvation? And then her voice. Gaby's. 'Ram, is that you?' I tried to move, kick out my feet against the stone, against the boxes. Desperate to call out to her. She had brought someone with her. An adult to help. My dad?

My dad.

It had to be. I kicked again.

'It's coming from in there,' I heard her whisper and her feet were hurrying closer. The door was pushed open and there she was, Gaby. I'd never been so glad to see anyone in my life.

'Oh my God, I knew you were here! That's why I came.' All the time she spoke she was throwing herself on the ground, pulling at the tape at my mouth. 'Oh, Ram, are you OK?'

As soon as I could speak it all came tumbling out of me. 'They're going to start a fire here tonight, Gaby. And there's acetylene cylinders here. They could explode. We've got to warn them, Gaby. We've got to get everyone out of here.'

She was fumbling with the ropes at my wrists now, gabbling herself. 'I know. Don't worry. Dan's here, he's going to help. Everything's going to be OK, Ram.'

And I looked up to see Big Dan coming in behind her. It was dark in the cellar. I couldn't see his face. I didn't need to. The bulk of the man, the hands, the way he walked.

I was looking at the Wolf.

Gaby stopped untying me, as if she felt me stiffen against her. 'What's wrong? It's only Dan. It's OK.'

She looked back at him and what did she see? The man who had lived in her house for almost a year? Generous, good to her mother. What did I see? The man who wanted to kill me. Who had tried to kill me so often.

The Wolf swayed on his feet. He saw nothing. The girl had disappeared from his vision. He saw only the boy, blackness all around him. He was consumed with hatred for him. The boy tried to stand up, staggered against Gaby.

'You,' the boy said. 'You're the one.'

'I'm the one,' he said. 'And now I've got you. This time you won't get away.'

The girl, Gaby – he heard her voice but could hardly see her – was puzzled, didn't understand what was going on. 'But, Ram, this is Dan, he's my . . .' She didn't know what to call him, so she called him at last what he'd always wanted her to call him. 'He's my dad.'

269

Too late. It was too late. Gaby knew too much now. No one knew of his other life. Not even Gaby's mum. He worked on the rigs, accounting for the big money he earned, accounting for the times he was out of town, on his own business. The Wolf's business.

'No, Gaby. This is the man who killed the man in the lift. Who followed me and tried to kill me.'

'You're talking rubbish, Ram.' Gaby came running over to him. 'I asked Dan to help me.' She looked up at him now. 'You're going to help, aren't you?'

The Wolf turned his eyes away from her. He couldn't think of her as Gaby now. She was expendable.

It was a joke really, that the boy had been down in Ellen's flat. He could have had him so easily. 'Yes, I'm going to help, I'm going to solve all his problems. For good.'

She stood up straight and faced him. She was a fiery wee thing, he had always liked that about her. 'Look, if you don't help us get out of here I'll tell my mum on you.'

The boy pulled her back to him. 'I don't think he intends you to tell anybody anything from now on, Gaby.'

It took her a minute to take it in. 'I don't get it. What's happening here?'

'He's the Wolf,' the boy said.

It was the moment that Eddie came running in. Coming downstairs to check on me, and finding his worst night-mare standing there to confront him. I could see fear,

270

not just etched on his face, but set there in stone. He stepped back when he saw the Wolf and swallowed. He glanced at me, saw I was unbound and with Gaby close beside me. Too stupid to take it in. He looked back at the Wolf. His voice was stammering. 'I . . . I caught him in here. I tied him up. Didn't have time to contact the Boss . . . or you. How did you get here?'

The Wolf didn't answer him, instead he drew his hand hard across Eddie's face and sent him reeling against the wall. Gaby gasped.

'Thought you could take over from me, eh, Eddie? You haven't got the brains.' Eddie slumped down the wall. I could see blood trickle from his mouth, but he said nothing. He just stayed down.

'I'll handle everything from now on,' the Wolf said.

He turned to me. 'You and me have got business to finish, eh, boy?' I moved away from him, but he grabbed me. 'You're not going to like what I've got in mind for you.' Then he dragged me close to his face. 'We're going to end this where it all began,' he said. 'I'm going to make you pay.'

Eddie whimpered. 'What about the fire?'

'There's going to be a fire, Eddie. I'll start it on the way out. Unfortunately, you're going to be one of the victims.' His cold eyes turned to Gaby. 'You too, honey. Sorry, but as they say in the movies, "You know too much."'

I began to struggle wildly. He was going to let her die, the girl he had classed as a daughter. What kind of animal was he?

Gaby ran at him and punched him wildly with her

fists. It meant nothing to him. With one hand he shoved her and she was sent sprawling back into the room. He dragged me out and pushed the door shut. He would have to wedge something there to keep that door shut, and when he did, then I would have my chance to run, to get help. But the Wolf already had all that figured out. He gripped my hair, yanked my head back and with one hand and a kick, one barrel was rolled against the door and then another.

Then he took a lighter from his pocket. He flicked it open and it lit up his features like a devil in the flame. He grinned at me.

'I thought for a while you were my nemesis. That you'd been sent to ruin me. But you're nothing, boy. Just a scratch on my backside.' He lit a rag, then another already soaked in petrol by the thoughtful Eddie, kicked them against the boxes by the corner. They would catch, and then the stacks of boxes would come alive with flames, and then the whole place would be consumed by fire rising to the dance floor where the teenagers sang and laughed. And then the fumes, it would be the fumes that would cause the panic first, and then the explosion. Simple, but effective.

I fought with everything I had, but he was strong and he hated me with more vengeance that I could imagine. Dragging me up from the cellar on to the alleyway above. He slammed down the hatch, punched me once and I slumped against him. Couldn't have helped anyone after that.

Zoe had gone to the disco by herself. She would never forgive Gaby for this. She'd tried to contact her since school finished and then had gone down to Heartbeat in the forlorn hope that Gaby would be waiting for her outside. Her spirits lifted when she saw Big Dan's car driving away. He must have dropped Gaby off, and typical of Gaby to go in without waiting for her friend. That was the only reason Zoe had gone inside. But Gaby wasn't there, and now she felt stupid standing on the sidelines, looking as if she was desperate for anyone to dance with her. None of the girls even came up to her to ask how she was. She felt stupid and angry and . . . was that Eddie? The one Ram told them about? It had to be. He looked worried. No, he looked *furtive* – that was more the word she was looking for. Yes, as if he was up to something. She tasted her Coke and hoped he hadn't been slipping alcohol into the drinks. And she thought of Ram again and wondered if Gaby had seen him. Or maybe Ram was somewhere far away by now.

So where was Gaby?

She saw that horrible boy Dev and his mates, and it looked like they were laughing at her. She would only stay another five minutes, she decided, and then she was going to go home and never speak to Gaby McGurk again.

Gaby and Eddie pounded on the doors, pushed with all of their strength, but it wouldn't budge. They could hardly hear anything. The room was practically sound-proof.

'I can't believe he'd leave me in here. I'm his family.'

'Believe it,' Eddie said. 'He's the worst. Works for every gangster in the country. Killing's just a job for him.'

'Well, Ram was one he couldn't kill!' she snapped.

'He will now. Nothing can save your boyfriend now.'

'He's not my boyfriend!' she said. Then, she stood still. Sniffed. 'I can smell smoke.'

Eddie panicked before her. 'We'll never get out of here!' He pounded again on the door, yelling at the top of his voice, 'Help!'

Lewis drew up outside the nightclub. He'd been driving about for hours, had gone for a cup of tea in a cafe, but he knew there was only one place he really wanted to be. Heartbeat. The Valentine disco was in full swing. He could hear the screams and the laughing and the singing. Could see, in the warm light inside, teenagers dancing and jumping about. Oh, to be young again, he thought, remembering his teenage years. It didn't take much remembering. It was only three years ago.

Heartbeat. Gaby had seen the dead man here hours before he died.

Everything came back to Heartbeat.

It was a beautiful crisp night. The temperature had dropped again, and the roads would be treacherous. Rain turning to ice. He drew in his breath. He loved the smell of the night air, even in town. The mix of pines and curries and cigarette smoke seemed to say all was right with the world.

The strong smell of smoke.

But that wasn't cigarettes.

Lewis got out of his car and stood looking up and down the street. The waterfront was dark except for the lights from the discos and restaurants. There was a definite smell of smoke coming from somewhere close by. He strode along the street, his eyes alert, watching for anything. He saw it just as he came to the corner of Heartbeat, looked down the side alley. Smoke. Not quite belching, but trails of it coming from the cellar at the side of the building.

Lewis sprang into action. He ran to the cellar, checked the hatch. Too heavy for him to lift. The priority was to get those teenagers out of the disco. He was on his mobile in an instant alerting the fire brigade, and even as he spoke to them he was running back round to the main entrance, shouting to the bouncers as he pushed his way inside.

'Get everybody out of here!'

The bouncers glared at him. They were always ready for trouble from Barry McKay's heavies, but not like this. They didn't know Lewis as one of the town's hard men. Didn't know him as policeman either. He'd been in the job for too little time.

'Who the hell are you?'

Suddenly, in that moment, Lewis became a policeman. A real policeman. Not a rookie. He drew himself up and barked out his answer. 'I'm a cop. There's a fire in your cellar. Get everyone out of here. Get them out calmly. The brigade are on their way.'

The men jumped to the sound of someone in charge. One of them ran inside the nightclub. Lewis turned to the other. 'Help me get that hatch to the cellar open.'

The teenagers were reluctant to leave. Didn't understand why they had to go. They were complaining, but laughing – in too good a mood to let anything spoil their night. Lewis recognised the boy Dev. He was making the most fuss about going.

'I better be getting my money back. I don't have to go if I don't want to. You cannae make me.'

The bouncer grabbed him by the collar. 'There's a blinking fire, son. You either leave, or you fry. Take your pick.'

So much for getting them out calmly. As soon as fire was mentioned, panic set in.

'He said there was a fire!'

There were screams, and they all began to push and shove each other. Some stumbled on the stairs. Lewis shouted, 'Get out. Right now! Move calmly towards the exit.'

It worked.

A girl hurried up to him, grabbed his arm. 'Is there a fire? Did you say there was a fire?'

Lewis recognised her, Gaby's pal. He recognised her too as the voice on the phone. She was a friend of Gaby's, but not the drama queen that Gaby was. Zoe.

'There is,' he said.

He watched her face crumple. 'The boy everybody's been looking for, the boy Gaby saw in the lift, he phoned Gaby from here today. Something's going to happen here. I think maybe it's this fire. And I don't know where Gaby is, but I think she might be here too.' She began to babble, but Lewis had heard all he wanted. Questions could be answered later.

He ran round to the cellar. Zoe was at his heels. He tried to pull at the ring on the hatch, but it was too heavy for one man. The smoke was belching out now, and Lewis strained himself pulling at the ring on the door. Seconds later the bouncer was by his side, a burly guy with muscles like iron bands. Together they hauled at the door, and inch by inch it came up.

They both fell back on the pavement as the thick black smoke surged up to escape. Lewis was about to jump down, but the bouncer held him back. 'There's nobody down there. Wait for the brigade.'

But Lewis couldn't take that chance. 'There might be,' he said, and he jumped.

His eyes nipped. He could see nothing. He stood for a moment, shouted hoarsely, 'Anybody here? Anybody here?'

There was a thump and a bang. He looked around, tried to see – saw nothing. Only black corners where anything could hide.

The bouncer jumped down beside him. He pointed to

one of the walls, stacked with barrels. 'There's a door behind there. A stockroom. Those barrels weren't stacked there earlier.' And now his voice seemed to say, there might be someone here too.

Lewis called again, louder this time. And he was answered with a faint scream. A girl's scream. Gaby. The men grabbed at the barrels. Pulled them down, hardly daring to breathe in the smoke, knowing it was winding its way round their throats down into their lungs. But they couldn't stop. They pulled the door open. Gaby fell against him, still screaming. Lewis grabbed her, lifted her. Eddie stumbled out behind her. Gaby's face streamed with tears. Lewis got her to the hatch. One of the boys, Dev, was standing above, looking down. 'Get her!' Lewis shouted. Dev did as he was told. Throwing himself flat and grabbing Gaby's arms. The bouncer was half-carrying Eddie. He was almost unconscious.

Suddenly Gaby was screaming. Lewis tried to comfort her. 'You're OK now, Gaby. We've got everyone out of the disco. The fire brigade's on its way. Everything's going to be fine.'

And still she didn't stop screaming. 'You don't understand.' She managed words at last. 'There's some kind of cylinders in there. Acetylene or something. I think they're going to blow up.'

My head swirled with pain as soon as I opened my eyes. All was darkness. I couldn't see where I was. Wish it had stayed that way.

He was suddenly there in front of me. The Wolf, with a face that oozed evil. Why did this man hate me so much?

'I waited till you came to. Didn't want you to miss the fun.'

It only took me a second to know what he meant. I heard the sound of the lift coming alive and the jerk as it began to move.

Up.

And then I realised where I was.

I was on top of the lift, and so was he, standing above me. Glaring down at me. Filled with hate for me.

I slid back, too near the edge. I almost slipped off. I tried to stand up, but there was nothing to hold on to. The cable was too far out of my reach. He was holding it. I was scared and couldn't hide it. The lift shuddered through me as it rose, floor by floor. Rising from the basement to the seventeenth floor. I tried not to look down. Tried not to imagine the drop below me.

He sneered. 'I finally figured out how you got away from me last night. There was no other way. The hatch on the lift must have been loose. I don't know how you climbed up here, but you managed it. Then you screwed it tight, eh? I should have had you then, but by God, I will have you now.'

I shuffled back again and froze, too near the edge. He saw my fear and laughed. A laugh that echoed and bounced from the walls to the floor to the roof. I looked up, could see the other lift sitting at the top floor.

He had no heart. I knew that when he left Gaby in the cellar. Gaby. Was she still alive? Had I stopped nothing?

At last I got to my feet, unsteadily, but if I was going to die, I would die standing. Not lying on the ground like a wounded animal. Up and up the lift went, and with every floor my terror grew. I thought of myself slipping, falling, tumbling down.

The lift shuddered to a halt at the sixteenth floor. No point calling or shouting. Help wouldn't arrive in time. Get out of this one, Ram, I thought. But I couldn't think of a way. This time I was finished.

He knew it too. He had won, at last.

And no one would ever know his secret – know he was the Wolf. He would slip back into the flat on the fifteenth floor, and pretend shock and horror at the fire, at the loss of his lovely little Gaby. I could almost picture it. Everyone would feel sorry for him, impressed by the way he would support Gaby's mum through the trauma. Maybe they would move away, and no one would ever find out that he was the legendary Wolf.

Yet, somehow I knew that even if the world did discover his secret, he wouldn't care. If he could never go back to Gaby's mother, or his old life – if like me he had to sink back into the shadows where he belonged – he wouldn't care about any of that. I could tell from the hate in his eyes. As long as he had got me along the way, nothing else mattered.

He reached out a hand, I shrank back from him and my foot slipped. I yelled and my voice rippled through the shaft in a ghostly echo.

'No escape,' he said. He was almost laughing. Mad with hatred. I had made him mad, insane with anger. And maybe that was my revenge. I would never know. I'd be dead.

The firemen stared at Lewis. 'Acetylene cylinders down in that cellar? Oh my God.' He yelled at his men, told them, then he looked back at Lewis. 'Cordon this place off. Evacuate the whole area – houses, factories, alert every business. Traffic will have to be diverted, and the train line runs along here. The trains will have to be cancelled too. If those cylinders explode, you don't even want to think about it.'

'OK, I'll get on to it,' Lewis said. He hurried back to Gaby. She was being comforted by Zoe. 'If it wasn't for this girl,' he said, 'I wouldn't have known you were here.'

More tears from Gaby. She clutched on to Zoe's hand. 'You're the best friend anybody could ever have, Zoe.'

Zoe was crying too.

Nearby, Eddie was singing like a bird. He wanted his

revenge on the Wolf, on them all. Gaby grabbed at Lewis's hand. 'You've got to get Ram, save him. Big Dan –'

'The Wolf,' Zoe corrected her.

Gaby nodded. 'The Wolf, he took him away. He's going to kill him.'

'But where?' Lewis asked. He wanted to help the boy, but he didn't know where to go.

Gaby was trying hard to think. 'He said, "I'm taking you back to where it all began." '

Lewis knew in that second exactly where the Wolf had taken the boy. Back to where it had all started. Back to a lift in Wellpark Court.

59

'Leave my boy be!'

The voice, loud and clear, sounded as if it had come from God himself. The Wolf, holding the cable, looked around, up and down. So did I, with nothing to hold on to, balancing myself with my feet. And suddenly, something, someone, was leaping from the darkness above. Leaping from the lift perched on the seventeenth floor.

The Dark Man. The man I had seen talking to Gaby. Leaping to my rescue.

My dad.

The Wolf turned on him, unafraid. Nothing was going to spoil this moment for him. The Dark Man, my dad? I could hardly believe it! He landed on the lift and it shook, and I stumbled and fell back.

My dad, here to save me.

He grabbed the Wolf and they began to struggle with each other. He punched hard, trying to make the Wolf lose his grip on the cable. At last his hand slipped and the man . . . my dad . . . punched him again, even harder this time. The Wolf stumbled, but with his foot he kicked out and caught my dad and brought him down hard on the surface of the lift. It shook so much I was afraid the cable would snap and we would all go plummeting to our doom. The Wolf was up in a flash, even taking time to kick out at me, trying to kick me over the edge. I rolled away, but clung on in terror, my nails scraping against metal. My dad (*my dad* – the words were like music) leapt to his feet. He was lean, where the Wolf was broad, but there was a power in his leanness, as if his muscles were made of taut steel. The wind whistled through the shaft, roared at them, egging them on, as they threw their fists wildly at each other. A blow caught my dad on the eye and nearly had him over, but he steadied himself and dodged the next blow.

He couldn't miss the next though. It landed hard against his head and sent him reeling. He fell, rolled, disappeared over the edge. I let out a gasp of fear. All I could see was his fingers clutching on to the rim of metal. My breathing seemed to stop. I wanted to reach down and help him, but I couldn't move. He was grappling at the edge of the lift for something else to hold on to. The Wolf ignored him, thought he'd got rid of him, and he turned again on me. I could see my dad moving, hauling himself up. The Wolf could see it too. He had to, yet he didn't turn back to him. And I realised, no one else mattered. The Wolf would plunge to his death happily, as long as he could take me with him. I edged back away from him. The Wolf reached out to grab me, grab me with those powerful hands. Together we would plunge down fifteen floors. Just one more inch and he would have me.

And suddenly my dad was on his feet. He gripped the Wolf by the shoulders and threw him so hard he lost his footing, began to tumble. Still he reached out for me, even in those seconds when he knew he was falling, he couldn't let me go, wanted me with him. I drew myself as far back as I dared, and it was as if the world began to move in slow motion. The Wolf did a dance, trying to regain his balance. It was no use. There was nothing for him to cling on to. Back and back he went, almost as if he was ready to fly. But I didn't look. I couldn't. Too much terror. There was no sound as he fell. No scream. Nothing. Just, moments later, a dull thud.

Lewis had never driven so fast. The siren wailed out a warning. Would he be too late, he wondered? He'd already sent out a call for back-up, and Guthrie and some other officers were there when he arrived. Lewis said to his sergeant, 'I think you need to ask him some questions,' pointing at Guthrie. They didn't need to. Eddie was already singing his song about the policeman who was paid by Barry McKay for information, and the CID officer too. Guthrie would be retiring a lot sooner than he expected.

There was just me and my dad in the dark of the lift shaft. 'Who am I?' I asked. I wanted to know my name, where I came from, how I had lost my memory.

'Time for answers later,' my dad said.

'Tell me something about myself.' I was trying to stand up.

My dad sighed. He held the cable tight and reached out for me. 'I'll tell you everything soon.'

I took a step forwards to his outstretched hand. 'I've been so scared.'

I admitted it at last. I wanted comfort. I wanted home. I wanted my dad so much.

Now I had it all, here, an inch from my grasp. 'I know,' he said. 'You're safe now.' He held out one hand to me, his other holding tight to the cable. 'Come to me.'

His voice was low and soothing, hypnotic. There was something in that voice that held me, like a spell. I moved closer. This was surely the voice I could trust. At last. He stepped closer too.

And the shadows fell across his face. It seemed to change in front of me. Change to something sinister, skeletal. The eyes sunk low, the cheekbones standing out starkly, the smile on his mouth twisted into a malevolent grin.

It was suddenly as if I was in another place. A room. I was hiding, listening. I could hear his voice, see his face with that same twisted smile. 'You can't stop us. We'll win in the end.' Who was he talking to? And where was I hiding? Then it was gone. I was back on the top of a lift in the dark. Another rush of memory, gone in an instant. But enough.

I had been suspicious for too long. I stepped back. 'No.'

And the voice changed. Patience at an end. 'Come to me!' This time an order.

'You're not my dad, are you?'

He didn't answer, but he didn't need to. He wasn't my dad. He was someone who meant me harm. Who had done harm already. It was all a lie. And that was the cruellest thing of all. For a moment, I had a dad. I had imagined him taking me home. My troubles over at last.

Someone there for me . . . and it was all a lie. It hurt so much it was like the knife of the Wolf through my body.

Nothing would make me go to him now. Ever. 'No,' I said again.

'You can't escape. We'll get you in the end.'

'Who is "we"?' I asked him.

'You really can't remember, can you?' He was still smiling. 'But the trouble is, you will one day, and we can't afford for that to happen.'

I took another step back.

That smile scared me. And suddenly I knew that smile had scared me before. I couldn't remember when or how. 'You don't understand.' He paused, said nothing for a long moment. Then what he said made my legs shake and my head swim. 'There is no escape for you. You're dead already.'

It was as if the world stopped moving. The blackness swirled around me like a shroud. I was dead?

I wouldn't listen. I turned my face from him. His voice still called to me. 'I've come for you.'

Dead? Was I dead? My head was filled with a silent scream. Was that why I had no memory? Why I could remember nothing? I wanted away from him, from here, but there was nowhere to go. I wanted away from this evil man, and I knew then the Dark Man was evil. He had pretended to be my dad, my saviour. I had wanted him to be so much. Now I wanted away from his words 'You're dead.'

No. It couldn't be. I couldn't be dead. I was flesh and blood. I felt pain, and anger. I was alive.

But I should have died in a fire. And how did I escape

death in the deep waters of the reservoir? Because I was already dead? No!

'Who are you?' I shouted at him.

'I'm Mr Death,' he said softly. 'And no one escapes death for ever.'

The other lift began to move above me. Coming down. I wanted so much to be away from here, from him. To think. But there was nowhere to go. I was trapped.

The lift was moving closer. Soon it would be level with the roof of this one. It would pass me. And suddenly I could hear Jake, almost feel him beside me. The perfect moment was almost here. Jump time. I saw the roof at my side. 'Go for it, boy!' I heard Jake say again, but I had been so afraid then. Too afraid. I was afraid now. But I was more afraid of something else.

Do you want to die, no name? Or live to fight another day? I knew the answer to that one. I was going to live.

I turned back to the Dark Man in the shadows. 'I'm not ready for you yet, Mr Death. You'll have to run fast to catch me.'

And I leapt. I flew through the air and I felt Jake's coat fly around me, billowing out like a parachute, and I felt his spirit shout out to me. 'Go for it, boy!'

I landed with a steady thump on the roof of the other lift, gripped the cable with both hands. I looked up. I had taken him by surprise. He stood, looking over the edge, and his face was angry, watching me. It was too late for him to jump down. The moment had passed as I knew it would. 'I'll get you,' he shouted. 'I'll be after you from now on. Every time you look behind you, I'll be there.'

But that would be another day.

EPILOGUE

By the time Lewis arrived at the flats, there was no sign of the boy. But the Wolf's body was found splattered on the basement floor.

Lewis got the credit for saving all those lives. Acting with a cool head in a crisis. It had been noticed in the right circles. He could see that CID job waiting for him in the wings. His mother was still annoyed he didn't get a medal.

Lewis tried not to smile when he thought of the boy. Just a boy, and yet he had got the better of one of the most notorious killers in the country.

He had done more than that. Because of that boy, Barry McKay was arrested. The town got rid of a cancerous growth. And the lives saved at Heartbeat, all those teenagers – the boy had been responsible for that too.

All because of the boy.

And they never did find him.

People whispered about him. Some said he'd never existed. He was a lie, a phantom. Gaby McGurk had made him up. Eddie had used him as an excuse. And Zoe wouldn't talk of him at all. The only other people who had seen him were Dev and his mates, and no one believed them.

Lewis thought the boy might become an urban legend himself, with stories told about him and spread from place to place. The boy who brought down the Wolf and saved a town.

Nemesis.

Zoe and Gaby stood at their lockers. They were the star attraction today. Gaby's exciting moment, her relationship to the Wolf and Zoe saving her best friend's life were all the talk of the school. That was beginning to get to Gaby. 'You didn't actually save me. You didn't literally lift me out of the cellar with your bare hands.'

That had been Dev, who was now acting as if he was a hero, and as if he and Gaby were an item.

In his dreams.

Zoe, however, wouldn't give it up. 'If it hadn't been for me, Gaby, Lewis wouldn't have known anyone was in that cellar.'

Gaby decided she would have to give in gracefully.

Zoe opened her locker. 'What's this?' She lifted out an envelope, addressed to her. It was a Valentine. 'Look what I've got!' She ripped open the envelope and pulled out the card. 'From a secret admirer.' Zoe looked up and down the corridor. 'Who do you think my secret admirer is?'

Gaby grabbed the card from her. She had a feeling she knew exactly who the card was from. Ram! Sending Zoe a Valentine. There was no stamp on the envelope. He must have sneaked back into the school. How daring was that!

Then a thought struck her. Maybe he had put a Valentine in her locker too. She yanked open the door. Her eyes glared with anger.

'What did you get, Gaby? Did you get a Valentine as well?'

'Not quite,' she said, lifting out a box. It contained a bottle of hair colour. Honeysuckle Blonde.

Now I could leave this town. I didn't know where I was going or how I was going to get there. Just keep running. Keep out of the clutches of Mr Death. One day I would find out the truth about myself. Snatches were already coming back to me. And how could I ever forget the Dark Man's words. 'One day you'll remember and we can't afford for that to happen.'

What did I know that made them so afraid? And who were 'they'?

So keep on running. I had no choice.

I walked the disused railway track out of that riverside town. The track would take me somewhere.

It might even take me home.